Praise for

MW00596660

GUARANTEED TO BLEED (#2)

"Set in Kansas City, Missouri, in 1974, this cozy mystery effectively recreates the era through the details of down-to-earth Ellison's everyday life."

– Booklist

"Mulhern's lively, witty sequel to *The Deep End* finds Kansas City, Mo., socialite Ellison Russell reluctantly attending a high school football game...Cozy fans will eagerly await Ellison's further adventures."

– Publishers Weekly

"There's no way a lover of suspense could turn this book down because it's that much fun."

– Suspense Magazine

"Cleverly written with sharp wit and all the twists and turns of the best '70s primetime drama, Mulhern nails the fierce fraught mother-daughter relationship, fearlessly tackles what hides behind the Country Club façade, and serves up justice in bombshell fashion. A truly satisfying slightly twisted cozy."

– Gretchen Archer,
USA Today Bestselling Author of *Double Knot*

"In this excellent follow-up to her debut *The Deep End*, author Mulhern continues to depict the trappings of a privileged community...that blends a strong mystery with the demands of living in an exclusive society. Watching Ellison develop the strength of character to break through both her own and her society's expectations is a sheer delight."

– Kings River Life Magazine

THE DEEP END (#1)

"Part mystery, part women's fiction, part poetry, Mulhern's debut, *The Deep End*, will draw you in with the first sentence and entrance you until the last. An engaging whodunit that kept me guessing until the end!"

– Tracy Weber,
Author of the Downward Dog Mysteries

"An enjoyable, frequently amusing mystery with a mixture of off-beat characters that create twists and turns to keep Ellison—and the reader—off-guard while trying to solve the murder and keep herself out of jail. The plot is well-structured and the characters drawn with a deft hand. Setting the story in the mid-1970s is an inspired touch...A fine start to this mystery series, one that is highly recommended."

– *Mysterious Reviews*

"What a fun read! Murder in the days before cell phones, the internet, DNA and AFIS."

– *Books for Avid Readers*

"Intriguing plots, fascinating characters. From the first page to the last, Julie's mysteries grab the reader and don't let up. When all is resolved and I read the last page, I wanted to read more."

– Sally Berneathy,
USA Today Bestselling Author

"Ms. Mulhern weaves a tidy tale of murder, blackmail, and life behind the scenes in the Country Club set of the 70s...an excellent mystery, highly recommended, and I eagerly await the next in the series."

– *Any Good Book*

CLOUDS IN MY COFFEE

The Country Club Murders
by Julie Mulhern

THE DEEP END (#1)
GUARANTEED TO BLEED (#2)
CLOUDS IN MY COFFEE (#3)

CLOUDS IN MY COFFEE

THE
COUNTRY CLUB
MURDERS

JULIE
MULHERN

HENERY PRESS

CLOUDS IN MY COFFEE
The Country Club Murders
Part of the Henery Press Mystery Collection

First Edition | May 2016

Henery Press
www.henerypress.com

Trade Paperback ISBN-13: 978-1-63511-021-0
Digital epub ISBN-13: 978-1-63511-022-7
Kindle ISBN-13: 978-1-63511-023-4
Hardcover ISBN-13: 978-1-63511-024-1

Printed in the United States of America

To Katie Mulhern, with endless love

ACKNOWLEDGMENTS

My everlasting gratitude to Madonna and Sally who held my hand, to Dash, Gersh, and Sunshine who kept me sane, and to my editors Rachel, Kendel, and Erin who made this a better book.

ONE

October, 1974
Kansas City, Missouri

Max, his short grey tail wagging impossibly fast, met me at the door with a did-you-ask-the-butcher-for-a-bone expression on his expressive doggy face. Of course, I had.

"Let me put the groceries away first."

He sighed as if I had my priorities backward.

I unpacked the bags, putting the cucumber in the sink to be rinsed, the potatoes in a basket on the counter, and the Tab in the fridge. Max whined softly, reminding me that he was waiting.

I scratched behind his silken gray ears and gave him his bone.

Brrnng, brrnng.

I answered the phone, stretching the cord toward the sink and the waiting cucumber. "Hello."

"Ellie. We have a problem." No greeting, no endearment, no inquiry as to my day. Daddy's words chilled me.

Horrible possibilities scrolled through my brain. "Is Mother all right?" Had the stress of planning a major event finally gotten to her? Had she suffered a stroke or a nervous breakdown? Unlikely. Mother ran her events with military precision. She ate stress for breakfast.

General Westmoreland could have learned a thing or two about organizing an army from Mother. Probably he could have learned about guerilla warfare as well.

I wish I had learned those things. Mother was all too willing to instruct me, but I had no desire to learn.

Who knew that long tall vases topped by balls made of pink carnations could look so phallic? The thought never occurred to me. It probably occurred to lots of the women who helped with the luncheon. No one said a thing.

They let me venture into battle with my flak suit around my knees.

That luncheon, remembered forever as Ellison's penis party, would never have happened to Mother.

"What's happened?" My voice sounded breathless. "Is Mother all right?"

"Your mother's fine."

Relief flooded my veins.

"But we need your help."

Dread replaced relief in my blood stream.

Help could mean folding six hundred napkins into swans. I proceeded with caution. "What is it?"

Daddy cleared his throat. "Your Aunt Sis has arrived."

As far as I knew, Aunt Sis came to Kansas City for weddings and funerals. We'd had neither in years. Well, not if you didn't count Henry's funeral in June. I didn't. "I thought she was in Majorca."

"So did your mother." Daddy used his driest tone—the one he saved for occurrences that interrupted his golf game or cocktail hour.

"But she's here? Now?"

"In the kitchen as we speak."

I pictured him in his study, surrounded by pecan paneling and pictures of his family. We smiled in those pictures, hid the problems, filled in the cracks and slapped on a coat of new paint. Aunt Sis was a crack that couldn't be filled. Why had she come to Kansas City now?

"How's Mother?"

"Stressed."

"You want me to take Aunt Sis?" It wasn't really a question.

"Please." Daddy didn't beg. At least not usually.

"Mother has Aggie." Taking on a houseguest without a housekeeper sounded like a recipe for disaster.

"You can have Aggie back. I'll hire your mother a temporary assistant—a Kelly Girl. Will you take Sis? Please?"

Daddy was brilliant. A Kelly Girl! We should have hired Mother a team of Kelly Girls weeks ago.

"Also, Sis has it in her head that she wants to go to a dinner theatre. If I buy the tickets, will you go with her?"

I swallowed a sigh. "Of course. What are you going to say about moving her to my house?" Foisting off a houseguest wasn't exactly polite.

"I'll tell her your Mother is terribly busy and you'd like to spend some time with her."

I hadn't seen Aunt Sis since my wedding. She'd jetted in from someplace exotic—Majorca or Cyprus—pulled me aside thirty minutes before the ceremony and told me not to marry Henry. She had no way of knowing what he'd become—a barnacle on the ass of humanity—she just thought he was boring. Her exact words were "dull as a lengthy sermon." Unfortunately, Mother overheard. The ensuing discussion was lengthy but not dull. The two dredged up four decades' worth of slights and hurt feelings and resentment at full decibel.

Daddy ended their fight by comparing them to fish wives.

Since then their only communication has been birthday and Christmas cards.

Until now.

"How long is she staying?"

Daddy grunted. Did that mean a night? A week? A month?

"How long?" I insisted.

"She hasn't said."

Peachy.

"I'll put her in the blue room for now."

"Thank you, Ellie. I owe you one."

Playing host to Aunt Sis couldn't come close to paying the debt I owed him. My throat tightened. "It's not a problem."

He chuckled. "You know how your aunt reinvents herself every so often?"

I made a noncommittal noise. My memories of Aunt Sis consisted of birthday gifts sent from afar and seemingly selected to annoy Mother—makeup when I was five, a lace (and completely unnecessary) brassiere when I was ten, and a Cab Calloway record when I was fifteen (Mother thought scat was something wild animals left in the woods). Then there was the year of the hookah— I still remember Mother's appalled expression (unmatched until she learned that I ran over my husband).

"How much trouble can she be?"

"You'll have to tell me what you think of the fish and the bicycle. Love you." With that, he hung up. I stared at the receiver in my hand. The fish and the bicycle? What had I gotten myself into?

I hung up the phone, climbed the back stairs with Max at my heels, and opened the door to the blue room. The room needed airing, the bed needed sheets and the dresser needed a bouquet of fresh flowers. I cracked the windows and grabbed neatly folded sheets from the linen closet. The flowers I'd collect from the garden later.

I'd just replaced the bedspread when the doorbell rang.

Max took off at a run. I followed more slowly. Aunt Sis must truly be driving Mother nuts if Daddy had bundled her out of the house and delivered her to me in less than fifteen minutes.

I donned a welcoming expression and opened the door.

Marjorie stood on the other side.

My smile morphed into slack-jawed shock.

Max whined softly.

"What are you doing here?"

"Is that any way to greet your sister?" She bent, picked up a Gucci suitcase, and brushed past me, stopping in the front hall to assess my house. "Did you paint? Is this the same color as the last time I was here?"

"No. I mean, yes. I mean, no, I didn't paint. It's the same color." Surprise had rendered me witless. "Mother said you couldn't come." Yet Marjorie was here, flawlessly made up and dressed as if she'd stepped off the pages of *Vogue* in a pair of decadent wool slacks and a silk shirt far too fashionable (unbuttoned) for my foyer. I suppose when you're married to the condom king of Cleveland, looking more chic than Halston's muse is probably the strongest armor available. My armor is designed by Diane von Furstenberg.

My sister dropped her expensive suitcase but kept her Hermes handbag hooked in the crook of her elbow. "I changed my mind."

"Does Mother know you're coming?"

"I thought I'd surprise her."

I gaped. Mother liked surprises the way Nixon liked Woodward and Bernstein.

Marjorie stepped forward and kissed the air next to my cheek. "It's lovely to see you."

"You too." I returned her air kiss and upped the ante with a half-hug.

"I can't wait to hear all the things you've been up to. Mother says you're dating Hunter Tafft."

Typical. Marjorie skipped right over multiple murders to ask about a man. "Not exactly."

A slight furrow appeared between her brows. "But Mother said—"

"Mother is wrong."

She tilted her head and smiled the superior smile of an older sister—one who was prettier, more experienced, more popular, and certainly better dressed. "Who's taking you to Mother's gala?"

My fingers smoothed the wales of my corduroys. "Hunter Tafft." His name somehow slipped through the tightly barred gate of my teeth.

"There you have it! You are dating Hunter."

"A date and dating are not the same thing." Why did I sound like my teenage self?

She lifted her gaze to the ceiling and shook her head slightly. "When it's a date to Mother's gala, they are."

I had a sneaking suspicion she might be right.

"Can your housekeeper take this upstairs for me?" She pointed to her suitcase.

"You'll have to take it yourself. Aggie is on loan." Then I remembered Aunt Sis. "I've already got someone in the blue room. I'll put you in the rose room."

"But the rose room has twin beds."

This was not news to me.

"I hate twin beds."

That wasn't news either. "You can always stay with Mother and Daddy."

Marjorie snorted.

"Where's Greg? Is he coming?"

"He's at home with the children." Her voice sounded flat, emotionless. Prudence's sly innuendos flashed through my memory. Uh-oh.

"Is he flying in for the gala? You're welcome here, but there's a new hotel on the Plaza—the Alameda. I don't think you've been there yet. I could book you a room."

"No."

"No, you haven't been there, or no, you don't want a room?"

With a chic flip of her wrist she flicked a stray hair back into place. "No, Greg is not coming."

"Why not?"

"I already told you, he's at home with the children."

"Did your *au pair* quit?"

"No."

"What about your housekeeper? Did she quit?"

"No."

"Then why isn't he coming?"

"Just drop it, Ellison."

There was trouble in Paradise. "Do you want to talk about it?"

"Drop. It."

We stared at each other. It would be a cold day in hell before Marjorie looked for succor or support from her younger sister. I got that. But her insistence on being superior meant we'd never be close. It also rendered her right (and maybe left) flank open to attack.

"You need a better answer."

She curled the corner of her upper lip and glared at me as if I was the problem. It was the kind of look one can only give a sibling. No one else would forgive it. I might not forgive it.

Max growled softly.

The front bell rang and we stopped glowering at each other. I opened the door to Daddy and Aunt Sis.

My mother's sister wore faded jeans, a loose white shirt that failed to hide her lack of brassiere, and flip-flops. Her grey-streaked hair was pulled back from her face in a ponytail.

I stared at Aunt Sis.

Daddy stared at Marjorie.

No one said a word.

Then Max shoved his nose into Sis's crotch and we all laughed, a nervous sound that belonged to people who weren't quite sure what to say.

Mother's sister grinned at me—"Ellie"—then pulled me into a hug.

Over Sis's shoulder, I saw Daddy positively gaping at Marjorie. She stepped forward and he hugged her.

"What are you doing here?" He put her through the same series of questions I had. And he got the same answers. "Is Greg at least flying in for the gala?"

"No. He's staying home with the children."

Daddy crossed his arms and scowled. "I realize Greg and your mother don't much care for each other, but he's willing to embarrass her by skipping her gala with such a weak excuse?"

"Greg didn't stay home to embarrass Mother."

"Then why?"

Marjorie's gaze traveled from Daddy to me to Aunt Sis then

back again. She adjusted the gold chains hanging around her neck. She patted her perfect hair. She chewed on the corner of her lip. "I left him."

TWO

After lobbing her grenade with all the insouciant elegance of a model walking a Parisian runway, Marjorie talked Daddy into lugging her suitcase up the front stairs. I carried Aunt Sis's.

The woman traveled with rocks...or maybe bricks. There was no way clothes weighed so much.

"I can carry that," she offered.

"Don't be silly." I hefted the enormous thing onto another step, then stopped for a rest.

"It's heavy." Aunt Sis was a master of understatement.

"It's nothing." Just last night I'd helped Grace study for a chemistry quiz, so I knew osmium was the densest of the elements—heavier than gold or platinum. Maybe my aunt had a suitcase full of osmium.

"Ellison, your face is turning red."

Maybe she carried rolls of quarters...or what was the currency in Majorca? Pesetas? Weren't hippie types supposed to travel light? I gathered my strength and climbed four steps quickly.

"What do you have in here, Aunt Sis?"

"Books."

"You couldn't ship them?"

She crinkled her nose as if the postal service was something distasteful. "I'm never in one place long enough."

My heart went out to all the porters, in all the stations, in all the cities. How many had herniated discs?

Aunt Sis peeled my fingers off the handle then lifted the case as if it was filled with cotton candy instead of multiple copies of

War and Peace. She traipsed up the remaining stairs with ease. I trudged.

Daddy, looking grim, stepped out of the rose room, dropped a kiss on my forehead, nodded to Aunt Sis, then started down the stairway. At the halfway point, he turned and said, "Enjoy the theatre."

"We will," said Aunt Sis.

That was optimistic.

Aunt Sis smiled. "I bet Marjorie would love to join us."

That was ridiculously optimistic.

Daddy made no comment. He just shook his head and descended the rest of the stairs. A few seconds later the sound of the front door opening reached us.

"Goodbye," he called. Then came the sound of the door closing.

"Perhaps Grace can join us," suggested Aunt Sis.

That was beyond ridiculously optimistic.

"It's a school night. If you'd like her to join us, we could postpone..." Forever.

"No, no. Just eager to meet her. Is this my room?" Aunt Sis pushed open the door to the blue room with the front of her suitcase. "I have a feeling I'm supposed to be at the theater tonight."

"A feeling?"

"I get feelings, Ellison. They come to me from the cosmos. I had a feeling you shouldn't marry Henry, and I have a feeling there's a unique experience waiting for me at the dinner theatre."

Aunt Sis was comparing my disastrous marriage to dinner theatre? I opened my mouth then shut it. That Henry's and my marriage had played out more like *Who's Afraid of Virginia Woolf* than a refurbished version of *Guys and Dolls* still rankled. But kicking Aunt Sis and her overburdened suitcase out before she unpacked—no matter how tempting—would be rude. Far ruder than her thoughtless comment. I pursed my lips and focused my gaze above her left shoulder.

"Your mother wears that exact expression whenever I annoy her."

I wiped my face clean—no pursing, no furrowing, no pretending to notice a stain on the wall above her shoulder.

"I'll just unpack and then we'll catch up." She surveyed the blue room with its Sister Parish elegance, cracked windows and fresh sheets, and sniffed.

That sniff...Aunt Sis shouldn't throw stones in the glass house of similarity. She had every nuance of Mother's sniff down.

"I was on my way to the garden to cut you some late blooming roses when Marjorie arrived. I'll do that while you unpack."

She inclined her chin and looked over imaginary readers, another one of Mother's habits. "Thank you, dear. Also, I'll need you to run a load of laundry for me."

I inclined my chin too. "I'll be happy to show you the laundry room."

She tilted her head and stared at me—the sort of considering look one uses when deciding upon a major purchase. *Yes, that Pucci dress is lovely, but is it worth the price?* The moment stretched.

After what seemed like an eternity, she smiled. "I'd appreciate that. Thank you."

I'd won? I'd won. And easily. Maybe Aunt Sis was less like Mother than I thought.

I took Aunt Sis to the Waldo Astoria. My friends who'd attended told me it was newer and nicer than Tiffany's Attic. Marjorie developed "plans" and couldn't join us. I didn't bother asking Grace.

We stood in the lobby, admiring the 1920s-style glamor. The owners had redone a movie theatre. I'd expected tacky. This wasn't. It was lovely.

Cassie LeCoeur waved at me from across the lobby. Sometimes that happens. You don't see someone for weeks on end and then you run into them in the oddest places. Poor Cassie. Being married to a man named Kinky LeCoeur must be a heavy cross to bear. Not that her husband's real name is Kinky. He introduces himself as Kenneth. Probably when they met in college he introduced himself as Ken. But to those of us who have known him his whole life, he'll always be Kinky. Mother says when one's last name sounds as if it might belong to a professional dancer, one must be extra careful when selecting first names. The LeCoeurs obviously never heard her wax lyrical on this point...or maybe she waxes because of what Bob and Mary LeCoeur named their children—Kenneth Keye (show me a bunch of high school boys who won't shorten that to Kinky) and his sister Candace, called Candy.

I waved back.

"A friend of yours, dear?" asked Aunt Sis.

"More of an acquaintance."

Cassie was with her mother-in-law and looked none too happy about it. I didn't blame her.

Aunt Sis squinted at them. "Is that Mary Laughlin?"

"Mary LeCoeur."

My aunt nodded. "Her maiden name was Laughlin. I must say hello." She pushed her way through the crowd, elbowing as she went.

I followed in her wake.

In her bell bottom pants and loose tunic, Aunt Sis looked like an aging hippie. Mary Laughlin LeCoeur looked like a woman whose carefully orchestrated ensemble had been purchased in its entirety at Swanson's.

Mary tried for an air kiss, but Sis pulled her into a real hug.

After a mere second, Mary pulled away and smoothed the wrinkles from her clothes. "What a surprise to see you, Cecelia."

"I decided to come home for a few weeks."

"I'm sure your family is delighted to see you." Mary offered me a tight smile, one that looked empathetic, you-poor-dear-you-got-stuck-with-your-crazy-aunt empathetic.

Was she really suggesting we were less than pleased with Aunt

Sis's arrival in front of Aunt Sis? I reached for my aunt's hand and squeezed her fingers. "We're thrilled she's here."

"Your mother must be getting excited about the gala, Ellison."

I nodded. Barely.

"John and I are benefactors. We just love the museum. History is so important."

"Have you seen the new exhibit?" Did she even know where the museum was?

Her cheeks pinked. "Not yet. But we will tomorrow night at the benefactors' party." She shifted her gaze to Sis. "What a treat that you could be here for the parties, Cecilia."

"Isn't it?" Aunt Sis's voice was as dry as one of Daddy's Friday night martinis. She might have spent most of her life swimming in other waters, but she still recognized the hidden currents in a simple conversation. "Ellie, we'd better find our table."

We nodded to Cassie and Mary then turned away.

A few steps across the lobby, Aunt Sis whispered, "When did Mary become such a bitch? She didn't used to be that way."

I shrugged. I barely knew the woman. It was Kinky I knew, and I hadn't done more than trade pleasantries with him in years.

We followed a uniformed girl into the theatre, were seated at a table for two, and ordered drinks.

Aunt Sis looked around—more gold, more glitz, more glamor. "I've never been to a dinner theatre before."

"That makes two of us."

"It's nice of you to bring me. Thank you."

"My pleasure," I murmured.

"Liar." With one word, she pulled my attention away from considering the color on the wall. Was it asparagus green or mushy-peas green?

"Pardon me?"

"You're lying." Her voice held a hint of laughter. "You'd rather watch paint dry than sit through this performance." She reached across the table and patted my hand. "I appreciate it. Thank you."

There was no point in arguing with her. She was right.

"You're welcome."

"You never know, you might enjoy it. Besides, it's important to do things one's never done. Especially for you."

"Oh?"

"You're an artist. You need to constantly expand."

Aunt Sis wasn't wrong. I donned a brave face. How bad could it be? "This should be fun."

A waitress delivered our drinks—Sazerac for Aunt Sis, wine for me—then climbed on stage with the other waiters and waitresses and broke into song. A show tune I think.

Aunt Sis opened her program and perused. "They're called the Hoochies."

"You're kidding."

She shoved the program toward me and pointed. "No. I'm not."

Mother could never come here. *Hoochie* was the disparaging word she used to describe a woman whose skirt was too short or sweater too tight. The girls on stage didn't look "hoochie;" they looked young and fresh-faced and thrilled to be entertaining us.

Aunt Sis leaned back in her chair. "So, Ellison, tell me what you're up to."

I took a sip of wine. "Painting, mothering, and keeping an eye on the bank."

"The bank?

"When Henry died he left controlling interest in the bank to Grace. Until she comes of age, I'm the conservator."

"What do you know about banking?"

"Nothing. I have very capable people in place—"

"You should spend your time painting. Creating. Sell the bank."

I shook my head. "It's not mine to sell."

Aunt Sis waved away my objections with one Auntie Mame like sweep of her arm. "Grace doesn't want to be tethered by a bank."

"Grace is sixteen. She doesn't know what she wants."

Sis blinked as if surprised that the artist in the family had disagreed with her.

"Didn't you used to date Randolph Walsh?" Now the artist questioned her. "He's a banker."

"He wasn't when I dated him." For a half-second the expression in her eyes softened to mist. She sat up straighter in her chair. "Your mother tells me you're dating a lawyer."

"Not really. We've gone out to dinner a few times. That's all."

"But he's taking you to the benefactors' party tomorrow night?"

I nodded.

"Good. I'll get to size him up." She held up a warning finger. "Remember, Ellison, you don't need him. A woman without a man is like a fish without a bicycle."

Aha! If Aunt Sis was quoting Gloria Steinem at Mother and Daddy's house, it was hardly surprising that they'd moved her out. In Mother's opinion, one she valued far more than a feminist's, a woman without a man was only half of what she could be.

"What brings you to Kansas City, Aunt Sis?"

"I wanted to see you and your mother." She looked me in the eye when she spoke.

So why didn't I believe her?

"The older you get, the more you reflect on your youth. Things you did right. Things you did wrong. Things that slipped through your fingers before you realized they were precious." She stared into the mid-distance for a moment then held up her near empty glass. "I need another drink."

The Hoochies finished their songs, exited stage left, and the curtain rose on a buffet table.

"A buffet?" In that instant, Aunt Sis sounded precisely like Mother. With two words she conveyed disapproval, superiority, and a willingness to take the whole operation in hand, thereby improving it drastically.

She swallowed the last sip of Sazerac then stood with a sigh. If the buffet was a cross to bear, she would bear it.

That sip of Sazerac had cost us. Already the line snaked through the tables. Eager patrons queued up for salad, various vegetables, rice pilaf, a chaffing dish filled with chicken breasts swimming in a white wine and butter sauce, an enormous basket of what looked like fried bread, and, at the end of the table, hand-carved roast beef.

The man with the carving knife had eyes that looked too big for his lean face, a mustache that drooped around the edges of his mouth, and a chef's hat that looked as if it should be a flak helmet. No way would I have ever given him a nine-inch carving knife. Still, he cut through the meat with an economy of movement that suggested long practice. That or an intimate relationship with knives.

The tall woman in front of us waxed lyrical about the apple fritters. She pointed to an enormous basket of fried bread and said to her friend, "Get three or four. Maybe five. If you don't eat them, I will."

The friend, a tiny woman playing Jeff to the tall woman's Mutt, nodded.

Mutt skipped the salad and the green goddess dressing, leaving plenty of room on her plate for fritters.

Aunt Sis and I took a step forward and picked up our dinner plates.

In front of us, Mutt and Jeff helped themselves to green beans and rice pilaf. Then Mutt took up the tongs for the fritters. One. Two. Three.

Aunt Sis watched her.

Four. Five. Six.

"How many can one woman eat?" Sis whispered.

Mutt must have heard her—she glared at us then thrust the tongs deep into the pile of fritters.

A mouse leapt from the basket seemingly aiming for Mutt's face.

Jeff screamed and threw her plate high in the air.

Mutt bellowed, "For the love of Mike!"

I squealed.

Aunt Sis, in a maneuver worthy of a gymnast forty years her junior, jumped off the stage and landed atop a table.

The mouse hit the floor and ran.

Who could blame the little creature? Especially when the man with the carving knife gave chase.

Those who hadn't seen the mouse screamed now. After all, there was a lunatic with a huge knife running around the stage shouting, "I'll get you, you little son of a bitch."

The steps bottlenecked and a few people followed Aunt Sis's lead and leapt off the stage. Sadly, they didn't land nimbly on tables. They brought tables crashing down in a symphony of breaking glass and falling cutlery.

Those not on stage rushed to the back of the theatre, pushing through the doors and crowding into the lobby.

Mutt pushed Jeff toward the stairs.

The mouse, seemingly tired of running around in circles, ran past the footlights and launched himself into the seats.

The man with the carving knife followed.

Louder screams ensued. As did the crash of more tables.

The stage had become the safest place to be. I stayed where I was.

A man, perhaps a manager, bellowed, "Vic, stop!"

If Vic was the man with the knife, he either didn't hear or chose not to listen. He held his blade poised and ready to chop the poor mouse to bits, or, at the very least, cut off its tail with a carving knife.

Aunt Sis still sat on a table, her foot in a butter dish, her gaze fixed on the man with the knife as if she'd never seen such a sight in her life.

The sound of a siren snuck past the screams and Vic's obscenity-laced promises of what he planned to do to the mouse. Thank God. The remainder of the audience pushed through the exit doors and someone, somewhere, had the good sense to turn up the house lights.

The change in ambiance slowed Vic.

It also revealed untold devastation. Broken tables. Women perched on chairs. Shattered glassware. A man still holding an enormous knife.

Then I saw him, a silhouette against the brighter lights of the lobby.

Vic must have seen him too. He dropped his knife and sank into a chair.

If the mouse saw Detective Anarchy Jones outlined in the doorway, he gave no hint. Instead he ran off to his mouse hole or maybe to the kitchen.

I almost wished I could run with the little fellow. Instead, I stood alone on a stage covered in broken plates and trampled food. I felt Anarchy's gaze on me. My cheeks warmed and I fought the urge to cool them with fingers that were suddenly ice cold.

I couldn't see his smile—confident, amused, and meltingly sexy—but I knew it was there.

I swallowed, smoothed my skirt, and wished I was someplace else—anyplace else—folding-napkins-into-swans else.

"Where's the body?" he called.

"There isn't one." My voice didn't carry as well as his did but at least it didn't shake. "How did you get here so fast?"

"There's a donut shop down the street."

I tilted my head. Was he joking?

"A patrolman stopped for coffee and noticed people running out of the theatre screaming about a man with a knife."

That would attract police attention.

"Ellison, who are you talking to?" demanded Aunt Sis.

"Aunt Sis, please allow me to introduce you to Detective Jones. Detective, this is my Aunt Cecilia."

Anarchy eyed the crazed man who'd dropped his knife on the floor and now had his elbows on his knees and his head buried in his hands. The man with the knife or Ellison, which would cause him more trouble? I could almost read his thoughts. He approached Sis. "It's a pleasure to meet you." If he was surprised to see a member of my family—other than me—sitting in the middle of a sixty-inch round, he didn't show it. *Inscrutable*, there's a word that describes Anarchy Jones. "Would you like some help?"

Sis removed her heel from the butter. "Is the mouse gone?"

"Yes," I called from the stage.

She extended her hand toward Anarchy. "I would be grateful for your assistance." She scooched toward the edge of the table.

"The mouse?" asked Anarchy.

Aunt Sis nodded. "That's what started all this." She put her hand in his, looked up at him and froze.

Anarchy Jones ought to be used to the effect he has on women. Tall, lean face, sandy blonde hair and brown eyes that manage—somehow—to be even more attractive than the first cup of coffee in the morning. Who could resist?

Maybe he didn't notice Aunt Sis staring at him slack-jawed and dazzled.

Anarchy doesn't miss much. He can't; he investigates homicides.

He'd investigated me.

I cleared my throat and pitched my voice to extra-loud. "No one is dead."

Anarchy's lips quirked as if I'd amused him. He led Aunt Sis to a chair. "Where are you from, ma'am?"

"I'm a citizen of the world. Please call me Sis." Her lashes fluttered a mile a minute. "All my friends do."

Oh dear Lord. Aunt Sis was *flirting* with Anarchy.

I tiptoed through the wreckage on the stage, avoiding mashed beans, a minefield of new potatoes and flattened fritters, descended the stairs, and approached my aunt.

"I told you," she said. "I told you tonight would be a unique experience."

"You were right."

"How do you two know each other?"

She nodded at Anarchy then me.

"Detective Jones investigated Henry's murder."

"I see." Aunt Sis rubbed her chin. When Mother did that, she was up to something. Was it a family trait? "So you're old friends?"

One of Anarchy's brows rose. As for me, the ability to form a coherent sentence up and left, departing faster than theatre patrons fleeing a mouse.

"You could say that," said Anarchy.

Around us, the room filled with uniformed police officers. One collected abandoned purses. Another put Vic, the would-be mouse killer, in handcuffs. Killing a mouse might not be illegal, but running through a crowded theater with a nine-inch knife was.

From her chair, Aunt Sis gazed up at Anarchy, her lips curled in an enigmatic smile. "Seeing as you and Ellison are old friends, would you do me a favor?"

"I'd be delighted."

"My sister is chairing a party on Saturday night. Would you escort me?"

What happened to fish and bicycles?

What happened to decorum? Aunt Sis had to be at least twenty years older than Anarchy—maybe more.

This wasn't New York; widows and women of a certain age didn't depend on charming gay men to take them to happenings. We didn't have walkers in Kansas City. And if we did, no one—NO ONE—would mistake Anarchy for a gay man.

He sent an absolutely unreadable—inscrutable—glance my way, bowed slightly, then said, "It would be my pleasure."

When Mother found out, she was going to have apoplexy. I might join her.

THREE

Mother held the benefactors' party at the museum. She'd have liked to hold the gala there, but there simply wasn't room.

In 1908, R.A. Long spent a million dollars on its construction. He built Corinthian Hall as a home, not a museum, but his daughters grew up and married, Long and his wife passed away, and, during the thirties in the depths of the depression, no one wanted to take on the upkeep of a seventy-room mansion.

Long's daughters gave the empty building to the Kansas City Museum.

Now instead of European antiques, Corinthian Hall housed stuffed polar bears and a concrete igloo, dioramas, and a trading post. Children loved it, and tonight it served up a very different backdrop for a very familiar party.

Mother, wearing Chanel in shades of copper, harvest gold and asparagus green, greeted people as they entered. Daddy stood next to her with a neat scotch in his left hand.

Guests filled the foyer. To the left, the beautiful remnants of a Louis XVI sitting room beckoned; to the right, a living room destroyed in the name of progress held artifacts. Sweeping stairs rose at the back of the foyer, paused at a generous landing, then split and rose to the second floor.

Aunt Sis and I stood halfway up the lower portion of the stairs.

"Who's the most interesting person here?" She surveyed the benefactors—the same benefactors who supported the symphony and the art museum and the hospital. Every face was familiar—at least to me. They might have secrets worthy of blackmail, but interesting? Aunt Sis was by far the most interesting person in the room. She'd sat with a swami in Nepal, lived abroad for more than a semester during college, and she didn't want to talk about gas prices, interest rates or how Dorothy and John Howland were getting divorced...again.

"I mean it, Ellison. Who should I talk to?"

I nodded my head toward the entrance where Mother greeted Hammie and Randolph Walsh. "You know them."

Sis brought her drink to her lips. "Indeed, I do."

I scanned the crowd below. "There's Libby Allerton. Didn't you go to high school with her?"

Sis focused on Libby. "Oh my. You leave town for forty years and people get older." She turned toward me. "I know lots of people here, Ellison. You don't have to babysit me. Go mingle. Your sister is."

I searched the crowd and found Marjorie. She wore a cream gown cut almost to her naval. It was a gown designed for a much younger woman to wear in a much more sophisticated city. Marjorie was chatting with Kinky. She looked up into his face. He looked down into her cleavage.

"Go on," said Aunt Sis. "Mingle."

If only she knew how parties sapped my energy.

"Go." She shoved me gently.

I descended the stairs and Joan Hanes grabbed me—literally. Her fingers circled my wrist. Damn. It would take a jackhammer to remove her.

"Ellison, I'm so glad I ran into you. Did you get my messages?"

"No." I used my free hand to scratch my nose.

"No matter." She waved aside the fact that I'd ignored four messages. "I need a painting for the school auction. When would you like to deliver it?"

Was she joking? I blinked, temporarily unable to connect the thoughts running through my head with my tongue. Probably a blessing.

Her grip on my arm tightened. "The auction is only a few

weeks from now so we'll need it right away. You can write up a description, can't you?"

"Joan, I don't have a painting to give you."

She wobbled slightly and steadied herself on the bannister. "Of course you do."

I didn't. I had a new dealer in New York, and I'd shipped every finished canvas to him. And after the way she'd *demanded* a painting, I wouldn't have given her one anyway. Had the woman never heard the word *please*? "I'm sorry, I can't help you."

"But I told everyone I'd get a painting. If you don't give me one..." Her voice trailed off, inviting me to imagine her embarrassment and damaged reputation.

"I don't have anything to give you." And I wouldn't if I did.

Joan's wide-eyed innocent look was just a shade too innocent. "You must have something." She drew out the last word.

I shook my head.

"You're lying." She spoke loud enough to draw attention. One or two faces registered shock. Prudence Davies looked gleeful. "Just give me a damn painting." She'd lowered her voice but not enough.

A murmur of interest swelled loud enough to draw Mother's attention. She glanced over her shoulder and shot me a look that said more clearly than words, "Do not make a scene at my party."

So be it, but it would be a cold day in hell before Joan Hanes got a painting from me. "I'll make a donation equal to the value of one of my paintings."

"I said I'd get a painting." Her brows drew together and her nostrils flared slightly. Why had she made such a promise? It wasn't as if we were close friends, and I didn't owe her any favors. "You have to do thish for me."

Thish?

Just how much had Joan had to drink? Where was her husband? I scanned the room. Alan (smart man) was nowhere in sight and the drink in her hand was empty—no surprise there. "Perhaps we could talk about this another time."

Her lip curled. "I need to report to the committee tomorrow."

If she wasn't attached to my arm like some art-sucking leech, I would have walked away. Instead, I lowered my voice. "Then tell them I said no." I pulled against her hold.

"Give me a painting, Ellithon."

There were easily fifteen people eavesdropping on our conversation. Could not one of them help me? A simple interruption was all I needed. I donned a damsel in distress look.

Nothing.

"Joan, my aunt is here alone, and I promised Mother I'd keep an eye on her." My escape line had the benefit of being true. I even glanced up the stairs where Aunt Sis and I had looked over the crowd. She was gone. I yanked my arm free. "Tell your committee I'll write a check." I stepped backward before she could catch me again.

"But—"

"It will be a big check."

"But—"

"Lovely to see you."

I fled the foyer and disappeared into the crowd in what was once the living room. Not good enough. A drunk Joan Hanes might pursue me. I cut through the stripped down dining room into the back hall, then climbed the dark servants' stairs to the second floor.

My hand closed on the doorknob to the landing.

A woman's voice, muffled by a door made to stand the test of time, reached me. "I did as you asked. No one found out about our son."

Not something I had any business hearing. I let go of the knob and backed up a few steps.

"Ellithon…" Joan's voice climbed the stairs.

Oh. Good. Lord.

Either I listened to a conversation that was none of my concern or I endured another conversation with a woman who wouldn't take no for an answer.

The decision was obvious. I climbed back into the shadows near the door.

"You must help." Even through the three-inch wood, I could discern the desperation in the woman's voice.

Another mumbled response.

"At least take the..." The rest of her words faded. Whoever was on the other side was moving away from the door.

I waited, counted to ten, counted to twenty, and cracked the door. The upstairs hallway stood empty and I ventured forth.

There it was again, that prickling on the back of my neck. I glanced over my shoulder and found no one. I was alone. The only other faces in the hallway belonged to the marble busts of Martha and Robert Long. They sat on plinths in the upper landing, their stony gazes turned toward the hall rather than the stained glass window. Neither of them looked particularly happy about it— roughly the same level of happy as Mother when Aunt Sis appeared at the party wearing a caftan (never mind that the gold abaya was Thea Porter couture).

When Aggie saw that caftan, she might wrestle my aunt to the floor for it—if I didn't beat her to it.

On the positive side, between Marjorie's plunging neckline and Aunt Sis's caftan, Mother hadn't complained one whit about my dress, a vintage Fortuny Delphos gown I'd purchased in a darling little shop in the Galleria Vittorio Emanuele in Milan.

I lifted the hem as I descended the stairs, unable to shake the feeling that someone watched me. I stopped and looked. No one. Just the backs of Robert and Martha's heads.

I reached the first landing and shifted my gaze to Mother's guests. Joan Hanes was nowhere in sight. What a relief.

Marjorie had taken my spot halfway up the lower staircase. Men circled her—John Ballew, recently divorced and looking as if he was enjoying life without Kitty, Quin Marstin, who was probably as interested in selling Marjorie a share in his hookah stores as he was her more obvious assets, and Kinky. Kinky had gone so far as to rest a possessive hand on her arm as if claiming the view of her cleavage for himself.

That wouldn't do. If Cassie saw, she might get the wrong idea.

I hurried down the next few steps then stopped and called, "Marjorie." I'd make up some excuse to remove her from her dubious circle of admirers...something.

They all looked at me—my sister, John, Quin, and Kinky. None of them looked pleased with the interruption.

Especially Marjorie—the wrinkle across the bridge of her nose coupled with her tilted chin and pursed lips told me we'd be having words later.

As if I cared. I smiled sweetly.

Her brows rose, her mouth dropped and she gasped.

In that same instant, Kinky launched himself at me and knocked me flat.

Bang!

It sounded as if someone had shot a cannon in the foyer.

Kinky lay on top of me, flattening my breasts, the scent of cigarettes and the scotch he'd just drunk filling my nostrils.

"What happened?" Mother's voice cut through the murmur of appalled voices. "Get off my daughter immediately." This she said so sharply, the hairs on Kinky's head probably split in two.

Kinky pushed himself off me with alacrity.

Everyone who'd been in the foyer stood at the bottom stairs, gaping. Everyone who'd been in either of the rooms off the foyer crowded into the foyer and joined in the slack-jawed staring. I lay on the stairs and wondered why the room was suddenly out of focus.

I extended my hand and encountered a shard of marble.

"What happened?" Mother demanded in a tone that said loud and clear she'd better not have to ask a third time.

Daddy pushed past her and joined me on the stairs. His were the arms that helped me to sitting.

"Are you all right, sugar?"

Sharp bits of white marble surrounded me.

"Fine." Not true. "Shaken," I amended.

Mother glowered. "What happ—"

"Something fell from up above. Kenneth pushed Ellison out of the way. He saved her life." Marjorie sounded almost as shaken as I felt. Almost. She somehow found it in herself to smile gratefully at Kinky. I probably should have smiled at him too but I just couldn't. My mouth still felt slack—too shocked to curve upward.

Mother climbed the stairs, carefully picking her way through shattered marble.

At the landing she turned and looked upward toward the second floor. "It appears a bust has fallen." Her gaze now searched the crowd below her. "Mr. Carstairs, how could an accident like this happen? My daughter could have been seriously hurt."

Her daughter could've been seriously killed. It seemed whiny to point that out, so I kept my mouth shut.

Mr. Carstairs was with the museum. A nicer, more ineffectual man never breathed. He stood at the bottom of the stairs wringing his hands—over my brush with death or the ruined bust I wasn't sure.

"How?" Mother's brows were drawn. Standing on the landing with that haughty expression on her face, she looked ready to pronounce, in Red Queen fashion, "Off with his head."

Mr. Carstairs swallowed loud enough for everyone to hear him. "Perhaps the vibrations from so many in the museum..."

Vibrations? Doubtful. Martha and Robert were heavy. It would have required an earthquake, or at least a healthy shove to send one of them over the bannister. I stared at the newels above me, someone had pushed the marble statue on purpose.

My hands shook. I folded them in my lap and stared at Robert Long's ruined visage. The marble seemed to have impacted several steps below me. If Kinky hadn't knocked me down, I might have walked under it.

I'd seen enough. I raised the heels of my hands to my eyes and held them there. If I rubbed, which I desperately wanted to do, I'd be covered in mascara. "I'd like to go home."

I uncovered my eyes and looked up at Mother.

Aunt Sis had joined her on the landing. Mother in her Chanel and white helmet of hair looked coolly elegant—ice queen elegant. Aunt Sis, wearing a boho caftan and sporting a greying ponytail looked cool. So different—yet they shared a certain set to their mouths, as if they took Robert Long's shattered head as a personal affront.

"I'll take you, sugar." Daddy stood and extended a hand toward me. "Frances, I'm taking Ellison home."

The set of Mother's mouth firmed to a near invisible line.

"Don't be silly, Harrington." Aunt Sis descended a few steps. "You stay here with Frances. I'll take Ellison home."

Mother's mouth relaxed. Slightly. At least her lips were visible.

"Do you think you ought to go to the hospital?" asked Daddy.

"No!" I'd spent far too much time in hospitals of late. Aside from a dull pain where my head had hit the marble stair, I was fine. I explored the area with my fingers and found a relatively small lump. "I just need an ice pack and an ottoman."

Daddy and Aunt Sis loaded me into the car. Aunt Sis drove me home, led me to the kitchen, sat me on a stool by the counter, poured a tumbler full of wine and put it in my hands.

I gave it back to her. "May I have water instead?"

She went to the fridge, pulled out a pitcher of water and poured me a glass. "That statue falling wasn't an accident."

"How can you be sure?" Aside from the fact that it was physically impossible for Long to have fallen over the edge.

"I was on the third floor. I heard the crash and then the sound of someone running. By the time I reached the second floor the hall was empty. I looked over the rail and saw the statue and some man. When he got up, I saw you. She held her right hand over her left breast. "My heart nearly stopped."

"Where did the person in the hall go?"

"They must have run toward the family stairs."

There were three staircases in Corinthian Hall—the majestic front stairs where Robert's bust had shattered, the servants' stairs that provided my escape from Joan, and the family stairs. Those ran from the first floor porte cochère all the way to the third floor.

The lump on the back of my head throbbed.

"Who wants you dead?"

I didn't have an answer.

Max and Grace wandered into the kitchen. Max rubbed his head against my leg. Grace asked, "What are you doing home?"

She didn't need to hear about my brush with death. "What do you say to your aunt?"

My daughter grinned. Just yesterday, Grace and Sis had taken one look at each other and settled into a relationship as comfortable as well-worn shoes. "Hi, Aunt Sis." She opened the refrigerator and surveyed its contents. "So, why are you home? I figured you'd be there till the bitter end."

"Your mother was injured."

Grace turned away from the fridge and regarded me, concern wrinkling her brow. "Are you okay?"

"It was just an accident." My expression dared Aunt Sis to disagree. "I'm fine."

"What happened?" she asked.

"A statue fell." I spoke quickly, not allowing Aunt Sis time to spout her attempted murder theory. Grace had been through enough. She didn't need to worry that someone was trying to kill her mother. "I've just got a bump on my head. That's all." I glanced at the clock on the wall. "What are you doing home? I thought you and Donna were going to a movie."

"It was sold out." Grace closed the refrigerator door. "We have nothing to eat."

Nothing but a refrigerator full of fruit, vegetables, cheese, cold cuts, and Aggie's chicken salad. "Is Donna here?"

She nodded. "She's spending the night."

No surprise there. "There are lemon coolers in the cookie jar." I kept a large supply of Donna's favorite cookie on hand.

Grace grabbed a plate from the cabinet and transferred most

of the contents of the cookie jar to it. "Thanks, Mom. You're sure you're okay?"

"I'm fine."

She picked up the plate of cookies and paused. "You'd tell me if anything was wrong, right?"

"Of course." My nose itched like hell. I tightened my grip on my glass of water and smiled at my daughter. "I'm going to go to bed early. I'll be fine in the morning."

Grace took her cookies and returned to the family room.

"You're not going to tell her?" I could hear the disapproval in Aunt Sis's voice.

"I am not."

"It seems to me the truth would be the best policy."

I snorted. An omission—especially one that kept worry wrinkles off Grace's face—was a better policy.

"She's a tough kid." That was indisputable. Between her father's death and recent events, Grace was a walking billboard for Nietzsche—that which does not kill us makes us stronger. "You could tell her."

I shook my head. "Not now." Not ever.

We stared at each other for a moment, then she shrugged. "She's your daughter. Who was that horrible woman who grabbed you in the foyer?"

"Joan Hanes."

"She looked very angry with you."

"I wouldn't give her a painting for a charity auction." Surely turning down her request wouldn't equate to attempted murder.

Aunt Sis took a long drink from the tumbler of wine. "Well, I'm going to call Detective Jones in the morning and tell him what happened."

Holy hell.

"I wish you wouldn't."

"Why?" Aunt Sis tilted her head as if she couldn't understand why I didn't want to call a homicide detective about an attempted murder.

There was a question I didn't care to examine.

I donned a look which I hoped said *please, please, please don't tell Anarchy about this*. "Maybe someone just wanted to ruin Mother's party. Maybe someone didn't like the expression on Robert's face. Maybe..." I ran out of maybes. "Please don't."

She huffed. "Fine. But if anything else happens, I'm calling him."

"Fair enough." After all, what could happen?

FOUR

Max woke me up. The last time the dog awakened me by pacing in front of the bedroom door, someone died in my hostas. I glanced at the clock and groaned. Three? Sleep is slow in coming when you're trying to figure out who might want you dead. At two, I'd finally come to the tired conclusion that Mother had more enemies than I did. No one tried to kill me with Long's bust; someone had wanted to spoil her party. Simple as that.

It had to be.

Max growled again, low and menacing. The sound sent a shiver down my spine, and I reached into my bedside table for my gun.

Once I'd thrown on a robe, my fearless pooch led the way into the hall. He walked slowly, deliberately, with a ridge of hair standing at attention down the length of his back.

Who was it who said, *déjà vu all over again*? Yogi Bear?

I followed Max to the dark kitchen, empty and silent except for a scratching sound on the outside door. My fingers tightened on my gun and my heart thumped in my chest. For a moment I didn't move. The certainty that the person making those scratching sounds meant me harm froze my limbs. A smart woman would have learned by now—call the police first; go downstairs second. Not me.

I swallowed around the dryness in my throat and yelled, "I called the police."

The scratching stopped.

"They're on their way." A justifiable lie if ever there was one.

"Why'd you do that?" My sister's slurry voice was loud enough to carry through a closed door—loud enough to wake my neighbors. Mrs. Hamilton next door *would* call the police, and I'd get a citation for making too much noise.

I put the gun on the counter, hurried across the kitchen and opened the door before Marjorie could yell anything else.

She stood on my back stoop with her dress askew, her mascara smeared, and her hair a mess. Vapors of sex and gin rose off her like mist from a lake at dawn. She clutched the front door key in her hand and gazed at me bleary-eyed, seemingly surprised the door had opened without her inserting the key in the lock.

Oh. Dear. Lord.

Max seemed to agree with my assessment. He growled deep in his throat and his doggy nose wrinkled.

"Where have you been?" My words and tone belonged to Mother.

"Out." Her word and tone belonged to a surly teenager. She held up her key. "This doesn't work."

"Wrong door." My whole body vibrated with tension. I'd nearly been flattened by a statue and she stayed out until the wee hours then scared me half to death? What was she thinking? "With whom?"

"None of your bithness."

An answer guaranteed to set my teeth on edge. But my sister was right. Her...her sex partners were none of business. I really didn't want to know who'd dropped her on my back stoop. Well, maybe I did—a little. I drew air deep into my lungs and straightened my spine. "I don't care who you sleep with. But as long you're staying with me, and as long as Grace is in this house, do not come home at three o'clock in the morning looking like some drunk floozy."

She stiffened, raised her chin, and looked down her nose. "I've never looked like a floozy in my life." Then she hiccupped.

Where's a hand mirror when you need it?

"You're acting like Mother."

Six months ago, such a comment might have wounded me. Now, it glanced off me unfelt. Mother and I might not see eye to eye on some things—most things—but she had her good points. Comparing me to her wasn't the insult that Marjorie intended.

"What happened to you?" I didn't mean that night. It was all too obvious what had happened to her—probably more than once. I meant in the larger sense. Where was my golden-girl sister who'd been touched with a magic wand of good fortune? She'd wanted and got a handsome, successful husband (yes, he sold and manufactured condoms with lurid names but no one is perfect). She had lovely, well-behaved children. She lived in an enormous house. She volunteered at the right places, sat on the right committees, and attended the right parties.

Aside from the condoms, Marjorie had the life Mother wished for both of us.

So why was she on my back steps stinking of gin and sex with a man not her husband, wiping her eyes and pretending that adultery was the moral equivalent of a speeding ticket?

Pity ate at the edges of my annoyance. "Come inside. I'll make us some coffee."

"Decaf?"

"Yes."

"Do you have cream?"

"Of course."

"And raw sugar? I only use raw sugar."

What the hell was raw sugar? Did she want to gnaw on sugar cane like the boy in the C & H commercial? Whatever raw sugar was, I didn't have it. It probably didn't matter. Marjorie was so far gone I could put salt in her coffee without her noticing. I nodded. "Of course, I have some."

"You're sure about the sugar? The raw stuff is healthier."

If you ask me, sugar is sugar. As for the pity I felt, it melted away like…like sugar in a cup of coffee.

I set her at the island, filled Mr. Coffee with decaffeinated grounds and water, and pushed his button.

"You want to tell me what you're thinking?"

"You wouldn't understand."

"Try me."

She rubbed her eyes and the circles of smudged mascara expanded. "Life isn't what I expected."

I said nothing.

"Don't judge me!"

"I wasn't." I was.

"You were too. You think I'm being whiny and self-indulgent."

If the shoe fits...

She dropped her head to her hands. "There has to be more."

So wife, mother and community volunteer wasn't enough for her. Fair enough. "Have you thought about getting a job?"

The look she gave me...I might have suggested she grow a third arm or have her face lift loosened. So, no job.

"It's so easy for you to say that. You have a skill." Was it resentment or liquor that put the edge in her voice?

"Get a skill. Go back to school."

My sister curled the corner of her lips and sneered at me. "You have no idea what it's like to be the sum of other people's parts."

Like Frankenstein? "What do you mean?"

She donned that put-upon look only older sisters can pull off. "I'm Greg's wife, Thea and Porter's mother, the Junior League's vice-president...When do I get to be me?"

"The kids will be in college soon."

"I am not waiting five years," she snapped.

"Well, I'm pretty sure sleeping with other men isn't going to help."

"What do you know?"

A lot. I knew that her adultery wouldn't just hurt Greg, but also my niece and nephew. I knew the man who dropped her off without making sure she was safely inside wasn't worth destroying her marriage. And I knew she couldn't fill a hole in herself with other people. I poured her a cup of decaf with cream and regular sugar and handed it to her. "I'm here if you need me."

Marjorie groaned.

Max growled.

"What?" I asked him.

He regarded me with amber eyes then sat himself in front of the back door.

"Nope, mister. You are not going out to chase squirrels in the middle of the night."

He growled again, deeper this time.

I crossed to the back door, locked it, and wagged a finger at him. "Absolutely not."

A light flared outside. I squinted and pressed my nose against glass that reflected the cheerful kitchen rather than revealing the happenings in my back yard.

The unexplained light raced toward me. What the—? The sound of breaking glass echoed across my patio followed by a burst of flames.

Max barked wildly.

I threw open the back door and ran outside. Fire climbed the side of my house like a trellis, bearing white and yellow roses of flame and acrid black smoke.

"Call the fire department!"

Max raced past me and disappeared into the darkest corner of the yard where his barks grew more frenzied.

I grabbed the garden hose, turned on the spigot and aimed what seemed a pitifully weak stream of water at the base of the fire.

Marjorie appeared, phone book in hand. "What's the number?"

Was she kidding? "Call the operator. She'll connect you." My sister was lucky the house needed the hose's spray. Otherwise she'd have found herself on the receiving end of a stream of water.

Bang!

A bullet ricocheted off the bricks.

I ducked. I cursed. And, were my house not on fire with my daughter inside, I would have run for cover. Instead I tightened my grip on the hose and took cover behind a wrought iron settee.

Marjorie disappeared into the house. Seconds later she was back, clutching my gun. She lifted the weapon.

"No! You might hit Max!"

She turned, regarded me with bleary, slightly crazed eyes, and squeezed the trigger.

The bullet whizzed well wide of me and headed toward Margaret Hamilton's house. Even above the fire, I heard glass breaking. The woman was going to hex me for sure.

"Put down the gun!"

"But..." Marjorie swung the .22 wildly and I crouched closer to the ground.

In the darkness behind us, Max offered up a last outraged bark. Whoever had tossed a firebomb at my home then shot at me was gone.

"Put the gun back on the counter. Please." A drunk woman with a fire arm could only make a bad situation worse. "Go wake Grace, Donna and Sis. Get them out of the house."

With a snap, crackle and pop, the window sill burst into flames. I aimed the water there. At least the smoke no longer seemed so thick and oily.

Grace and Donna appeared in the backdoor, their faces marked by fear. "The noise woke us. What happened?" asked Grace.

"What can I do?" Aunt Sis stood next to her.

There was only one hose. "Make sure Marjorie put my gun down and see if she called the fire department."

The distant sound of sirens suggested someone had.

"What else?" asked Aunt Sis.

"Go meet the firemen in the front yard. Show them where to come." She went and I lifted the nozzle and sprayed water at a second floor shutter that was smoking as if it intended to burst into flames. Thank God I lived in a brick house. Thank God whatever had hit the house hadn't sailed through a window. Thank God Mother wasn't here.

Two out of three ain't bad.

Mother and Daddy charged around the side of the house.

Daddy's salt and pepper hair stood up in tufts and Mother's hair was a bit flat on the left side. Daddy saw us and his tight expression relaxed. Not so for Mother, the expression on her face somehow combined outrage and extreme annoyance.

"What happened?" she demanded, her tone suggesting I was somehow to blame.

"Someone firebombed the house." Marjorie sidled past Grace and Donna and joined us on the patio then hiccupped. Loudly.

Mother stared at her for a few seconds then added deep disapproval to her expression. "Where have you been?"

"Out."

"With whom?"

Their conversation sounded all too familiar.

"I reckon that fire is out, Ellie." Daddy stepped forward and took the hose from my hand. "Why don't you sit down?"

Because if I sat, I might not be able to get up again. I was familiar with adrenaline rushes. When this one passed, I'd be weak as a kitten. "Who called you?" I asked. "How did you know to come?"

Daddy jerked his chin toward Margaret Hamilton's house. "She says someone shot at her."

"Marjorie was returning fire. She shot wide." Very wide. Wrong direction wide.

"Returning fire?"

"Someone shot as us." My sister giggled. "Ellishon hid behind the settee."

Really, Marjorie should never drink.

Daddy glanced at the lacy iron of the settee then held up his hand for silence.

Marjorie donned a sullen (or maybe shullen) expression. The look on Daddy's face—well, it was almost as disapproving as Mother's. And all that disapproval landed on me. "Let me understand this. Someone threw a Molotov cocktail at your house?"

"Yes." Clear, assured, succinct—that was me.

"And even though you knew there was an arsonist in your backyard, you ran outside and grabbed the hose?"

"Yes." Still clear, less assured, very succinct.

"And someone shot at you?"

"Yes." More of a mumble now.

"That's when your sister returned fire?"

I barely nodded.

"So, just tonight, there have been two attempts on your life?"

I didn't answer.

Mother scowled, no doubt remembering the disruption of the benefactors' party.

"What's the name of that detective? Smith?"

"Jones." Mother pronounced Anarchy's name as if it was a flesh-eating disease.

"We need to call him."

Oh dear Lord. Daddy and Aunt Sis were on the same page. Anarchy was as good as called.

Daddy shifted his gaze to Marjorie. "Marji, go inside and clean yourself up."

She stared at him for a moment, her mouth hanging open. Daddy cajoled or charmed or sweet-talked, he didn't give orders. Especially orders not softened by *please.*

"Now." It was a voice from our childhood. One reserved for missed curfews and boys he didn't like. "Wash your face and put on something decent."

Marjorie's chin trembled. She turned on her heel, stumbled, clutched at the smoke blackened wall, and disappeared inside.

Daddy shifted his gaze to Grace and Donna who wore short nighties. "Girls, go get your robes. Grace, while you're upstairs, make sure your aunt finds the bathroom. Go on, the firemen will be here any minute now."

Mother looked positively horrified, someone-just-presented-her-with-a-dead-rat horrified. "She's tipsy."

"Frances, she's three sheets."

Mother's lips thinned to nothing. She looked at me and said, "How could you let this happen?"

"How could Marjorie getting sauced possibly be Ellison's fault?" asked Aunt Sis. Three firemen stood behind her. They wore hats. They carried axes. And they looked almost disappointed that they didn't have a chance to use them.

"It's not her fault," insisted my intrepid aunt.

"Stay out of this, Sis." Mother's voice matched her expression with a slight adjustment. Not just one rat. A whole platter of rats.

Daddy held up his hands in a peace-making gesture. Mother ignored him. "What have you done?"

She meant me.

"First someone pushes a statue over the bannister and spoils my party and now they've tried to burn you alive. What have you done?"

"Nothing."

She snorted, her disbelief apparent in the air she breathed.

Fortunately, another fireman chose to drag a heavy hose around the corner of the house. For a moment, we all stared at him.

Unfortunately, the staring soon ended, and Daddy strode toward the back door and the phone.

"Where are you going?" Mother asked. "We're not done here." She had to be truly and utterly furious if she was willing to have this discussion in front of four curious firemen.

"I'm going to call Detective Jones."

"My date?" asked Sis.

"Your date?" The tone of Mother's voice should have been a warning.

Aunt Sis ignored the warning. "He's escorting me to your gala. Ellison introduced us."

Max chose that moment to return from his adventures in the backyard. He was muddy. He was wet.

And he shoved his muddy, wet nose deep into Mother's most private parts.

Not just rats. Not even a platter full of rats. A heaping platter of rotting rats, garnished with snakes and spiders. That was the look Mother gave me.

FIVE

It turns out that not even my father, who plays golf with the police commissioner at least twice a month, can get a homicide detective out of bed when said homicide detective is not on call. He can, however, get a marked police car with two policemen inside parked in my driveway.

I didn't complain about either result.

I was glad the policemen were there. I was glad Anarchy wasn't. He complicated things.

Grace, Donna, Sis and I trudged back up the stairs to the sound of Marjorie's snores and headed for our rooms. My bed called to me like the sirens called to sailors. Like Odysseus, I overcame temptation and went instead to the bathroom and stripped off my nightgown and robe. They stank of smoke, and tiny holes marked the spots where cinders had landed. Trash. Expensive, Italian, La Perla trash.

I climbed into the shower and washed the smoke from my hair and body. The adrenaline that had sustained me through the fire washed down the drain with the shampoo bubbles. I patted myself dry, crawled into bed and slept.

Five minutes later—it felt like five minutes, in truth, four hours later—someone knocked on my bedroom door.

"Come in," I croaked.

Aggie appeared, coffee mug in hand. "Detective Jones is here to see you."

I groaned and reached for the mug.

"What happened last night?" Aggie is an observant type, she

studies things, notices details. Right now she was observing me, and if the furrow in her brow was any indication, she was worried about what she saw.

"Someone threw a firebomb at the house. When I went outside and grabbed the hose, he shot at me." That was undeniably what happened, but it felt off, wrong.

"He?"

"Or she," I conceded. "Is everyone else still asleep?"

Aggie nodded and her earrings, dangling and purple, bobbed. The furrow remained firmly in place.

"Would you please tell Detective Jones I'll be down in a few minutes?"

"Of course." She wrinkled her nose. "It smells like smoke in here."

"I left the clothes I was wearing in the bathroom."

She crossed the room, opened the bathroom door and a wave of odor broke upon us. My eyes watered.

"I don't think I can save these."

Her voice sounded choked.

"No," I agreed. "Throw them away."

She scooped up my ruined clothes and left.

I swung my legs out of bed and headed toward the bathroom. What had I been thinking leaving my smoke saturated clothing in there? Everything from the towels to the shower curtain would have to be washed. I grabbed my toothbrush and glanced in the mirror.

A crazy woman stared back at me. A crazy woman who'd stolen Phyllis Diller's hair (Phyllis Diller's hair on an epically bad hair day). Granted, my hair was longer than hers, but the strands stood out from my head at odd angles, tangling and twisting and turning like pipe cleaners. It was a back-comb experiment gone bad, an electrocuted bouffant, a—I shook my head—a demented cross between Ronald McDonald and Hamburglar.

I reached up and touched it. This was not a brush out. This was a scarf-covered trip to the salon. With Anarchy Jones waiting for me downstairs, this was a disaster.

I shouldn't care. I shouldn't. But Anarchy Jones always seemed to catch me at my worst.

I brushed my gritted teeth, tied a scarf around Medusa's locks, donned a caftan and descended the front stairs.

Anarchy waited for me in the foyer, his hands wrapped around a cup of coffee.

His gaze flew to my hair—maybe my face, but probably my hair. "Good morning."

Not hardly. "Shall we sit in the living room?" I chose the corner of the couch, crossed my ankles and folded my hands in my lap.

"Do you want to tell me what happened?" He sat down next to me.

No. But I did it anyway. I told him about the statue, about the fire, even about the prickling on the back of my neck at the grocery store.

A scowl created little commas at the edge of his mouth and a wrinkle appeared between his coffee brown eyes, but he didn't say a word, not until I'd finished talking.

"Any idea who might want you dead?"

I shook my head. "None."

He rubbed his face with the palm of his hand. "We'll need to arrange protection."

"Protection?" I squeaked.

He nodded.

"In the meantime, let's go out back and you can show me what happened."

I didn't argue. A trip through the kitchen meant more coffee in my cup.

We stood on the patio and stared at the wall of my house. Smoke and soot had turned the carnelian hued bricks to ebony.

Anarchy's scowl deepened. "So someone threw—" he bent and picked up a piece of broken glass with his fingertips "—a Molotov cocktail at your house and you ran outside." There it was, the judgmental tone I'd been expecting.

"I did. I grabbed the hose."

"Grace was inside?"

"I sent Marjorie to wake her." A teensy-weensy bit of acid might have made its way into my tone.

The corner of his lips twisted slightly. "Where were you standing?"

Since the firemen had shoved my patio furniture onto the lawn, telling Anarchy I'd stood near the settee would be useless. I closed my eyes and recreated the patio as it had been before the fire. The settee had sat in front of the kitchen windows.

I walked to the spot. "Here. I was here."

"And then someone shot at you?"

I nodded.

"You say the bullet hit the house?"

"It did."

Anarchy didn't respond. Instead, he approached the blackened bricks near the window and studied them. After a moment, he turned. "You're sure this is where you were standing?"

"Positive."

"Humph." He took a step toward the door and studied those bricks instead. He took another five or six steps before he found what he was looking for. "Here."

"What?"

"This is where the bullet hit." Anarchy tapped the wall.

"Thank heavens they were a bad shot. They'd missed me by several feet.

He rubbed his chin and his eyes searched the yard as if the mysterious gunman still lurked among the blue spruce. "I think we should go to the museum."

"I can't."

He tilted his head as if he couldn't quite believe I'd told him "no."

He should believe it. There was no way I was going anywhere but Salon Kunz. After that, my presence was required at the ballroom. Mother wanted me on hand to triple check the seating chart with the table assignments—a task that promised hours of untold misery.

"It's important."

So was Mother's gala. I patted the scarf that hid my hair. My trip to the salon was even more important.

Anarchy strode across the patio, planted his feet immediately in front of me, and stared at me. "Someone is trying to kill you."

Good thing the would-be killer was inept. I raised my shoulders then let them fall.

The commas bracketing his mouth deepened. "Aren't you concerned?"

Of course I was, but if I acknowledged the icy fear that had taken up residence in my heart, it would spread. I took a sip of deliciously hot coffee and shook my head. "There has to be some other explanation."

Anarchy closed his hand around my arm then turned and pointed at the bullet hole in my house. "Someone set a fire to get you outside then shot at you."

I knew that. I'd been there. I just couldn't believe it. "Maybe they were shooting at Marjorie."

"Why would someone shoot at Marjorie?"

"No idea. But I have no idea why someone would shoot at me either."

With his free hand, Anarchy rubbed the furrow between his brows then shifted his gaze back to me. Emotions flitted across his face. Annoyance. Irritation. Exasperation. And then something softer. "I don't want anything to happen to you."

A smart reply raced to my lips then stalled there.

Every so often—rarely—when Anarchy looks at me, his eyes warm. They were warm now—delicious, first-cup-of-coffee-in-the-morning warm.

He brushed an escaped strand of hair away from my face and my cheek tingled where his fingers touched my skin.

The world around us faded like a watercolor painting left out in the rain. The soot, the brilliant leaves—burnt umber, orange-red, gamboge, and the Tyrian purple of the now-trampled pansies planted in my hosta beds dimmed.

Something sparked between us, more electric than lightning, more seductive than Marjorie's plunging dress ever dreamed of being.

My mouth went dry. My heart went wild. My feet stayed firmly planted. They should have run.

Anarchy's hand closed around the nape of my neck and brought me closer to him. Close enough to smell the mint on his breath. 1 thanked God I'd taken the time to brush my teeth.

His lips barely touched the corner of my mouth—a butterfly kiss that was ticklish and chilling and exciting enough to make my stomach plunge and soar and swoop.

My head failed me. It turned and met Anarchy's lips full on. Firm lips. Warm lips. Lips I had no business kissing. I sighed and my free hand—the one not clutching the coffee mug like a life-preserver—reached up and touched his hair. Soft. Thick.

His arm reached around me and brought me flush with his chest—all hard-muscled plains covered by an ugly plaid shirt. At that moment, I was willing to overlook the unfortunate plaid. After all, my blood fizzed like Champagne and, after nearly two years of celibacy, I ached for a man's touch. I closed my eyes, parted my lips and melted into him.

His hand at my neck pulled at the scarf in my hair.

He shouldn't do that. He should just kiss me. I tilted my head farther.

The scarf slipped away.

Every muscle in Anarchy's body tightened (I know. I was pressed against them).

His hold on me loosened.

I opened my eyes.

Anarchy's gaze was fixed on my head. He stepped away. "Ellison—" his voice sounded choked, as if he'd had a shock or was trying very hard not to laugh, "—what happened to your hair?"

All that swooping and soaring in my stomach ended. Instead,

my other organs plunged. The fizz in my blood went flat as tap water.

I grabbed my scarf from his slack fingers, somehow overcame the need to kick him in the shins, and tied the length of cloth back around my head where it belonged.

"I didn't mean to offend you."

If seduction tingled, rejection stung.

I took a giant step backward—away from intimacy, away from trust, away from Anarchy. "I'm not offended." My voice was tight and bitchy. "Not at all." I patted my scarf. "If you'll excuse me, I have an appointment." I turned on my heel.

"Should I ask Aggie where to put my things?"

I whirled around and faced him. "Your things?" My heart perched unsteadily at the edge of an abyss.

"I'm your protection."

Just a few words—but the right words to send my heart, stomach and even my spleen careening. Those organs had designated spots within my body. They needed to stay in those spots.

Anarchy Jones over morning coffee? Anarchy Jones before I went to bed at night?

"You can't stay here."

"You'd rather move into my apartment?" That eyebrow again. Arched. Amused. Assured.

"I'd rather have a police car parked in my driveway."

"Then your father shouldn't have called the police commissioner and demanded that I protect you."

I could fix that. I marched into the kitchen, picked up the phone and dialed. My parents' number rang, and I stretched the phone cord until I reached Mr. Coffee.

Anarchy leaned in the doorway, his arms and ankles crossed. For a half-second, my teenage self saw James Dean—cool, arrogant and crush-worthy. I blinked and returned to reality—being a mother on the cusp of forty with a police officer in her kitchen.

I poured more coffee into my cup.

Flora, Mother's long-suffering housekeeper, answered the phone. "Hello."

"Good morning, Flora, this is Ellison calling. May I please speak to my father?"

A moment later my father picked up the phone. "Ellie, how are you?"

"Fine, Daddy. Did you ask for Detective Jones—" I glanced at Anarchy. He didn't look James Dean cool, he looked Steve McQueen cool. "—to protect me?"

"I did."

"To stay—" My voice was too squeaky. I took a deep breath. "To stay at my house?"

"I did."

"I think having a police car in the neighborhood might be a better idea."

Anarchy, the new King of Cool, rolled his eyes.

My father simply said, "No."

"But—"

"No buts, Ellie. He'll keep you safe until they catch whoever wants to hurt you."

"Daddy." I set my tone to wheedle on the charm-your-father dial "I'll be fine. I already have Sis and Marjorie staying with me. Please call the police commissioner and tell him that Detective Jones' talents would be better used catching the perpetrator."

"No, Ellie. I want him protecting you. I trust I'll see you both this evening. Your mother has a list of errands for me a mile long; I'll talk to you later. Goodbye, sugar."

I hung up the phone and took a restorative sip of coffee. "You can't stay here."

"Your father wants me here."

"My father doesn't make the mortgage payments on this house. I do. You cannot stay."

Anarchy pushed away from the doorframe. "You are in danger."

"So find the person who wants to hurt me."

He stepped toward me. "Half the police force is working on that."

"I'm sure they'd appreciate your assistance."

"Why don't you want me here, Ellison?"

There was a question to keep me up at night. One interrupted kiss on the patio and I'd melted like peppermint ice cream covered in hot fudge sauce. One interrupted kiss and I'd forgotten everything I knew about how very undependable men were. Thank baby Moses in the bulrushes that my hair had stunned Anarchy, giving me time to come to my senses. I put the empty coffee mug on the counter and crossed my arms. "I just don't."

"That's not good enough."

"It is for me." I left him standing in the kitchen.

Twenty minutes later, I drove to Salon Kunz all too aware of the detective following me.

Kunz put me in his chair, slipped the scarf off my hair and stared. "Oh mein Gott!"

Heads turned. As if the ladies in the styling chairs had any room to judge. Half of the women staring at me (the older half) had their hair wrapped around tiny pink rollers and were surrounded by noxious clouds of ammonia chemicals strong enough to induce tears.

"What have you done?" Kunz demanded. He covered his eyes with his hand.

"Just fix it."

Without shifting the hand hiding my disastrous hair from his delicate sensibilities, he raised the other hand and snapped his fingers.

Immediately, a shampoo girl appeared. Her nametag read "Wendy".

"Take her to the bowl. Extra crème rinse."

Wendy was too well-mannered to gawk at my hair. The customers dotting Kunz's ridiculously chic salon were not. I donned a tight smile and followed Wendy to a line of black leather chairs that leaned back into black porcelain sinks.

She washed my hair, poured half a bottle of crème rinse onto my head, then ran a comb through the tangled strands.

Even with my head bent back into a porcelain bowl, the murmurs of interest from the front of the salon reached me. They were that loud.

When Wendy raised me to sitting, I saw what the fuss was about. Anarchy had claimed a chair in the reception area and stretched out his legs. He'd even picked up one of Kunz's glossy magazines filled with stylish hairstyles.

My teeth clenched.

"I'd do his hair anytime." Wendy wore a dazed, dazzled look, a look that said a cross between James Dean and Steve McQueen was lounging in reception and she wanted to be his groupie.

I said nothing.

With a lingering look over her shoulder, she led me toward Kunz's chair in the center of the salon. I nodded to several of Mother's friends, smiled at a few of mine and air-kissed Libba's cheek. Anyplace else, I would have stopped and told her about the fire. Not here. Kunz did not like being kept waiting. At all. His hissy fits were legendary. And frankly, I had enough problems without adding an angry German wielding a sharp pair of scissors.

"Call me," she said. "I want to know what you're wearing."

I nodded then hurried to Kunz's chair and climbed in.

He trimmed.

"I hear you were hurt last night at the party."

"A small accident."

He poured some miracle concoction onto my head then showed me the bottle. "It will add body and shine and softness. I will send you home with some, yes?"

"Yes." A bathroom full of expensive, miraculous hair care products was one of the costs of sitting in Kunz's chair.

He blow-dried.

I looked in the mirror. My hair had body. My hair had shine. I touched a strand. My hair felt soft. Perhaps this miracle product really was miraculous. Or perhaps that half a bottle of crème rinse

Wendy had poured on my head had something to do with the transformation.

Libba rose from Jacque's chair (yes, all the stylists were European—or at least pretended to be), and mimed a phone to her ear.

I nodded.

Kunz swept my hair into a twist, secured it with a few pins, put a bottle of hair miracle into my hands and sent me on my way.

Hammie Walsh rose from Emilio's chair and we walked to the front of the salon together. "Just a few hours away. Your mother must be excited," she said.

"She is. Thank you so much for supporting the event." Hammie and her husband had made a contribution just shy of sizeable. I smiled at her and ignored the police detective who'd looked up from his magazine.

"Well, of course, dear. It's such a worthy cause. All those adorable little children..."

Did she know what she was supporting?

"You go ahead." She waved me forward. "I'm sure your mother has given you a to-do list a mile long."

"Thank you." I pulled my checkbook out of my purse and laid it on the receptionist's desk.

Lynn, the receptionist, had a phone plastered to her ear and a pencil in her hand. "Yes, Mrs. Cooper, we have you down for next Tuesday at three." She tapped the pencil tip against an entry in a calendar so complicated it would give Einstein a headache. Maybe it had given Lynn a headache, her eyes were red-rimmed. "We'll see you then."

She hung up the phone and offered me a watery smile. "Just the trim and blow-dry today, Mrs. Russell?"

"And this." I set the bottle full of miracles next to my checkbook

Lynn patted her hair, a shade of bottle red that verged on purple. "We've been selling a lot of that lately."

I bet they had.

"With that, your total is $25."

I wrote a check and handed it to her.

Hammie picked up the bottle and studied the label.

"Thank you for the plant," said Lynn. She wiped her eyes with a tissue. "That was very kind of you."

I'd heard over the bridge table that Lynn's husband had cancer. Sending a Swedish ivy and a note expressing my thoughts and prayers seemed the least I could do.

Hammie looked up from a careful reading of the label. "That's right, I heard your husband was sick." She cocked her head like a curious robin. "Has he died yet?"

My jaw dropped.

Anarchy's magazine dropped.

Lynn stood up, sending the appointment book and a handful of pencils to the floor. With a shaking hand, she pointed toward the door. "Get out."

Hammie puffed her chest and lifted her chin. "I was just asking a question."

Lynn's voice rose, attracting attention. "You rich bitch. Who the hell do you think you are? Get out."

"Well—" Hammie brought her hand to her chest as if she'd been mortally wounded "—I'm sure Kunz won't approve of your name calling."

Lynn leaned over the edge of the counter. "Get out or I'll kill you."

Hammie paled, raised her chin another notch and walked to the door. She paused and looked over her shoulder. "Don't plan on working here after today." The door slammed behind her.

Lynn collapsed into her chair, tears streaming down her cheeks. "He only has a few weeks left—" her voice broke. She hiccupped. "I don't know how I'm going to live without him." She buried her face in her hands.

I snuck behind the desk and wrapped an arm around her shoulders. "Hammie didn't mean it. She didn't. She was just born with a sterling silver foot in her mouth."

"I could kill her." Lynn wiped her eyes. "I mean it; I really could."

Obviously she didn't know there was a homicide detective present.

Anarchy picked up the fallen magazine and put it on a side table. He stared at Lynn with his forehead creased and concern writ large across his face.

Those wrinkles probably would have been deeper if he'd known what was coming.

SIX

Some women might swoon at the sight of Anarchy Jones in a tux.

Not me.

I recovered the ability to breathe after only a few seconds.

My lungs might have inflated faster if he wasn't standing at the bottom of the stairs staring at me like I was a ray of sunshine after a month of rain.

I closed my eyes, shutting out his smile.

"Who—" Marjorie paused for breath "—is that?"

With my eyes still closed, I said, "Anarchy Jones. He's Aunt Sis's date." I didn't add that he'd taken up residence in the studio apartment in the carriage house. Given my sister's recent exploits, it didn't seem wise.

"Why are your eyes closed?" she asked.

Because Anarchy looked more mouth-wateringly dangerous in a tuxedo than James Bond. "No reason." I opened my lids and stared at Marjorie.

Oh. Dear. Lord.

The neckline of her dress plunged to her waist. Unmistakably Halston. Gun-metal blue, barely-there Halston.

I don't care for Halston. Swimming into a dead body clad in one of his designs has put me off him. Probably forever.

She pursed her lips. "You don't like my dress?"

She looked like an aging call girl, but what I thought didn't matter. "Mother's head is going to spin off her neck when she sees you."

Marjorie grinned. "As long as she doesn't vomit pea soup."

While the thought of Mother as Linda Blair possessed by a demon was amusing, Marjorie exposing her…melons as if they were produce marked for a quick sale was not. "Tomorrow, when this is over, we should talk."

"Fine." She shook her head as if she was already dismissing my opinions. "Now, introduce me to our aunt's date."

We descended the stairs. "Marjorie, this is Detective Jones. Anarchy, this is my sister, Mrs. Blake."

"Don't be so formal, Ellison." Marjorie extended her hand. She also took a deep breath and arched her back. "Please, call me Marjorie."

When I was sixteen, I glanced out the front window of my parent's home and saw my boyfriend and my sister kissing—kissing as if they were performing tonsillectomies with their tongues. I broke up with him and didn't speak to her for three months. Finally, Daddy intervened—I think the death glares at dinner gave him indigestion. Marjorie's excuse—that she wanted to prove to me that Bill couldn't be trusted—was absurd. She was the one who couldn't be trusted. With a sister like her, who needed enemies?

And now she'd set her sights on Anarchy. Acid green vines appeared from nowhere, wrapped around my heart, my lungs, and my stomach. They squeezed and twisted and sent starter shoots to my fingers, curling them into claws.

To his credit, Anarchy didn't seem to notice that my sister's breasts puffed like pigeons less than a centimeter from his chest. "A pleasure to meet you." He extended his hand and took a step backward.

"All mine." She said the words as if she were declaring intent.

Heat seared the vines to ash. Heat closed my claws into fists. What was she thinking?

What was I thinking? A cat fight in the foyer? I loosened my taut muscles.

Ding-dong.

"Is that my date?" Aunt Sis's voice floated down from the second floor.

Her date was already here. Chances were good this one was mine.

Marjorie slipped past Anarchy and opened the front door. "Hunter." Her voice sounded as seductive as warm brandy on a cold night. She rose on her toes and her arms circled his neck. Her barely covered body molded to him like cling wrap.

"Lovely to see you, Marjorie."

"Isn't it?" she purred. Since he was seeing—and feeling—most of her, maybe it really was.

The vines made a reappearance, so too did the need to yank Marjorie away from a man.

Maybe Marjorie and I shouldn't wait for tomorrow to have that talk. Maybe I should say something about her dress and the way she threw herself at men this very minute. I opened my mouth but Aunt Sis's hand on my arm stopped me from speaking. She'd come downstairs without my noticing.

"Don't," Aunt Sis whispered. "Not now."

Probably good advice. I ignored it. "Marjorie," I said through gritted teeth. "May I see you in the kitchen for a moment?"

Aunt Sis sighed.

Marjorie released her tentacles and Hunter stepped inside.

My breath caught all over again.

Hunter Tafft combines Cary Grant's charm and good looks with a level of charisma that defies description. He has prematurely silver hair, a golden tan, and very white teeth. In a tuxedo, he is perfection.

Perhaps living with perfection is wearing. He is thrice divorced.

A fact that Mother brushes aside like a bit of cottonwood fluff. In her mind, I am the fourth Mrs. Hunter Tafft.

Aunt Sis glanced at her watch then at me. "Don't you think we should be going? Your mother will have a hissy fit if we're late."

My aunt was right, but I jerked my chin to the back of the house. "Marjorie. Kitchen."

She followed me down the hallway. "What?"

I knew without looking that she'd put extra sway in her hips in case Hunter or Anarchy were watching. With my lips tightly sealed, I held open the kitchen door.

She stepped inside and I let the door swing closed behind her.

"What is it?" Marjorie demanded.

"Stay away from Anarchy." My voice shook with unexpected emotion.

She planted a hand on her silk jersey clad hip. "I see. Does that mean Hunter is fair game?"

"No!"

"So they're both off limits?" She licked her lips as if she'd just tasted something delicious and had every intention of going back for a second helping.

Damn straight they were off limits. At least to my sister.

A saturated shade of crimson clouded my vision. I raised a flattened palm, ready to slap the sexy pout off Marjorie's glossy lips, and stopped myself. Just. Instead, I fanned my flushed cheeks. Truth was, I had no claim on Anarchy or Hunter. If either, or both, of them wanted to look down my sister's dress and gaze at her toes, I had no right to stop them. I took a deep breath and held it for a few seconds. "They're not off limits, but you should be. Last time I checked, you were still married."

Her eyes thinned to mere slits. "That is none of your business."

"Figure out what's important to you, Marji. If it's your family, then stop screwing around."

"Oh, lighten up."

I responded with an eye roll that would have done Grace proud.

She crossed her arms and her breasts nearly escaped the confines of her dress. "Which one do you want? Both? Or is it just that you don't want me to have them?"

I didn't know *if* I wanted a man in my life, much less which man. This wasn't about Hunter or Anarchy. It was about something bigger. "Why would you hurl yourself at my date? We're adults now. Who does that?"

She snorted. "Try being unhappy for years on end."

"I have. And you didn't answer my question."

"You want them to look at you instead? Stop dressing like a nun."

Was she referring to the rather austere lines of the nutmeg brown Bill Blass I'd chosen? The front might say "nun" but the back plunged. I smoothed the fabric against my hip. "Just answer me."

"You get to date and go out and—"

"You think dating is fun?" Incredulity made my voice squeak. I drew a breath deep into my lungs. "Men scare the bejesus out of me." In my experience, they broke vows, broke hearts and broke trust. When it came to men, I was as skittish as a new foal. But this wasn't about men, this was about my sister wounding me on purpose. "Why throw yourself at Hunter like that?"

She rubbed her bare arm, patted an invisible strand of hair back into place and glanced around the kitchen, her gaze landing anywhere but me. "You take things too seriously, Ellison. You really do need to lighten up."

She wasn't going to answer. Damn.

If I were to paint how I felt, my brushes would create a monochromatic landscape in shades of gray. For a bit of visual interest, I'd add a leafless tree reaching its bony limbs toward the leaden sky. That tree—desolate and lonely. I bit my lips and closed my eyes for an instant—more to block out my sister's derisive glare than to stop a well of tears. Counting to ten seemed like a good idea, so I did that too. Then I took a deep breath and opened my eyes. "You can move out in the morning."

We stared at each other for a moment then she lifted her chin. "Fine."

The kitchen door swung open and Aunt Sis peeked her head in. "Girls, we need to go."

"We're ready." Marjorie swept past me without a glance.

Aunt Sis shook her head. "This promises to be a fun evening."

Exactly what I'd been thinking.

*   *   *

It was hardly a surprise that Marjorie chose to ride to the gala with Aunt Sis and Anarchy. That left me alone with Hunter, grinding my teeth in the front seat of his Mercedes.

Hunter, bless him, kept up a stream of small talk as he drove.

I looked out the window, silent and fuming.

"Let it go, Ellison."

"Pardon?"

"It's obvious you're furious with Marjorie, but for tonight, let it go."

I cut a glance his way. Perfect profile. Hands at ten and two. Eyes on the road. Three failed marriages. And no wonder. He didn't understand women at all. I snorted softly.

"There will be plenty of tension tonight with your mother wanting everything to be perfect. Don't let the problem between you and Marjorie add to it."

The problem? Was that what he was calling having my sister press her breasts through his chest and into his spine?

I said nothing.

"It's rather sad."

He looked my way.

The black mood that had settled on my shoulders like one of Mother's fox stoles lifted its head and stared at Hunter with beady eyes. "Sad?"

He nodded and returned his gaze to the road. "You've made something of your life and she's jealous."

This time, my snort wasn't soft. Marjorie and I had been handed the same tools—to whit, a copy of *Emily Post's The Blue Book of Social Usage,* a recent *Social Register*, a lifetime of listening to Mother repeat her expectations for us, and a closet full of pretty clothes.

We'd done exactly what was expected of us. We got married.

True, Mother had approved of my husband and barely tolerated Marjorie's. Of course, my late husband turned out to be a cheating, lying blackmailer. But at least he didn't manufacture condoms.

We pulled up in front of the hotel Mother had chosen for the gala and a doorman helped me out of the car. Hunter handed his keys to the valet and we stepped inside.

Mother had transformed the lobby. An igloo similar to the one children played in at the museum stood in the lobby. The igloo at the museum was made of concrete. The one in the lobby was constructed from Styrofoam blocks. Men in bear suits stood ready to startle patrons. Davy Crockett carried a musket and wore a coonskin cap.

"Wow," said Hunter. "Your mother went all out."

Mother swept toward us, reviewed my gown, then air-kissed my cheek. "Ellison, you look lovely."

"Doesn't she?" Hunter slipped an arm around my waist.

Mother positively beamed at him. "And you look dashing."

"Thank you, Frances. I am in awe of what you've created."

A satisfied smile touched Mother's lips. "Just wait until you see the ballroom." She scanned the lobby until her gaze landed on a man weighed down with camera equipment. "I thought we'd get a picture since we're all together. Hunter, you must join us." She resumed her scanning. "Now, where has your sister got to?"

Mother wanted Hunter in a family picture? That was about as subtle as clubbing him over the head and dragging him to the nearest preacher.

"Perhaps Hunter doesn't want to be photographed," I suggested.

"Don't be silly, Ellison. Of course, he does. If he didn't, why would he bring you early?" She reached out and patted his arm. "Isn't that right, Hunter?"

Hunter is too smart a man to argue with Mother. "Is that Marjorie coming out of the ballroom?"

It wasn't. It was Cassie LeCoeur. But I could see how he might be confused. Her dress was also blue...also revealing.

I pointed to Marjorie. She stood among a cluster of committee members who'd arrived early to carry out Mother's final orders. If my sister noticed their sideways glances at her exposed flesh, she didn't respond. Instead, she smiled sweetly, as if she was delighted to be making small talk with women whose husbands she'd been flirting with—outrageously—just last night.

"Go fetch her, Ellison. We need to get that picture."

Hunter's grip on my waist loosened. "I'll go."

Mother and I watched him cross the lobby, then she turned to me, her indulgent expression a thing of the past. "No bodies tonight, Ellison. I mean it. Stay out of the coat room, don't go to the ladies' room alone, and don't you dare venture inside that igloo."

Find a few corpses and all of a sudden you get painted with a very unpleasant brush. "It's not as if I killed anyone."

"But you find them when they're dead." Icebergs are warmer than the expression in Mother's eyes. "Don't find anyone tonight."

It wasn't worth pointing out that someone seemed to want me dead, that the rest of her guests were probably safe. "I'll do my best."

"See that you do." She swanned off toward the photographer, paused and looked over her shoulder. "Come along."

Hunter sent Marjorie but took himself to the bar.

Mother arranged me, Marjorie, Daddy, and Aunt Sis to her satisfaction (she did not ask Anarchy to join our family picture) then inserted herself into the center. We all donned smiles for the camera, froze while the photographer snapped shot after shot, then separated.

I accepted a drink from Hunter, who magically arrived as soon as the pictures were done. Together we crossed the lobby to the tables where the silent auction items were displayed.

Mother and Daddy greeted guests.

Aunt Sis and Anarchy stood on the edge of the room and watched expensively clad people fill the lobby.

Where Marjorie went, I didn't know. Nor did I care.

L'Air du Temps, Johnny Walker and cigarette smoke swirled together and mixed with the clink of ice in glasses, the rustle of silk and satin and velvet and the genteel conversations of people who had seen each other just that afternoon on the golf course.

We stopped by the painting I'd donated just long enough for Hunter to place the opening bid.

"Thank you." No matter how well my paintings sell, I always worry that mine will be the sole auction item without a bid.

"I intend to win." He smiled at me and for a moment I didn't know if he was talking about the painting or something else entirely.

It was an unexpected waft of air on my bare back that made me shiver. I'm sure of it.

We moved on.

"This could be interesting." Hunter tapped a bid sheet for philharmonic tickets and dinner for two at the American Restaurant. "Would you care to join me?"

My friend Libba saved me from answering. "There you are!" She made it sound as if I'd been hiding.

I hadn't been.

She offered Hunter a half-smile. "May I steal Ellison for a moment?"

He flashed his teeth. "Of course."

Libba grabbed my elbow with an icy cold hand. "I have a problem."

"Oh?"

She nodded vigorously. "My date is dead—"

My heart stopped.

"—drunk."

Lub-dub. Lub-dub. My poor heart resumed its beating and I relocated the ability to breathe. "The bar has been open for less than twenty minutes."

"He picked me up three sheets."

"And you drove with him?"

She shook her head and scowled as if I was missing the point. "Limousine."

"Where is he?"

"Apparently, he threw up in the men's room then passed out."

I refrained from comment. Libba has epically bad taste in men. This is something she knows, something she bemoans regularly. "Let's find the manager."

We located a manager, arranged to have Yancy Arnot moved to a hotel room immediately and slipped the helpful man a fifty.

Libba groaned.

"What?"

"Your mother's seating charts. She'll kill me if there's an empty spot at the table."

Mother—because what's a party for seven hundred people without adding a bit of a challenge?—had decided to offer a choice of meals. Guests could select beef tenderloin, grilled salmon or a vegetarian option. "You know people lie," she had explained.

I was all too aware of that. "What do you mean?"

"They order salmon, see the beef, and change their minds. It causes no end of trouble for the chef."

A lesser woman might have given up, allowed a free-for-all of guests claiming beef when they'd ordered fish. Not Mother. Place cards were the answer. Place cards for seven hundred guests. A "B," "S," or "V" written in the corner under the names would alert the server to the proper meal.

She completed a seating chart for seven hundred faster than most people can complete a round of golf.

And now my best friend was going to throw it off.

"Someone has to be in the ballroom," I said. "We'll have them pull Yancy's place."

Women on a mission, we wove through the crowd, smiling politely, avoiding being drawn into conversations, our eyes fixed on the closed doors.

The locked doors.

Mother wanted a "reveal" and the doors had been locked to keep the curious in suspense.

"I know another way in," said Libba.

She led me around a corner, down a corridor and through a

door clearly marked "Staff Only." Another turn or two and we were in.

The ballroom stood empty.

Libba gaped at the decor. "Your mother works miracles."

I didn't argue. "What's your table number?"

"Sixty-two."

There's a science to placing tables. Obviously, the largest donors get the best tables, the ones closest to the dance floor and stage. But what about donors who give the same amount when there's only one first-row table left? Is a second-row center table better than a table adjacent to the dance floor but just to the right of the stage? These are the questions that give ball chairmen sleepless nights.

We found table sixty-two on the second row, not exactly center, but close.

"Now what? There's no one to help us," said Libba.

I scanned the ballroom and saw a door that led back to the cocktail hour closing behind someone. A door that should have been locked.

"Let's find the kitchen," I suggested. "There's bound to be someone there."

We didn't have to. An official looking man in a black bow tie and matching vest entered the ballroom and glowered at us. "The ballroom is closed."

"Yes, of course. I'm Mrs. Walford's daughter, Mrs. Russell. My friend's escort is unable to attend this evening. We'd like his place removed from this table."

The man approached and I read his nametag.

"We'd be most appreciative, Hector." I reached into my clutch, withdrew a twenty and handed it to him. "His name is Yancy Arnot."

Hector took the bill and nodded. "I'll take care of it."

Libba and I returned to a lobby that had filled to bursting in our absence. Hunter stood near the silent auction table with Mother's hand on his sleeve. He smiled when he saw me.

"There you are, Ellison." Mother looked mildly put out. "Wherever have you been?"

"Small problem. Taken care of now."

"No one dead?" Mother does have a sense of humor. She just keeps it well hidden.

"Not yet."

She actually smiled at me. "I was just telling Hunter that no one seems to be bidding on the ski trip to Vail."

Hunter patted Mother's hand where it rested on his sleeve but looked at me. "I'll bid if you agree to go with me if I win."

"How could she refuse?" Mother gave me a looked that said clearly I'd best not refuse. "There are two bedrooms, Ellison. It's not as if Hunter is asking you to—"

"I'll go." The words flew out of my mouth faster than Franz Klammer could ski down a beginner's slope. There was no way on God's green earth I was going on a ski trip with Hunter Tafft. But asking Libba to outbid him was easier than arguing—or letting Mother finish her sentence.

The three of us walked over to the empty bid sheet and read, "One week in a two-bedroom luxury condo in Vail. Week of December 12. Valued at $400."

No one had ventured the opening bid of $200.

Hunter's eyes twinkled and I felt a twinge of unease just south of my stomach. He tapped a gold pen against the bid sheet. "Now, if I win, you promise you'll go with me?"

There was no chance he'd win. Libba owed me. "I promise."

He wrote.

Mother peered over his shoulder. "Oh!" Then she giggled. Giggled like a sixteen-year-old girl. "Ellison, you need to have your skis waxed."

I bent and looked at Hunter's bid.

Two thousand dollars.

SEVEN

A trumpet blared a fanfare and servers opened the doors to the ballroom. A cold mist blew out at the guests, circling their ankles, peeking beneath their skirts. Delighted shivers abounded.

Mother can do wonders with dry ice.

Libba charged through the mist. Hopefully, Hector had removed Yancy's place. I didn't blame her for checking.

The rest of the guests entered at a more relaxed pace.

The ballroom looked like an Inuit's vision of luxury. Northern lights played across the ceiling, pristine white tablecloths draped to a carpet sprinkled with sparkling glitter, silver Chiavari chairs surrounded the tables, and snowdrops and crocuses bloomed in the center of the tables.

Hunter and I wove our way through the crowd toward the dance floor. "We're at table sixty-seven," I said.

Except, we weren't.

Marjorie was. Aunt Sis and Anarchy were. Kinky and Cassie LeCoeur were. Tibby and Martin Davis were. Jinx and Preston George were.

Not us.

Someone had moved us.

Someone who wanted to flirt with Anarchy without my glare burning through her poor excuse for a dress?

I scowled at my sister.

Was Marjorie deliberately ignoring me? She seemed entirely too enthralled by whatever Kinky was saying to her.

He seemed enthralled by the not-thereness of her dress.

Poor Cassie seemed pale and miserable. Her hand on the top rung of her chair shook. Maybe she was struggling not to slap the come-hither look off Marjorie's face. I know I was. "This isn't our table," she said.

Kinky spared her half a glance. "Our place cards are here." He yanked Cassie's chair away from the table. "Sit."

"But—"

"Just sit, Cassie."

She sat.

"You're over here, Ellison," Libba called.

I locked my teeth together (ground them together) and took the high road. A confrontation would mean a scene. A scene would embarrass Mother. Mother embarrassed would mean a year of hell. Besides, Mother had worked so hard to make this evening a success. I wasn't going to be the one to spoil her party. I swallowed my annoyance. "Apparently we're at Libba's table."

We found our place cards. Mine was next to Hammie Walsh's. She looked up at me and smiled—a real smile, not the usual polite stretching of lips. "What a treat that we get to sit together."

With a grunt of effort, her husband lifted halfway from his seat.

"Please, don't get up."

He sank back into his chair. "Nice to see you, Ellison."

"You too, Mr. Walsh."

"You make me feel old, dear. I think it's time you called me Randolph."

With his shock of white hair and Palm Springs tan, he looked very much like a mister but who was I to argue? "Thank you, Randolph."

Hunter pulled out my chair and I sat. He claimed the seat next to mine.

Hammie rubbed her throat as if it pained her. "It's so nice that your aunt and your sister could attend."

"Isn't it?" My voice was drier than the ice Mother had used to create mist.

Hammie looked at me sharply then coughed. Not a discreet your-sarcasm-is-showing cough but an I've-smoked-a-pack-a-day-for-most-of-my-life cough. Finally, the hack subsided. She took a sip of water and asked, "How long has it been since Marjorie came for a visit?"

Not long enough. "I believe she brought the children in July but I missed her. Grace and I were in Europe."

Hammie coughed again. From the sound, I could only assume her lungs were as sooty and blackened as the back of my house.

Randolph regarded her with a furrowed brow and patted her on the back.

"Can I get you anything?"

"No, no. I'm fine." Hammie cleared her throat. "I seem to have a tickle." She lifted her near-empty water goblet to her lips and drained what was left in the glass.

"Would you like mine?" I held out the glass that had been set at the upper right of my place.

Hammie rubbed her throat. "Thank you, dear. Don't mind if I do."

She took the glass from my hands and gulped as if she'd just played eighteen holes on a broiling afternoon.

Hunter touched my arm and I turned away from Hammie's imitation of a thirsty camel.

"How long has it been since you've been skiing?" he asked.

That bid.

Two thousand dollars.

My mouth went dry at the thought and I wished I'd kept my water.

"Last winter we went to—"

"It burns!"

I turned back to Hammie.

She half-dropped my glass onto the table and covered her mouth with one hand, her throat with the other.

"What's wrong, dear?" asked Randolph.

"It burns!" Hammie's voice was raw, its pitch hysterical. She moved her hand away from her mouth. Blisters circled her lips and bubbled on her skin.

Someone at the table gasped. It might have been me.

Hammie stood, stumbled a step or two away from the table, and collapsed onto the glitter-strewn carpet.

Randolph half-rose from his seat. "We need a doctor!"

There was one at the next table.

Dr. Glen Franklin rushed toward us, took one look at Hammie and said, "She's allergic to something. Call an ambulance. Now."

"I'll call." Hunter strode toward the ballroom doors, people seemed to part for him. Probably a good thing since Hammie seemed to be convulsing.

Randolph, Glen and I knelt on the floor. Hammie clutched her throat. "I can't breathe."

"We need help!" Randolph yelled.

Randolph wasn't wrong. Glen caught babies for a living. He'd probably forgotten everything he ever learned about adverse reactions years ago. Nevertheless, he did whatever it was doctors do when they had no idea what to do. Randolph held his wife's hand.

Neither man seemed to be making much of a difference.

I climbed onto a less than steady Chiavari chair and scouted the ballroom for an emergency room doctor or an allergist. The chair wobbled and I extended my arms for balance.

Our crisis had made hardly a ripple in the noisy ballroom. Guests chatted, table hopped, and drank, undisturbed by our drama. Not even those at the tables closest to us realized there was a problem.

Mother sat at one of those tables. Anarchy sat at another. They both stared at me perched atop my unsteady chair. They both wore I-knew-something-awful-would-happen-and-Ellison-would-be-right-in-the-thick-of-it expressions. They both stood and moved toward me, thunder upon their brows.

"What are you doing?" Mother couldn't have sounded more scandalized. I might as well have streaked naked through the ballroom.

"I'm looking for a doctor."

She opened her mouth, noticed Hammie and the obstetrician on the floor, and snapped her lips shut.

"Bruce Collins is three tables over." An ear, nose and throat doctor had to know more about a closing throat than Glen Franklin.

"Get down from there." Low-pitched with all the subtlety of a buzz-saw—that was Mother's voice.

Anarchy offered me a hand and I descended from the chair.

Poor Hammie sounded as if she was breathing through a very small, very clogged cocktail straw. Her face, the part of her face not disfigured by blisters, was tinged with blue.

"What—" Mother glared at me as if I was personally responsible for Hammie's distress "—happened?"

"She's dying!" Randolph squeaked in a pitch usually reserved for teenaged girls screaming at movie stars or musicians.

The obstetrician on the floor next to Hammie didn't argue.

"Help her!" Tears formed in Randolph's eyes. "Please. Help her."

Anarchy Jones donned his cop face—hard-edged, suspicious, and intimidating. "We need a surgeon."

Mother brought her hand to her heart. "A surgeon?"

"Emergency tracheotomy. Does anyone have a pen?"

Mother swayed on her feet.

For a moment it looked as if she might join Hammie on the glittery carpet but she straightened her shoulders, eyed the ballroom full of people, then shifted her gaze to her dying friend. "Fine. I'll get you one." She disappeared into the crowd but she went the wrong way.

Bruce Collins was to the left.

I ran to his table and tapped him on the shoulder. "We need you!"

To his credit, Bruce didn't ask questions. He stood and followed me back to table sixty-two where Glen was shaking his head and Randolph was shaking.

Glen shook his head. "It's too late."

Too late? It couldn't be too late. I'd been talking to Hammie not five minutes ago. Except her chest wasn't moving and the desperate rasp of her breathing had stopped.

I fell to my knees next to Randolph and dared put my hand on his shoulder. Silent sobs racked his body. With his right hand he rubbed his chest and then his left arm.

"Glen. Bruce." I jerked my chin toward Randolph, who showed symptoms of a heart attack.

Both men shifted their attention to someone who needed them. Together they helped Randolph into a chair.

Anarchy touched my arm, pulling me away from a discussion of Randolph's possible heart attack. "What did she eat or drink before this happened?"

"Nothing. Just water." I pointed to the two water glasses at Hammie's place. "See?"

"Where did the second glass come from?" he asked.

"It's mine. She drank all of hers and still had a tickle in her thro..." My voice died. The ability to speak slaughtered by the expression on Anarchy's face.

"This is a crime scene." Anarchy's voice was as dangerous as his expression. He turned his rather scary gaze on Glen and Bruce.

Glen opened and closed his mouth like a goldfish. Bruce flushed.

Mother rushed back to the table, pale, regal, and pen in hand. "I have a—"

"She's dead." If Virgil himself had taken Randolph by the hand and led him to the gates of Dante's inferno, the poor man couldn't have sounded more hopeless.

Mother stared at Hammie for a moment then shifted her gaze to the full ballroom before settling her icy stare on me.

Anarchy, who didn't know how to read Mother's mind, didn't realize she'd just affixed blame for the destruction of her gala on me. If he had, perhaps he wouldn't have said, "This is a crime scene. No one touches the body or the table. Make sure of it." Then his hand circled my wrist. "You're coming with me." He dragged me past a few tables.

I pulled against him. "Wait. What? Where are we going?"

His narrow-eyed, dangerous expression hit me right between the eyes. "She died after drinking your water. We're calling for backup."

I stopped dead in my tracks, processing the idea that poison meant for me had killed Hammie. Nearly pushing a statue on top of me was one thing—it spoke of sudden anger or a spur of the moment decision—but poison? It couldn't be. He was wrong.

Anarchy tugged on my arm. "I have to make that call, Ellison. Come on. Now."

"Problem?" Hunter's voice combined urbanity and possessiveness. So did the expression in his eyes.

Anarchy tugged again. "Someone tried to kill Ellison."

I jerked my head. Anarchy was wrong. He had to be. I looked at Hunter as if he could change the last few minutes. "The allergic reaction—" I crossed my arms over my chest. "Hammie died." Over the course of five words her death became real. All the air whooshed out of my lungs and stars danced around my head—a galaxy waltzing past my eyes.

Hunter's hand on my back was warm. "You need to sit down."

I did. My legs had lost the strength to hold me.

Hunter turned toward the nearest table. "Martin, Ellison isn't feeling well. Would you mind giving up your chair for a moment? Please?"

Hunter and Anarchy helped me to Martin Bishop's chair. Someone offered me water.

I pushed it away. Closed my eyes.

Hammie was dead. I'd been talking to her, she'd coughed, drank two glasses of water, and died.

I felt stares—felt them as actual touches. Some were concerned. A few were gloating (delighted to see me—or Frances Walford's daughter—in distress again). Most were curious.

Hunter knelt on one side of my chair, Anarchy on the other.

Their stares felt different from the rest. That difference...I shifted in my chair, opened my eyes. "Does anyone have any scotch? I just need a sip."

Martin Bishop (bless him) put a half-empty old-fashioned glass in my hand. I drained it.

"I have to call this in." Anarchy looked at Hunter. "You'll take care of her."

Hunter answered with a curt nod. "I will."

They stared at each other for another few seconds—some silent, testosterone-fueled communication I couldn't hope to understand.

"I'll be back," said Anarchy.

Hunter grimaced. "I know."

Anarchy strode away.

I sat and stared at the empty scotch glass.

"Ellison—" Hunter brushed a strand of hair away from my cheek "—what do you need?"

I needed to stop finding bodies—although strictly speaking, I hadn't found Hammie's.

I glanced around the ballroom. The ripples of distress that had started at table sixty-two had spread. Everyone knew something was wrong. Mother's party was ruined. Not just ruined. Ruined in tragic fashion. And she blamed me. "I think I'd like another scotch."

Things really couldn't get any worse.

Why? Why? Why do I keep thinking things like that?

EIGHT

The magic of northern lights on the ceiling, silvered tree branches dripping crystal icicles, and glitter strewn across the carpet—all that faded. That's what happens when you're locked in a ballroom with seven hundred restless people.

Glamor turns tawdry in no time at all.

Of course, watching both Hammie and Randolph being wheeled out on gurneys didn't exactly add to the party atmosphere. There's nothing less glamorous than dying by asphyxiation or having a heart attack. At least Randolph was headed to the hospital and not the morgue.

And then there was Mother. She stared at the ballroom as if its existence was an affront. She looked ready to murder someone. Maybe me. Maybe Anarchy. Definitely Anarchy. He was the one who'd insisted every person in the ballroom be interviewed before they could leave.

Her guests, CEOs and doctors and lawyers and their wives, were now murder suspects—or at least material witnesses.

Mother's lips were so pinched she was in danger of giving herself permanent wrinkles. Thank God she was pretending I didn't exist. I sank lower in my chair and longed for something alcoholic.

The hotel staff had wheeled in a few portable bars but the lines for a drink were nearly as long as the line to talk to the police. Hunter braved a line for me. Maybe for himself as well. When he arrived at the table, his drink looked more scotch than water.

He handed me a glass of amber-hued escape. "I have a few clients here."

A few was probably an understatement.

"They want me to be there when they talk to the police. It won't take long. Will you be all right?"

I sipped, nodded, and sipped again.

Somewhere on the other side of the ballroom, a woman had hysterics.

The lines around Mother's lips deepened.

Hunter dropped a kiss on the top of my head and disappeared into the restless crowd.

Just when I thought I'd get a moment's peace, Aunt Sis claimed the chair next to mine. She'd somehow commandeered a whole bottle of scotch so I didn't complain.

I held out my glass and she topped me off.

"Mother is never going to forgive me." I drank.

She patted my knee. "How could she possibly blame you?"

I snorted softly.

"Don't be silly, Ellison. They may look annoyed now, but these people are thrilled. Being interviewed by the police is the most exciting thing that's ever happened to ninety-nine point nine percent of the people in this room. They'll dine out on tonight for decades. This party will live forever. Frances will get over her snit when she realizes that."

I stared at my aunt. Did she really not understand? There was an enormous difference between a party remembered because it was perfect and a party remembered because someone died at the dinner table. Not just died—died horribly. Mother's gala might live forever—but it would live in infamy. Whoever wrote *I wonders* for the society magazine was going to have a field day at Mother's expense. I felt my own lips pinch.

Aunt Sis leaned forward. Her eyes glittered and her breath smelled strongly of Johnny Walker. "I mean it. Everyone is secretly thrilled. The closest any of these people have come to walking on the edge is voting for George McGovern."

Aunt Sis was wrong. My late, lying, cheating, no-good husband had proved that. His legacy included a safe stuffed with files on our friends and neighbors. Those files included scandalous predilections, infidelities, theft, and even a secret baby. Just try having a conversation with your insurance man when you know his underwear is probably lacier than yours. As soon as it got cold enough to justify a fire in the hearth, I planned on burning everything. Until then, only Hunter and I knew of their existence. I didn't reply to Aunt Sis's specious claim. Instead I sipped my scotch and longed to be tucked safely in bed.

Marjorie wandered over. Apparently even she realized that shameless flirting at a crime scene was *de trop*. She sat on the other side of Aunt Sis.

Aunt Sis nodded a welcome then brushed some glitter from her caftan. "It was very handy having a homicide detective here, don't you think?"

Because you never knew when you might need one?

Marjorie snorted, saving me the trouble.

"I think he's charming." Aunt Sis offered me a telling look.

Charming?

Handsome? Definitely.

Bossy? Absolutely.

Charming? I knew for certain that Mother wasn't charmed.

My neck prickled, the same something-wicked-this-way-comes feeling I'd had at the grocery store. I looked over my shoulder at a room full of people. Joan Hanes glared at me, probably upset because I'd managed a painting for Mother's auction but not hers. Prudence Davies didn't glare. She looked as if she was battling a thoroughly inappropriate grin, one that would reveal her horse teeth and her dislike for me and my family. Truly, her parents should have named her *Schadenfreude*.

"Here's your drink, Marjorie." A man's voice claimed my attention.

Kinky stood next to my sister. He offered her a very full glass of clear liquid with two limes floating in its depths then dropped his hand to her bare shoulder.

"Thank you." She leaned against him.

His hand slid from her shoulder to the back of her neck.

True they'd known each other since they were four, even dated each other in high school, but their actions spoke of intimacy and not of Kinky angling for another gaze down the front of Marjorie's dress.

The prickling on my neck grew more...prickly. I looked behind me again.

Cassie LeCoeur wore a look that might have turned a more aware husband to stone.

Oh dear Lord.

I turned back to my family. "Aunt Sis, have you met Kenneth LeCoeur?"

Kenneth removed his left hand from my sister, transferred his drink, and held out his right hand. "Pleased to meet you..." His voice faltered. I'd done a poor job with introductions and he didn't know her last name.

My aunt extended her hand. "Call me Sis. Everyone does." She wore the polite mask that will get its wearer through most any situation—even a there's-just-been-a-horrific-death-and-my-married-niece-is-carrying-on-with-a-married-man (what a shame they're not married to each other) situation.

"Marjorie tells me you live in Majorca," said Kinky.

"I keep a house there." Polite but cool, that was Aunt Sis.

"I'd like to visit Spain. I've never been." Kinky snuck a not very sneaky look down the front of Marjorie's dress.

Really? He wanted to ogle Marjorie's breasts and talk about vacation plans? Hammie had died not thirty feet from where we sat.

Aunt Sis tsked. She sounded enough like Mother to make Marjorie jump in her chair. She sounded enough like Mother to drag Kinky's avid gaze away from my sister's bosoms.

"Have your travel agent book you into a hotel on the beach." Aunt Sis's gaze landed on Kinky's wedding ring. "I'm sure you and your wife would enjoy it." Her polite mask morphed to downright chilly.

Mother and Aunt Sis are as different as a Chanel suit and a Thea Porter caftan, but when it comes down to it, the cloth they're cut from is the same.

"Is your wife here?" Aunt Sis made a show of looking around the ballroom. "I'd love to meet her. I can offer her all sorts of recommendations." Something in her voice made it sound as if those recommendations might include advice on what to do with a wandering husband.

A dull flush rose from the crisp white collar of Kinky's tux and stained his cheeks. "She's around somewhere."

She was twenty feet behind us, probably wishing she could snatch Marjorie bald-headed and take a pair of pruning shears to Kinky. In her shoes, that's what I'd be thinking. Poor Cassie. Perhaps she could take comfort in the fact Marjorie leaned forward and offered an unimpeded view of her cleavage to every man she met. Gold bands be damned.

But having a husband who flaunts his dalliances can curdle one's soul. I know firsthand.

Kinky extended his hand. "It was nice meeting you, Sis." He jerked his chin in my direction. "Ellison, always a pleasure." Then he walked away.

Aunt Sis still wore her polite mask. She crooked a finger at Marjorie and my sister leaned toward her. "Have you lost your mind?" Aunt Sis asked.

Marjorie blinked. Three times.

A moment passed.

"I'd like an answer." Aunt Sis put both her bottle and her glass on the table, leaned back against her chair, crossed her arms, and waited.

Marjorie stared at the crocuses blooming in ersatz snow. "We're not..."

When we were kids, Marjorie's left eye would twitch whenever she fibbed. It didn't twitch now.

Either she'd improved her lying skills or I'd been wrong and she and Kinky were not dallying.

Yet.

"If you're not, you're thinking about it." Aunt Sis took a long drink of scotch. "You're risking everything—your husband, your children, the life you've built, for that?" She tilted her head in the direction Kinky had disappeared. "Grow up, Marjorie."

"You don't understand." Marjorie's voice was small.

"I bet I do." Aunt Sis waited for a response. When Marjorie said nothing, Aunt Sis waved her arm in an expansive gesture. Too bad that hand held a glass of scotch. She didn't seem to notice that a quarter of its contents mixed with the glitter on the carpet. "Life is passing you by. Other people are living and you're just existing."

Marjorie's shoulders stiffened but she remained silent.

"You were the one who was supposed to have a successful life but your sister is living one. She's famous and, now that her husband is dead, men surround her like bees to honey. Jealousy has either rendered you stupid or blind. Maybe both."

Marjorie's lips quivered.

I reached out and touched my aunt's arm. "This isn't the time or the place."

She shook me off. "She has to hear this. Marjorie—" Aunt Sis positively speared my sister with her gaze "—if he leaves his wife, you get to spend the rest of your life with a man you know will cheat if given the chance. If he doesn't leave her, you've destroyed your marriage for nothing."

My sister grabbed a napkin from the table and daubed at her eyes. Was she hiding tears or twitches? "There is nothing between us."

I wasn't sure I believed her. Nor, apparently, was Aunt Sis. She regarded my sister with an expression that could only be called "baleful."

A man cleared his throat.

I looked up at a uniformed police officer.

"Mrs. Russell?" he said.

"Yes."

"Detective Jones would like to speak with you and your mother."

"Together?"

"Yes, ma'am."

Damn. All things being equal, I'd rather watch Aunt Sis scold my sister. All things being equal, I'd rather swim into a corpse than spend time with Mother in her current mood.

I took another fortifying sip of scotch and stood. "There's my mother." I nodded in her direction.

She stood alone, as cold and remote as a marble statue—if marble statues could seethe. Mother was definitely seething.

The poor man approached her and said something I couldn't hear.

She answered.

He ran a finger under his collar and paled.

We followed the now pasty police officer through the ballroom. I swear, a cold wind blew off her shoulders, freezing all around her.

He led us through the lobby and to a small office.

"Please—" Anarchy, who sat behind a desk, stood and waved his hand toward two chairs "—have a seat."

Mother perched on the edge of her chair and shifted her gaze from the grass cloth covered walls to the neutral carpet to the just-shy-of-nice desk. "Whose office is this?"

"I believe they make it available for guests."

Mother glanced again. Her gaze pausing on a tiny bit of scuffed veneer and a miniscule bubble in the wallpaper.

I sat back in my chair. It wasn't remotely comfortable.

"I have a few questions," said Anarchy.

Mother inclined her head, offering her permission.

"I understand you had a detailed seating chart," said Anarchy.

"That is not a question." Mother sat rigid as a two-by-four. The view down the length of her nose must not have pleased her; the corner of her lip curled as if it longed to sneer.

"Did you have a detailed seating chart?"

"I did." She added a put-upon sigh.

"So every guest was assigned a seat?"

"Every guest was assigned a table," Mother corrected.

"But there were place cards."

"Only so the waiters knew what to serve. I assigned ten people to a table and made sure that the correct cards were placed. I don't know how they were placed."

"How they were placed?"

Mother pursed her lips. "I didn't arrange the tables." She shifted in her seat and her lips curled in a bitter smile. "I let the cards fall where they may."

"Meaning?"

"Meaning I have no idea where the cards were placed on the table."

Anarchy rubbed his chin "Who was supposed to be seated at table sixty-two?"

"I'd have to consult my chart." Mother was being deliberately difficult. She knew the table at which every person in the ballroom was seated—or was supposed to be seated.

"Mother..." My voice was low but audible.

She ignored me.

"Yancy Arnot got drunk," I blurted

Two sets of eyes stared holes right through me.

For a moment no one said a word, then Anarchy asked, "Why is that important?"

"Because he was seated at table sixty-two. Libba and I snuck into the ballroom and asked a man named Hector to remove his place."

"How did you get in?" Anarchy rested his forearms on the desk and leaned toward me. "The doors were locked."

"Libba chaired a luncheon here not long ago. She knew how to get in through one of the staff entrances."

"Were you supposed to be seated at table sixty-two?" Anarchy's brown eyes were as serious as...well, they were as serious as a heart attack.

"No." Mother and I answered in unison.

"Then who moved you?"

I glanced at Mother. She still resembled a two-by-four—stiff shoulders, stiff spine, stiff face. I swallowed. A moment passed.

"Ellison, someone is dead. It could very easily have been you. Who moved your place card?"

"I don't know." I had my suspicions.

Mother didn't exhale her next breath, she hissed it. That and she looked at me with a glare that could freeze a water hazard solid in seconds flat.

I held up my hands. They shook. I dropped them back to my lap. "I don't know." If I vocalized my theory, Mother would have my head.

"But someone moved your card?"

"Yes." I wriggled in my uncomfortable seat. The itching of my nose was the real problem

Mother hissed again. She must have shared my thoughts. I was dangerously close to airing dirty laundry in front of a police detective. I could hear her thoughts—*not our kind, dear.*

I chose my words carefully. "Marjorie and I had that argument at the house. She might have moved my card so..." *so that she could flirt with Anarchy.*

"Who was supposed to be at table sixty-two?"

"Cassie and Kinky LeCoeur."

Mother confirmed this with a near imperceptible nod.

"When did Marjorie move the cards?"

"I'm not sure she did."

He leaned farther across the desk. "Did you see anyone in the ballroom besides Hector?"

"Someone left as we entered."

"You don't know who?"

"No."

"How many people know about the staff entrance?"

"Dozens."

Anarchy sat back and rubbed the bridge of his nose.

"Any idea who might want to kill you?"

Mother hissed a third time.

"No one," I insisted. "Isn't it possible that Hammie was the intended victim? You saw her at the salon. She wasn't always considerate..."

"What happened at the salon?" Mother's voice was so cold it was a wonder her words didn't hang in the air like breath on a winter's morning.

My stomach clenched. "I'll tell you later."

"Tell me now."

"Hammie asked the receptionist if her husband had died yet."

Mother nodded as if Hammie had asked a legitimate question. "Then what happened?"

"Lynn called Hammie a rich bitch and kicked her out of the salon..." My voice faded. Lynn had also threatened to kill Hammie. The idea was simply ridiculous. There was no way Lynn would leave her dying husband's side, sneak into a ballroom, and poison a woman who'd been rude to her. Except...Lynn's reaction hadn't been entirely rational. I glanced at Anarchy, tried to read his unreadable expression.

With all the table hopping, that glass could have been meant for anyone.

Anyone.

But it had ended up in front of me.

NINE

Max's growl awakened me.

I lay in bed, my eyes sealed shut, and groaned. Whoever was lurking around my house at—I squinted at the clock—five in the morning would pay. Enough was enough.

I hauled myself upright and looked out the back window. Anarchy's car was not parked in the drive and the light he'd left burning in the carriage house still lit the window.

Damn. He was probably off investigating Hammie's death.

I crossed to the front window and looked outside. I even watched the street for a moment in hopes that a police car would drive by.

Seconds ticked by.

Nothing.

"Shhh." I laid a quieting hand on Max's head then picked up the phone and dialed the operator. "I need to speak with the police," I said softly. "Central Division."

The operator transferred me.

"This is Ellison Russell calling."

"How can we help you, Mrs. Russell?"

"My dog is growling."

The woman with whom I was speaking said nothing. Her silence spoke volumes.

That silence was the reason I usually grabbed my gun instead of the phone. "I believe there may be an intruder at my house."

"Yes, ma'am." She used a you're-the-fifth-crazy-woman-to-call-me-this-shift tone.

"Please notify Detective Anarchy Jones. He'll want to know."

I traded the receiver for my .22.

Max, who'd been waiting by the door, made a doggy sound that translated quite clearly to "finally."

I stepped into the hallway and followed my intrepid pooch down the front stairs.

He led me to the kitchen.

It was déjà vu all over again.

Except this time I heard voices—a man's and a woman's.

Marjorie and who? I strained to hear more.

"Don't ask again...mumble, mumble, mumble...already said no." The man's voice was hardly discernable.

It was still louder than Marjorie's. Her response sounded a lot like the adults in a Peanuts cartoon. "Wah, wah, wah, wah."

I flipped on the kitchen light and unlocked the back door.

Silence.

That was easily remedied. I let Max out the back door.

He took off at a run.

Marjorie shrieked.

I pulled a stool away from the island counter, put my gun within easy reach, and sat down to wait.

A moment later the back door cracked and Max trotted inside, sat, and gazed at a jar on top of the refrigerator—the only place high enough to foil his ongoing goal of gorging on dog treats. The dog has hidden opposable thumbs; there is no other explanation for his ability to access things he shouldn't. One of these days I'm going to walk into the kitchen and see him atop a step-ladder with his paw in the dog treat jar. Today, thank God, was not that day. Max whined softly. Obviously he believed his bravery should be rewarded with a dog biscuit.

He wasn't wrong.

"Would you get him a treat, please?" I called to Marjorie. "They're on top of the fridge."

Except it wasn't Marjorie who walked through my back door.

Aunt Sis wore her hair loose and a kimono wrapped tight. She also wore an expression that looked guiltier than Tricky Dick's. "Good morning, Ellison."

Had the whole world gone mad?

"Who were you talking to?" I asked.

Aunt Sis turned her back on me and reached for Max's treat jar. "No one."

"There was a man outside."

She delivered a biscuit to Max's waiting mandibles, replaced the jar, and turned to face me. "You're mistaken."

"There was a man."

"There wasn't." She favored me with a haughty stare.

I used one of Mother's ploys. I raised an eyebrow. "I heard him."

My aunt's hauteur melted away and she scratched her nose.

As if I needed confirmation that she'd been lying. "Who was it?"

She straightened her now drooping shoulders. "None of your business."

"If he's sneaking around my backyard, disturbing my rest, it is my business."

"Let it go, Ellison." She yanked Mr. Coffee's pot off its warmer and turned on the tap.

The back door flew open and Anarchy Jones rushed in. He still wore his tux, but he'd loosened the collar of his shirt and his bow tie hung loose. Stubble darkened his jaw and his coffee brown eyes snapped. "Are you all right?"

"Fine. False alarm." I was suddenly uncomfortably aware of my sheer silk nightgown and mussed hair. If I'd bothered looking in a mirror before coming downstairs, I'm sure it would have shown me last night's mascara smudged into raccoon eyes. I wiped under one eye and glanced at my finger. Smudged with black. Perfect. "Aunt Sis went outside to get some air and Max heard her. When he growled, I got spooked."

"Oh?" It was Anarchy's turn to raise a brow.

Fortunately, decades of dealing with Mother have inured me to such tactics. True, my nose itched. True, the temptation to tell him about Aunt Sis' rendezvous was dreadful. But I held strong. My nose remained unscratched; Aunt Sis' secret remained unshared.

"It's my fault," said Aunt Sis. "I couldn't sleep after last night, so I went outside and sat on the patio."

Really? That was the best she could do? The patio furniture had been pushed into the grass and the patio itself looked like...well, it looked like a crime scene—a crime scene covered in soot. Aunt Sis was entirely soot free.

As if realizing her mistake, she turned away and poured water into Mr. Coffee. "Ellison, where are the filters?"

"The drawer to your left."

She pulled one out. "Do you know what happened to Hammie, Detective?"

"Not yet."

"But you're sure she was murdered?" Aunt Sis opened the canister that sits next to Mr. Coffee. Her hand shook and some of the grounds fell on the counter. "It's terribly upsetting."

"Nothing is confirmed but I assume she was poisoned and—" he favored me with a narrow-eyed stare "—I assume that the poison was meant for Ellison."

"You know what assuming does?" The words slipped past my filters unchecked.

Anarchy grinned, the kind of grin that could make Gloria Steinem advocate for ceding control to a man—as long as that man looked like Anarchy Jones and delivered on the wickedness promised by those curved lips. "Assuming might just save your life."

I shifted my gaze to my aunt (who did not possess a melting grin).

"What if Hammie was the target? Or what if whoever was supposed to be in that seat was the target?"

"Who was?" asked Aunt Sis. "I mean, who was supposed to be seated there?"

"Mother didn't have a traditional seating chart. Just table

assignments. The place cards were meant to designate the meal not where someone should sit."

Anarchy reached inside his tux and withdrew a folded piece of paper. "Your friend Libba and Yancy Arnot, Cassie and Kenneth LeCoeur, Tibby and Martin Davis, Anne and Hedrick Walmer, and Hamilton and Randolph Walsh were all at the table. I assume you know them all?"

Of course. "I do."

"If you're not the intended victim, and Mrs. Walsh wasn't, then who was supposed to die?" Anarchy's expression dared me to come up with a reasonable alternative, but try as I might I couldn't think why anyone would want any of those people dead.

The Walshes seemed blameless. As did everyone else at the table. But someone who was supposed to be at table sixty-two knew something or had done something worthy of murder.

Discovering that secret moved straight to the top of my priority list.

"How is Randolph?" The pitch of Aunt Sis' voice sounded off.

"He'll be fine. The doctors have diagnosed severe anxiety and not a heart attack. He'll be released later today."

Aunt Sis leaned against the counter. "That's a blessing."

If it was such a blessing, why was she holding on to the edge of the counter so tightly her knuckles turned white?

"Walsh tells us there is no way someone would want to kill his wife." He looked at me. "You are in danger."

"You keep saying that, but the poison could have been meant for anyone."

"Correct me if I'm wrong, but aren't you the only person at that table who'd already lived through two attempts on your life in as many days?"

"He's right, Ellison."

Aunt Sis was a Judas.

At least Mr. Coffee would never betray me. He made comforting my-pot-is-almost-full sounds.

My aunt opened a cabinet and withdrew three mugs. "Coffee?"

After the three hours of sleep I'd managed, her offer was tempting. So was more sleep.

Anarchy rubbed his stubbled jaw. "Please."

That decided things for me. "I'm going back to bed." I rose from my stool and pretended I didn't feel Anarchy's gaze tingling on my skin. "I'll see you in a few hours, Aunt Sis."

"Sweet dreams." Anarchy's voice was just rough enough, just mocking enough. It dared me to dream of him.

"That hardly seems likely." I grabbed my gun, left them all—Aunt Sis and Anarchy and Max—in the kitchen, returned to my room, and fell into bed.

I didn't expect to sleep. Hammie was dead. Anarchy believed I was the intended target. My aunt had a secret rendezvous in my backyard. Anarchy was staying in my carriage house. I'd kicked my sister out of my house. Anarchy looked like sin incarnate in a tux. Mother was so angry with me she might never forgive me. Had the auction closed? Was I committed to spending a week in Vail with Hunter Tafft? All those thoughts should have kept me staring at the ceiling. I closed my eyes and didn't open them for five blissful hours.

The smell of bacon lured me from my bed.

God love Aggie; she'd come to work on a Sunday. This called for a huge bonus. Normally on Sundays, Grace and I fended for ourselves. That usually meant take-out pizza in front of the NBC Sunday Mystery Movie or *Kojak*. Tonight, given that I had a house full of guests, I'd planned on upping my game with Chinese.

I washed my face, brushed my teeth and hair and threw on actual clothes before I headed to the kitchen—after all, there was no telling who'd be clustered around the island.

Just Marjorie.

"You cook?" I asked.

"Don't you?" My sister wore capris and a sweater. How nice that she possessed clothing capable of covering more than twenty percent of her body. She should wear it more often.

"Not really."

"Eggs and bacon?" She grabbed a hot pad holder and pulled out a loaf pan that filled the air with the scent of banana bread. "I left this in the oven to keep it warm."

"Where's Aggie?" My housekeeper allowed me to make coffee in my kitchen and here was my sister...baking.

"No idea. I thought she was off today. Sit down and I'll fix you a plate."

Remaining stiff and standing should have been easy. My sister had switched place cards and put me next to a woman who was murdered (although arguably Marjorie couldn't be blamed for the murdered part). And, while I didn't exactly know if I wanted a man in my life, I did know I didn't want her flirting with the candidates. She'd flirted, but not because she was interested in Hunter or Anarchy. She'd flirted to hurt me.

Try remaining stiff and standing when your stomach is rumbling and someone puts down a plate of bacon, eggs and your favorite quick bread. Then, just to gild the lily, that someone pours you a cup of coffee and adds the exact right amount of cream.

I sat.

"I'm sorry about last night." Marjorie did her best to look contrite. Her forehead wrinkled. Her brows drew together. And her puppy dog eyes were nearly as melting as Max's.

"Which part?" Did she think a fabulous breakfast and an apology could make up for everything? I took a bite of banana bread...maybe it did.

"All of it. I shouldn't have flirted with Hunter or Anarchy. I shouldn't have switched your seating card. I shouldn't have come home drunk the other night."

She meant it. At that moment.

"When you changed the seating cards, who had my seat?"

"Detective Jones asked me that."

"What did you tell him?"

"I don't know."

I stared at her, a forkful of eggs suspended halfway to my mouth. "You don't know?"

"Originally, I moved myself to table sixty-two and I moved the cards around. When I realized there would be six women and four men, I put myself back at our table and moved you and Hunter."

"Why move in the first place?"

"You were so angry at me…"

She had that right.

"And I knew you had every right to be." She scratched her shoulder. "It made me itchy."

"You have absolutely no idea who was supposed to be seated next to Hammie?" I confirmed.

"None."

I ate in silence.

Marjorie sipped her coffee.

"Do you still want me to move out? I can. I hear the new hotel on the Plaza is quite fabulous."

After the apology and the banana bread there was no way I could kick her out. "Stay."

Marjorie's eyes looked misty—or maybe it was a trick of the light.

"What happened to us?" she asked. "We used to be such good friends."

Maybe the mist was real.

Maybe time's passage had added a golden hue to her memories or maybe all that mist in her eyes had blinded her to our actual pasts. I remembered constant arguments over everything from socks to boys.

She looked at me as if she expected an answer.

Um…We'd just mended our fences. Why was she bringing up the past?

"Something smells amazing." Grace bounded into the kitchen and saved me from answering.

"Do you want some banana bread?" asked Marjorie.

"You cook?" Grace sounded surprised enough to be insulting. It wasn't as if I couldn't cook at all. Hand me a box of Bisquick and I could make a mean pancake.

"I do."

"Mom can't." See if I made her any more pancakes.

"I can't paint." Marjorie handed Grace a plate with fresh-sliced bread on it. "I don't have an artistic bone in my body."

Grace bit into Marjorie's bread, closed her eyes and groaned.

Perhaps I should have learned to mix batter instead of paints.

"Did Mom tell you? She has a new dealer in New York. We're going up for a show in November." The pride in Grace's voice made me glad I couldn't make a muffin.

"She didn't tell me. Congratulations, Ellison."

Grace grinned. Marjorie smiled. My own lips curled.

The phone rang.

"I'll get it." Grace somehow teleported herself from the far side of the island to the kitchen phone in the time it took me to blink. She snatched up the receiver. "Russell residence."

She listened for a moment then said, "She's right here. I'll put her on." Then she held out the phone to Marjorie.

My sister wiped her hands on a tea towel.

"It's Uncle Greg."

Marjorie's face paled and she backed away from the phone. "I'm not here."

She obviously was. What's more, Grace had said as much.

Right there. That was why I couldn't get past the years and scars that stretched behind Marjorie and me. She'd just asked my teenager to lie.

I took the phone from Grace's hand.

"Greg, it's Ellison." I regarded Marjorie with disgust. "How are you?"

"Fine." Greg didn't sound fine. He sounded dead tired. "May I talk to Marjorie? Please?"

Truthfulness or family loyalty? What was more important? "She took Max for a walk. May I have her call you?"

Greg's laugh was as bitter as yesterday's coffee. "That's the best you've got? You're a terrible liar, Ellison."

How is one supposed to respond to a comment like that?

"Tell her my plane just landed. I'll be at your house within the hour."

"I'll tell her." Just what we needed. More drama.

I dropped the receiver back on the cradle and regarded my sister. "Greg's flight just landed. He's on his way here."

Marjorie wiped her hands again, patted her hair, and swallowed audibly. "I guess I should go clean up." She glanced at the pans on the stove. "Do you mind?"

Her wanting to primp for her husband was a positive sign. Maybe their marriage wasn't irreparably broken. "Go." I shooed her toward the back stairs. "I'll clean this up." It wasn't the first time Marjorie had left me with a mess.

"Thank you."

She ran up the stairs.

I washed dishes.

Grace dried. "So I heard last night was eventful." My daughter is a master of understatement.

"Your grandmother may never recover."

"Poor Mrs. Walsh."

Hammie Walsh definitely wouldn't recover.

"Who told you?"

"Aunt Sis. She also told me that Anarchy thinks you were the intended target."

"Did she?" Aunt Sis wouldn't tell me who she'd met in my backyard but had no trouble spilling the beans about me to Grace? And since when did Grace call Anarchy by his first name? "Detective Jones is mistaken. Who would want to kill me?"

Grace looked at me with serious eyes. "Just be careful. Promise?"

I tossed the sponge into the sink and pulled her into my arms. "Promise."

My daughter's scent is a mix of girl and woman, Love's Baby Soft and Tame Créme Rinse. I breathed her in. She let me hold her for almost thirty seconds. She might have tolerated my hug longer but the doorbell rang.

She pulled free of my arms and hurried toward the front door. I followed more slowly.

"Hi, Uncle Greg." Her voice was bright and confident. So why did unease rumble through my stomach.

I stepped into the foyer. "Greg, how lovely to see you."

My brother-in-law looked like hell. His skin held a grayish cast, someone had left suitcases under his eyes—large suitcases, and, like Anarchy, stubble colored his jaw. Unlike Anarchy, the stubble did not add to Greg's sex appeal. Instead, the whiskers on his cheeks made him look like a tired old man.

"Grace," I said. "Go tell your aunt that Uncle Greg is here."

She took the stairs two at a time.

Greg and I stared at each other, neither sure what to say. "May I get you a cup of coffee?"

He nodded.

"Mooooom." Grace's voice carried down the stairs.

"There's fresh coffee in the kitchen," I said to Greg. "Help yourself. I'll be right in." I climbed the front steps.

Grace met me at the top. "She's gone!"

"Who is gone?" She wouldn't.

"Aunt Marjorie. She's not in her room. Her purse is gone."

I went to the nearest window and looked out onto the drive where my car should have been parked. It wasn't. Marjorie was gone and she'd left me with another mess.

TEN

Twenty years ago, when Marjorie and Greg were married, he possessed a sort of devil-may-care charm, a grin that said no one who made condoms for a living could take life too seriously, and a youthful vigor that suggested he was his own best customer.

Twenty years had cost him dearly. The charm, the grin, the vigor—all gone. Instead, a middle-aged man with a slight paunch and sad eyes sat slumped at my kitchen counter. "She left."

It wasn't a question, but I nodded anyway.

He rubbed his stubbled jaw. Had he not had time to shave before boarding the plane? And, I blinked, was that—just visible through his open collar—a gold chain nestled in his chest hairs?

A watch. A wedding ring. Maybe a signet ring. That was the sum total for acceptable jewelry on a man.

Greg's hands moved from his jaw to his cheeks, pushing loose skin until his eyes were lost in the creases. "Damn."

"What happened?" How had the couple who'd once seemed so happy come to this?

He dropped his hands to his lap and his gaze followed them. "It's all my fault."

I doubted that. Seriously. The proper implosion of a marriage takes both a husband and a wife. "Do you want to talk about it?" I crossed my fingers that he didn't.

He shifted his gaze to the depths of his near empty coffee cup.

"More coffee?" My voice sounded new penny bright—far too cheerful to address a man whose wife had just snuck out of the house rather than talk to him.

He nudged his mug my direction.

I refilled it. "Cream?"

"Please."

Could I be in the clear? No embarrassing revelations. No sordid secrets. Cream bloomed like algae in his cup. "Tell me when to stop."

"Stop." He reclaimed his cup. Took a sip. Swallowed. "I asked for an open marriage."

Oh. Dear. Lord. I returned Mr. Coffee's pot to its warmer. Jamming my fingers in my ears and singing, "La-la, la-la, la," never seemed so attractive. Somehow I refrained. "Oh."

He lowered his head, ran his fingers through his thinning hair, then looked up at me. "Can every woman in your family do that?"

"Do what?"

"Fill one word with so much disapproval that disdain sloshes over the rim and runs down the sides."

Oh. That. Yes. Mother's first lesson.

He ground the heels of his hands into his eyes. "Don't look at me like that, Ellison. I'm not a monster."

Did I dare say "Oh" again?

"Marjorie and I got married when we were twenty-two. I thought experimenting with other people might bring us closer together."

Oh.

"She wasn't excited about the idea at first, but I convinced her."

That must have been some conversation. "Something went wrong?" Imagine that. My idiot brother-in-law, who was apparently in the midst of an epic mid-life crisis, probably thought he'd be able to sleep around, not feel guilty, then come home to a wife who kissed him at the door before putting dinner on the table.

"We weren't prepared for the emotions." He wasn't prepared for the emotions.

"Oh?"

I swear, I couldn't help but say it.

His lips thinned but, unfortunately, he kept talking, his voice somehow sharper. "We went to one of those parties…"

Henry took me to one of those parties. A glass fishbowl filled with car keys. People drinking too much to get over their inhibitions. Women with numb expressions in their eyes because they'd taken too much valium just to get through the night. I left in a cab.

Apparently Marjorie had not.

If the sour look on Greg's face was any indication, Marjorie hadn't endured, she'd enjoyed.

"I think this is a conversation you need to have with your wife." Not me. I'd heard more than enough.

"You have to help me win her back."

Oh?

"I need her. The kids need her."

He'd opened Pandora's box and now he wanted me to stuff everything back inside?

"Greg, you two need counseling. You don't need me meddling in your affairs."

"She won't talk to me." A tear gathered on his lower eyelid then rolled unchecked down his cheek. "Will you at least get her to talk to me?" More tears joined the first.

A grown man crying in my kitchen? The second one this year. Was there something about me that invited men to reveal their feelings? If so, I needed to figure out what it was and change it.

All things being equal, I'd rather triple bogey an easy par with Prudence Davies watching than endure the raw emotion emanating from Greg. Sadly, no one offered me a choice.

"Greg—"

"Please, Ellison. I need your help."

I handed him a tissue.

He wiped his eyes and sniffled as if he was four instead of forty. "Please?"

How could I say no? "I'll talk to her."

"Thank you."

He stood, towering above me, reached out a hand as if to pat me on the shoulder and—

"Freeze." Anarchy pointed a gun at Greg.

Revealing more intelligence than he'd shown since he walked through my door, Greg froze.

"Anarchy," I said. "Please meet my brother-in-law, Greg Blake. Greg, this is Detective Jones."

The two men stared at each other. By the slight curls of their lips, I surmised that neither was particularly impressed. At least Anarchy lowered his gun.

"Do you often have policemen with guns in your kitchen?" There was the Greg I knew. Slightly starchy. Slightly snobbish. He'd even squared his shoulders.

"More often than you'd expect," I replied.

Anarchy holstered his gun.

"He just wanders in whenever he feels like it?"

Talking about a man with a gun as if he wasn't there probably wasn't the smartest move, but at least Greg sounded like Greg.

The skin around Anarchy's eyes tightened so much he looked a bit like Dirty Harry. Greg might not sound like Greg for long.

"Anarchy is staying here."

"Oh?" Turns out Greg can pour a lot of disapproval into one word as well.

"Someone might be trying to kill me."

"What did you do?" My brother-in-law sucked in his paunch, puffed up his chest and looked as if he was ready to take charge—of the situation, of my kitchen, of my life.

"Nothing," I snapped. What is it about men that makes them think women are just sitting around with tragic, helpless looks on their faces waiting to be saved?

My would-be hero drew his brows together. "I should probably stay here."

All four bedrooms and the carriage house were occupied. Either Grace gave up her room and slept with me—a solution that was less than optimal for both of us—or I put him in with Marjorie.

That gave me pause. My sister wouldn't appreciate my moving her estranged husband into her room and after the way she'd behaved…"You can't."

"Oh? You have four bedrooms." Greg counted on his fingers. "You, Grace and Marjorie. I'll stay in the fourth."

"Aunt Sis is in the fourth. The house is full. There's a new hotel on the Plaza. We'll get you a room there."

"Where is he staying?" Greg jerked his head toward Anarchy who leaned against the counter and watched us with an amused expression on his lean face.

"The carriage house."

Greg jerked his chin toward Anarchy. "He can move out."

Anarchy roused himself to speak. "No. I can't."

"Blood is thicker than water, Ellison. I'm family."

"Which is why I know you'll understand when I tell you, you can't stay here."

The silence that followed was as itchy and uncomfortable as a Shetland sweater against bare skin.

Anarchy lounged.

Greg glared.

I silently cursed my sister.

"Fine," Greg huffed. "Can you put yourself out enough to give me a ride to the hotel?"

"She'll call you a cab." If anyone, anywhere, had a desire to split strands of hair against something razor sharp, Anarchy's voice was their answer.

Twenty endless minutes later, Greg was gone.

I closed the door on my brother-in-law and Anarchy said, "We need to talk."

Indeed, we did. "You cannot keep barging into my kitchen acting as if you're ready to shoot someone."

"I am ready to shoot someone."

"Not in my kitchen!"

He bit his lip as if suppressing a laugh. "Is it the barging, the potential shooting, or the blood on the floor that bothers you?"

"All of them."

"Let me understand." He crossed his arms over his chest. "You're upset I want to protect you?"

Not exactly. I was upset because he thought I needed it. In my own kitchen. Power matters. And in Anarchy's scenario, the rescuing hero had all the power; the damsel in distress had none. A big, strong man who wanted nothing more than to protect me sounded good in principle. But the reality—my reality—was that to move forward with my life or be any kind of role model for my daughter, I couldn't play the damsel. Try explaining that to a man who reaches for his gun first and asks questions later. "Just drop it. What did you want to talk about?"

"The Medical Examiner thinks Hammie was poisoned with Cantharidin."

"With what?"

"Cantharidin." He spoke slowly, enunciating each syllable.

"I understand what you said. I just don't know what it is."

"Spanish fly."

His explanation wasn't helping. "What?"

"You've never heard of Spanish Fly?" He covered his mouth with his hand as if hiding a smile. "Some people think it's an aphrodisiac."

"Oh?"

"They're wrong. It's a poison. Mrs. Walsh's throat was so blistered she couldn't breathe."

I sat on the stairs. "How awful."

"Probably better than what would have happened once the poison hit her internal organs."

I pondered that for a moment then shuddered. "Where does one get Spanish Fly?"

"It's derived from a Spanish Fly."

"So Spain?"

"Yes. But it's available anywhere. Some people take it for...In small doses it..." His cheeks darkened. Whatever Spanish Fly did, Anarchy was embarrassed to tell me.

I sank my elbows onto the stair above me, leaned back, and waited.

He mumbled something.

"I'm sorry. I didn't hear what you said." Turning the tables on Anarchy, even for a moment, was delicious.

"I said it gives men long-lasting erections."

My gaze, quite of its own accord, traveled to Anarchy's...to the general vicinity of Anarchy's...(I couldn't help it; it was at eye level since he stood and I sat). Then, showing heretofore undetected intelligence, my gaze darted away as if it feared getting caught looking. "I see." My cheeks warmed and I spoke to my knees.

"I'd like to speak with your aunt. Is she here?"

"Why?"

"Last time I checked, Majorca's in Spain."

"You just said that Spanish Fly was readily available everywhere."

"I need to speak with her, Ellison." Any amusement he might have felt at my general ignorance of aphrodisiacs had disappeared, replaced by a serious expression and cop eyes.

I stood. "This is ridiculous. Why would Sis kill Hammie Walsh? She hadn't seen her in decades until a few days ago." I planted my hands on my hips. "Besides, I thought you were convinced someone was trying to kill me."

"I have to consider every possibility."

"And one of those possibilities is that my aunt murdered Hammie?" I flexed my fingers then closed them into fists. Every muscle in my shoulders tightened. "She didn't do it."

"Let her tell me that."

"Tell you what?"

Aunt Sis descended the stairs like a queen descending from a carriage—chin up, posture perfect, a gracious smile on her lips. She paused a few steps above us and looked down upon us as if we were her subjects.

"Anarchy wants to ask you some questions about Hammie's death."

Still the queen, Aunt Sis granted permission with an elegant wave of her hand.

"Of course."

"How long have you known Mrs. Walsh?"

Aunt Sis stared into the near-distance. "Since high school, so at least forty odd years."

"Is that how long you've know Mr. Walsh?"

"Longer. We went to grade school together. Ellison, dear, I don't suppose you'd get me a glass of tea?"

"Of course."

"And, Anarchy, wouldn't you be more comfortable sitting? Would you care for some tea?"

"No, thank you."

"Just the one tea, Ellie. We'll be in the living room."

I went to the kitchen, poured tea over ice, then put the glass, a few slices of lemon fanned across a butter plate, and the sugar bowl on a tray. Aunt Sis was up to something; she was behaving like Mother.

People donned masks when they had something to hide. So what was Aunt Sis hiding?

I carried the tray to the living room and put it down on the coffee table in front of the love seat where Aunt Sis perched with her ankles crossed and her hands folded in her lap. She looked nothing like the woman who'd snuck in my backdoor in the wee hours. Her nose wrinkled and she scowled as if she could read my mind, then she reached for the glass and took a sip.

"Hammie and Randolph got married young. Of course, their families had known each other for years. And it didn't hurt that Hammie's family was in the lumber business and Randolph's was in residential development."

"An arranged marriage?" asked Anarchy.

"Heavens, no. Such an idea is archaic." Aunt Sis put down her glass with a shade too much force. "Their marriage was a convenient one."

Randolph had practically keened when Hammie died. No

matter what Aunt Sis said, theirs was more than a convenient marriage.

I waited for Anarchy to point that out. Instead he said, "You didn't come home after college. Why not?"

"I wanted to explore the world." Aunt Sis swept her arm across the front of her body as if every country and wonder on earth lay scattered across my living room carpet.

It was the story I'd always been told. So why didn't I believe her now? Perhaps it was her impersonation of Mother or the stiffness of her spine or the way she used the tips of her fingers to smooth the skin near the corner of her left eye. Whatever it was, I sensed she was lying.

Dread circled my feet as if determined to trip me as soon as I took a step.

Damn it. A sudden, very real urge to hit something took hold of me. Not the expensive down pillows that littered the couch. Not even the pillows on my bed. I needed to take out my anger on something hard.

I backed toward the door. Dread (or Max's pully-rope thing) tripped me. I fell to the carpet.

"Are you all right, dear?" Aunt Sis looked at me in a perfect mirror of Mother's what-has-Ellison-done-now look.

"I'm fine. I tripped." I hauled myself off the carpet and walked toward the door.

"Where are you going?" asked Anarchy.

"The club."

"The club?" Was he mocking me?

"Yes. The club. I want to hit golf balls."

"I'll come with you." He rose from his chair.

At least one of those golf balls would be a stand-in for Anarchy Jones. "They won't let you on the course."

"Why not?"

"No denim allowed."

"I'll change."

"Do you have golf clubs?" More golf clubs resided at my house than in most club shops, but there was no reason to share that fact.

"I do. We can stop by my house and get them."

"I need some time alone."

"When we catch the killer, you can have it."

"I can take care of myself."

His gaze strayed to the dog toy that had sent me thumping onto the carpet. If he said "Oh?" I was going to get my gun and shoot him.

He held up both hands.

As if a simple—meaningless—ceding gesture could placate me.

"I know you can. I just haven't hit golf balls in a long time."

"Ellison." Aunt Sis was still channeling Mother; she looked down the length of her nose. "Don't be ridiculous. If Anarchy wants to join you, let him."

"Fine." A whole bucket of balls with Aunt Sis's face on them waited for me—called to me.

Which is how I ended up on the practice tee with Anarchy Jones.

ELEVEN

We had the practice range to ourselves, the sky being heavy with bruised clouds and the air weighted with impeding rain. It was the sort of raw fall afternoon that portends winter—complete with a chilly breeze.

The weather didn't matter. Only the *thwack*. When a club face hits a golf ball just right, the result is a soul satisfying *thwack*.

Thwack. Anarchy's ball cut through the air like a hot knife through butter before hitting the grass and bouncing along to the very end of the practice fairway.

He could play golf. I hadn't really believed him.

"Nice shot," I said.

He grunted, bent, and selected another ball from the bucket that sat near his feet.

I teed up my own ball, firmed my grip on the club, imagined my negative emotions shooting from my fingers along the length of the shaft, and swung.

Thwack. Music to my soul.

My ball had more loft than Anarchy's. It fell well short of his.

I teed up another, went through the same exercise but added Marjorie's face to the golf ball.

Thwack.

This shot cut through the air. Still not as far as Anarchy's, but closer.

"You're a golfer," he said.

I wasn't. I just found hitting golf balls therapeutic. "No short game." The patience required to line up a shot that didn't *thwack* eluded me.

He hit another shot, the ball landing within feet of his first.

We swung in silence, each hitting our way through a bucket of balls. I went back for a second.

"So this is how you deal with stress," he said when I returned.

I pulled a three-iron from my bag. "One of the ways. Hitting a tennis ball can be pretty satisfying. I also paint."

He glanced around the empty golf course, the chilly wind carried leaves on its currents and threw them at us. "Why didn't you paint today?"

"Too much stress." And anger. "Anything I painted would be muddy."

I dropped a ball onto the close cut Bermuda grass, imagined it was Greg and firmed my grip on the club.

Thwack.

Greg sailed down the fairway.

"You're imaging those golf balls are people, aren't you?" Anarchy can be too observant.

"That was my brother-in-law."

"Have you hit me?"

"Of course not." My nose itched so badly it actually twitched.

The wind snatched up Anarchy's laughter and spun it around me.

"I'm not trying to interfere in your life, Ellison. I'm keeping you safe."

There it was again—that easy assumption that I needed someone to protect me. That I lacked the skill or intelligence to take care of myself. I dropped another ball onto the turf and imagined it was a police detective.

Thwack. The ball flew a country mile.

"That was me, wasn't it?" he asked.

I smiled tightly and dropped another ball.

The *thwack* of the club face meeting the ball got lost in a louder sound. I looked toward the heavens. Thunder?

Anarchy looked toward the clubhouse, dropped his driver on the ground, and took off running. "Stay here!"

Not thunder. A gun shot.

Stay here? Alone on a windswept golf course? I'd worn a red sweater. If someone was shooting, I might as well have worn a target.

I hurried up the hill toward the parking lot.

The pro-shop staff stood outside with their heads cocked to the side as if the wind might whisper in their ears what that loud sound was and where it came from. One of them, a nice young man named Ryan, stepped forward. "Are you sure you want to go up there, Mrs. Russell? That sounded like a gunshot. You should probably stay with us."

There it was—the easy assumption that I needed male protection.

"No, thank you." I climbed the rest of the way to the parking lot.

On I trudged.

Fortunately, Henry's Cadillac was parked near the cart path. I pulled the bags off my aching shoulders and leaned them against the side of the car. Then I stretched, rolling my neck and extending my arms. Better.

The trunk key slid easily into the keyhole. I opened the trunk and lifted the first bag. That's when it caught my eye.

British racing green with the top down and rain only minutes away.

Damn it. Marjorie had been doing this since we were kids—taking my things then losing them or leaving them in a place they'd be ruined.

I hefted the other bag into the trunk and slammed the lid.

My sister was quite possibly the most self-centered, irresponsible person on the planet. I strode toward my Triumph, rehearsing a whole conversation in my head—all the things I'd say to her and all the things I wanted to say but wouldn't.

Was she blind to the people she hurt?

Was she so addled by her need to feel wanted that she didn't see the damage she left in her wake?

Was that my yellow rain slicker tossed on the ground?

Were those her legs?

I ran.

A saturated crimson stained the cadmium yellow of my coat.

"Marjorie!"

She lay face down and unmoving.

"Help!" The wind shredded my yell.

Then I felt it. The prickle on my neck.

I spun around.

The parking lot was empty save for cars—Mercedes and Cadillac and Volvo sedans clustered near the clubhouse entrance. Given the emptiness of the golf course, the men's grill had to be full of football fans.

The prickle got worse. My skin crawled.

Whoever had shot Marjorie was still nearby. My fingers turned to icicles. My mouth went dry. My blood roared in my ears.

Who knew that we could be so alone only a few hundred feet from the clubhouse?

I crouched on the damp pavement next to my sister and picked up her wrist. My hands shook so badly it took me a moment to find her pulse. Thank God. "Help!" I rose from my knees and yelled again. "Help!"

If I ran to the clubhouse for help, would whoever was lurking out there shoot at me (I was wearing a red target on my back) or would they wait until Marjorie was alone and finish her off?

Now was the time I needed a hero. Where the hell was Anarchy?

"Help!" I yelled louder.

How many steps to the clubhouse doors? If I made it there, stuck my head inside, and screamed, would the prickler kill Marjorie in my absence?

Would she die if I didn't go for help?

"I need help," I screamed into the wind.

Ryan, who'd suggested I stay with the gaggle of men at the pro-shop, appeared at the top of the cart path. God bless him.

I waved my arms and he ran toward me.

"Call an ambulance! My sister's been shot."

His steps halted, he stared at the bright stain on Marjorie's back, and his lower jaw dropped.

"Now!"

He moved. Too slowly. Apparently the sight of blood had rendered him stupid.

"Go!"

He went.

A sound—something sharp—carried across the lot. A gun? A car door? My imagination?

I scanned, saw nothing, and knelt on the pavement next to my sister. Marjorie looked as gray as the concrete beneath her. I snatched her hand and held it in mine. "Someone has gone for help," I told her—or maybe I just told myself. Marjorie was unconscious. Still, I kept talking. "I know it hurts, but you'll be fine. The ambulance will be here any minute now. You'll love the hospital. Everyone's so terrified of Mother that it's like staying at the Ritz." I wiped my eyes with my free hand. "Just you wait and see. Another pillow, Mrs. Blake? Warm blanket, Mrs. Blake? More ice for your water, Mrs. Blake?"

Marjorie didn't respond.

I clasped her hand more tightly and leaned close to her ear. "Don't you dare leave me, Marjorie. There's no way I can deal with Mother on my own. I need you." Tears wet my cheeks and my stomach hitched and knotted and rebelled. "Do you remember that time we were kids and Mother made us wear matching dresses? You were so embarrassed to be dressed like your baby sister that you smeared strawberry jam down the front. I wanted to be just like you so I did the same. Mother was apoplectic." Furious didn't begin to cover Mother's response. Her head had completed a three-hundred-sixty-degree rotation then levitated off her body. She never bought us matching dresses again. I laughed at that memory—a splintered, broken sound. "Don't leave me. Hold on, Marji."

Where had the golf pro gone to ask for help? Timbuktu?

I could run for the clubhouse. The prickling had disappeared. Except I couldn't. What if she died? Alone. I couldn't leave her. My throat swelled and my jaw ached. She couldn't leave me. "Marji, you better stay with me."

The doors to the country club flew open and men spilled into the parking lot like water from a tap opened too wide. First among them was Anarchy Jones.

It took all of five seconds for him to analyze what had happened. "Did you see anyone?"

"No."

He knelt on the other side of Marjorie and held his fingers against her wrist. "Hear anything?"

"No."

The men who'd abandoned their football game watched us as if we were tennis players volleying for the championship. Their heads swiveled with each question and answer. Four lawyers, two accountants, one insurance man, six business owners, two trust fund cases, and three ad men. Not a doctor among them.

"I think whoever shot her was in the parking lot when I found her."

"Why?"

"A prickling on my neck."

To his credit, Anarchy did not roll his eyes.

The sound of a siren reached us and the gallery's heads swiveled as one. The vehicle raced up the long drive.

"Whoever shot her was here," I insisted.

Anarchy glanced around the windy lot and his expression tightened. "Whoever it was, they're gone now."

Were they? How easy would it be to shoot Marjorie then slip back inside the clubhouse? I'd been too busy talking to Marjorie to watch all the doors.

I looked more closely at the men who surrounded us. They

ranged from middle-aged to old but shared a certain well-heeled air that had little to do with the corduroy pants and cashmere sweaters they wore. Was the prickler among them? No one looked like a murderer. Then again, those Scooby Doo cartoons Grace watched when she was little had it all wrong. In real life, one didn't pull a mask off a monster and find a man. Nope. In real life, one pulled a mask off a man and found a monster.

The cluster of men made way for the medics who rushed to Marjorie's side and somehow pried my hand from hers.

Within the time it took to *thwack* a golf ball, she was on a gurney and loaded into the ambulance.

"I'm going with her." I fisted my hands, ready for an argument with Anarchy.

He didn't argue.

"In the ambulance," I added.

Anarchy flashed his badge at the medic. "Take her with you."

"But—"

Anarchy cut him off with a look.

"This way, ma'am."

I followed the medic to the back of the ambulance, climbed in, and tried to stay out of the way.

The door slammed shut behind us and one of the EMTs sliced through my ruined raincoat, pulling it away from my sister body. Beneath she wore a V-neck sweater. That he sliced through that as well. Her bra gave him pause. It was black and lace and racier than anything I'd ever seen.

If Mother saw that bit of lingerie, her head was going to levitate off her shoulders again.

The medics switched from English to a language I didn't understand—BPs and numbers and vitals.

I bowed my head and negotiated deals with God. I'm not sure if he cared about my donating paintings to school auctions, but it didn't hurt to offer.

We arrived at the hospital and they whisked Marjorie inside. I followed more slowly, allowing myself a moment to adjust to the antiseptic smell and fluorescent lighting. I really had hoped to avoid hospitals for at least a few years.

I'd managed a few weeks.

The woman behind the ER intake desk looked at me, waiting. She had a tired look in her eyes, one that said she'd seen every illness and heard every sob story.

"My sister was just brought in."

She picked up this paper and that one, constructing a ream for me to fill out.

"She was shot."

"Do you have her insurance card?" The woman sounded bored.

"No. But she's Frances Walford's daughter." That at least caught her interest. She picked up papers faster.

"I need to make a few calls," I said.

"There's a payphone in the waiting room."

"My sister was shot. I left my purse at the crime scene."

She stared at me, apparently unable to make the connection between no purse and no change for telephone calls.

"I don't have any money with me."

Mother saved her from the necessity of explaining to me that hospital phones were for hospital use.

Frances Walford blew through the emergency room doors like a hurricane. "Ellison! Jim Ward called me from the club. What happened?"

She was in five-star general mode which meant she didn't want an answer. She wanted action. Within two minutes, everyone from the hospital president to the head of surgery had been contacted. She arranged for a private waiting room and insisted on an update.

That no update was available—"She's in surgery, Mrs. Walford"—just annoyed her.

She turned that annoyance on me. "What were you two doing at the club? It's disrespectful. Hammie's hardly cold."

"I was hitting golf balls."

She sucked in her cheeks. "Why?"

"Because I like hitting golf balls, Mother."

Her lips thinned. "What was Marjorie doing there?"

I shook my head. I had no idea.

"Who shot her?"

"I don't know." I recounted finding Marjorie in the parking lot.

"She was driving your car?"

"Yes."

"And wearing your coat?"

"Yes."

"I bet that bullet was meant for you."

My heart, my lungs, my ability to move through time—they all froze.

Could Mother be right? Much as I hated to admit it, she often was. A tsunami of guilt washed over me.

"Do you know her number?" Mother regarded me as if she expected an answer, as if she hadn't just pushed me down a bottomless well of recriminations.

My brain was numb. "Pardon?"

"Do you know your sister's phone number? Someone should call Greg."

"He's in town. He's staying at the Alameda." Another wave of guilt hit. I should have called him first thing. "He came to see Marjorie but as far as I can tell—" sneaking out of my house to avoid him being a fairly good indication "—she doesn't want to talk to him."

"Greg is in town?"

"As of this morning."

"Here?"

"Yes, Mother."

"They're estranged?"

I nodded.

"And Marjorie's been shot. Where's that police detective you insist on encouraging?"

"At the crime scene. Why?"

"I was wrong, dear. That bullet wasn't meant for you. Everyone knows that the spouse is always guilty."

How quickly she forgot. "I did not kill Henry."

She patted my knee. "Except for you, dear. No one could think you capable of murder."

Was that a compliment or an insult?

"Why would Greg kill Marjorie?"

"You said it yourself. They're estranged." She squared her shoulders and her neck seemed to lengthen. "If she dies, he gets her money."

"He has plenty of money of his own."

Mother snorted softly. In her estimation, Greg's money—being of the newly minted and slightly naughty variety—was worth less than Marjorie's.

"Mother, if he planned on killing Marjorie, why would he let me know he was in Kansas City?"

Mother opened then closed her mouth, apparently unable to argue with such logic.

That was how Daddy found us. "It took forever to find a parking space. Any news?"

"No," said Mother. "But I think Greg shot her."

So much for logic.

"That or someone wanted to kill Ellison and shot Marjorie by mistake."

Daddy stared at her as if she'd grown two heads. "That's enough, Frances."

My father doesn't often make pronouncements, but when he does, he expects them to be respected.

Mother fell silent.

I stared at the overcooked oatmeal hue on the walls.

Daddy settled into one of the chairs.

A minute ticked by. Then another.

I stood.

"I'll just go call Greg. Someone should let him know his wife is in the hospital."

Mother muttered something. It might have been *he put her there.*

I took the high road and ignored her. "Daddy, do you have any change?"

He deposited a pocketful of coins in my palm.

I escaped the little room and my parents' worry, took a deep breath of antiseptic air and found a phone. My finger circled the dial, rotating the zero hole.

An operator answered.

"Hello, would you please connect me with the Alameda Plaza?"

A moment later I was talking to someone at the hotel. "Would you connect me to Mr. Blake's room, please?"

The phone rang and rang until finally it rolled back to the front desk. "Would you take a message for me?"

"Yes, ma'am. Ready when you are."

"This is Ellison Russell calling for Greg Blake. Please tell him his wife has been hospitalized."

I had the hospital's address and number memorized—that's what happens when you end up in the same place too often—and gave it to the young woman on the other end of the line. Where was Greg?

I called home.

No one answered there either.

I had no choice. I returned to the private waiting room.

Daddy stood outside the door. "Someone came by. Your sister's still in surgery but things are looking good."

Thank God. I'd made a bargain with him. The auction would get its painting per the terms of our agreement.

"Your mother has gone to arrange things."

Things meaning a private room with a view.

I nodded, not trusting my voice.

He handed me his handkerchief, perfectly folded and slightly warm from being in his pocket.

I wiped my eyes. The Irish linen came away smudged with wet mascara. I wiped again.

"What's happening, Ellie?"

I handed him back his hankie and straightened my spine. "I don't know."

He took my hand, led me back to the waiting room and sat me in a chair. "Let's talk this through."

Too bad I'd returned the hankie. I used my fingers to wipe the dampness under my eyes. "It started with the bust of R.A. Long."

"You didn't see anyone?"

"Not a soul. I was watching where I was going."

"Which was where?"

"Marjorie. She was talking to Kink—Kenneth LeCoeur, Quin Marstin, and John Ballew. I was only a few feet away when Kenneth knocked me out of the way."

Daddy rubbed his chin. "If you repeat this, I'll say you're lying. Your sister has the worst taste in men of any woman I've ever met." Daddy wasn't much of a Greg fan. Unlike Mother, he didn't object to the condoms. Daddy just plain didn't like him. It made for uncomfortable Christmases.

But the worst taste? I didn't reply. Not given the man I'd married. People who live in glass houses...

"What exactly happened at your house?" he asked.

"Marjorie got home late. We were up in the kitchen chatting. I glanced outside and saw a light in the backyard. Fire. Someone threw a Molotov cocktail at the house. When it hit the bricks, I ran outside and grabbed a hose."

"And someone shot at you."

I nodded. "It took them a moment but yes. They didn't come close to hitting me."

"Last night?"

I didn't reply. There were no words. Hammie's terrified expression as she clutched her mouth was too fresh in my mind.

"And now someone has shot your sister."

I closed my eyes but the damp snuck past my eyelids.

Daddy pressed his handkerchief back in my hands.

"Thank you." My voice was thick with unshed tears.

"She had on your coat and was driving your car?"

"Yes."

"I don't believe in coincidences," said Daddy. "Someone is trying to kill you. We need to figure out who it is."

"There's no reason for someone to kill me," I insisted.

"Maybe they don't need a reason."

They did. In my limited experience, people killed to save their reputations or protect someone they loved. They killed for money or love or jealousy. Try as I might, I couldn't match any of those motives with wanting me dead.

Daddy wrapped his arm around my shoulders and pulled me into a side hug. He smelled of Irish Spring soap and a forbidden cigar. "We'll figure this out, sugar."

If we didn't, someone else—maybe me—might end up like Hammie.

TWELVE

The hours spent in a hospital waiting room are spent in a twilight world. Time doesn't move at its customary speed. Instead, every minute drags as if each second is hauling a lifetime's worth of pain and suffering behind it.

Time moves even slower when the people in the waiting room include Mother and Daddy, the son-in-law Mother suspected might have shot her daughter, me, and Aunt Sis, who arrived in a flurry and developed a case of nervous hiccups. Who could blame her? The silence was toxic.

An orderly appeared at the door and cleared his throat. We all half-jumped out of our chairs.

"You can see your wife now, Mr. Blake." The young man offered Mother an apologetic smile.

As if a half-smile could stop Mother.

She rose from her chair and smoothed her skirt—a soldier adjusting her armor for battle.

Daddy caught her wrist. "Wait, Frances. We'll see her shortly." Daddy jerked his chin at Greg. "Go. Tell her we'll be in soon."

Greg followed the orderly into the hall and the door swung shut behind them.

George Washington probably looked at Benedict Arnold the way Mother looked at Daddy.

"Frances. Sit down." Daddy's voice brooked no arguments.

Mother sat, her displeasure evident in the tiny, tight lines around her mouth. The depth and number of those lines suggested there would soon be hell to pay.

Poor Mother. First a ruined gala and now a daughter in the hospital—add to that her husband embarrassing her in front of her daughter and sister. I steeled myself for something ugly.

"There's no need for you to be here, Sis. You should go home." Having lost one battle, Mother was apparently looking for a fight she could win.

Hiccup. "So I could wait by the phone?" Aunt Sis settled more deeply into her chair and the Naugahyde squeaked in protest.

The chairs at my house were more comfortable. And, given Mother's mood, Max was definitely better company. I'd happily go and wait by the phone. But in her current mood, there was no telling what Mother's retribution might be if I left.

"I've spent enough time—" *hiccup* "—in hospital waiting rooms to know it's better not to be alone."

Mother's lips pinched at the implied criticism. "You could have called."

"If I had, would you have come?"

The color of Mother's cheeks was answer enough. "Go home, Sis. I have my *husband* with me."

What was I? Chopped liver?

"If it's all the same to you, I think I'll stay." Did Aunt Sis not see the glint in Mother's eyes? Mother wouldn't be happy until she drew blood.

With a lift of her manicured hand, Mother hid a yawn. "I'd think you'd be tired of hospitals."

I glanced at Daddy and tilted my head. What were they talking about?

He answered me with a miniscule shrug.

Either he didn't care or he wasn't telling. He definitely wasn't getting involved. He disappeared behind the pages of the sports section.

"You'd think. But here I am."

Mother held herself erect as if she was enjoying high tea at the Ritz instead of sitting in a waiting room filled with Naugahyde chairs and particle board side tables. "We all make choices."

Aunt Sis loosed her hold on the chair, folded her hands in her lap, and matched Mother's perfect posture. She even matched Mother's sour pickle expression. "Some things are not a choice. Some things just happen."

What in the world? What had happened?

"You think?" Mother sounded almost snide.

Hiccup. "You think the person who gets cancer chooses it?"

Mother's lip curled. "We're not talking about cancer." Somehow her shoulders and neck looked even stiffer than they had when she'd been giving Greg the stink eye. "I'd think with all your travels you'd have discovered karma."

Aunt Sis paled. "Following that logic, what did you do to get Marjorie shot?"

Now Mother paled.

Is there a sister alive who doesn't know how to push her sister's buttons?

"It's a good sign that they're allowing Marjorie visitors so soon." My voice sounded weak, unable to dispel the animosity sparking between my mother and aunt.

Mother and Aunt Sis ignored me. They were far too busy glaring at each other.

Daddy's newspaper rustled.

"You cannot compare my situation to yours." Mother had lost her well-modulated cadence.

"Can't I?" Aunt Sis drew out *can't*. "Who are you to judge?"

"I'm the one who did everything right. I did everything asked of me and more. You—" Mother crossed her arms across her chest as if the gesture could hold in all her secrets "—didn't."

What had Aunt Sis done or failed to do?

Aunt Sis leaned slightly forward in her chair. "You think following all the rules gets you some sort of special pass? Grow up. Life is messy. People—" Aunt Sis snorted "—people other than you, color outside the lines. And they're happier for it. Look at Ellison."

I wished they wouldn't.

All heads swiveled. Daddy lowered his paper.

"You forced her into marrying that dreadful man."

"Aunt Sis, that's not fair."

"Don't defend her, Ellison. You're enormously talented. You could have moved to New York and been the toast of the city. Instead you married that vile Henry Russell."

"So, according to you, I forced my daughter into marriage?"

"If the shoe fits," said Aunt Sis.

"I wouldn't have Grace if I hadn't married Henry." My feeble attempt at peacemaking landed on the linoleum unnoticed.

Well, the peacemaking part went unnoticed. Aunt Sis favored me with a look worthy of Mother and said, "You don't have to be married to have a baby."

"Something you know all too well." Mother's voice was venomous. And loud.

"Enough!" Daddy rose from his chair. "Frances, they can probably hear you on the pediatric ward. As for you, Sis—" my father's brows drew together "—it's a good thing Ellison is the only one in here. Remember, it's never too late for a scandal. I'm going for coffee. When I get back I expect you two to have worked things out."

Daddy used to say the same thing when Marjorie and I fought. It never worked. He strode to the door, cast a last warning glance over his shoulder and disappeared.

How could he just leave me with them? I like coffee—I love coffee. I could have gone with him.

Maybe he left me to make sure their hands, all four curled with tension, didn't end up around each other's throats.

"Could we do this later? Please?" I glanced from one furious woman to the other.

"It's fine, Ellison. Your mother gets her wish. I'm leaving." Aunt Sis stood in a swirl of aubergine caftan, wounded feelings and anger that had apparently been festering for decades.

Mother said nothing. Not until Aunt Sis walked out the door. "I didn't force you to marry Henry."

True, she hadn't held a shotgun to my back and marched me

down the aisle. But her belief—everyone's belief—that marriage was the only pathway to a happy life had certainly given me a nudge in the kidneys. Add to that a girl's starry-eyed infatuation and marriage was inevitable. The woman I was now would never have married Henry. The girl I was then didn't possess the strength of character to stand up to both society's expectations and Mother.

"Water under the bridge, Mother. Besides, I have Grace." She was a fabulous consolation for nearly twenty years spent with the wrong man. I drew on some of that newly developed strength of character and asked, "Did Aunt Sis have a baby out of wedlock?"

"Don't be ridiculous." Mother said the words so fast they sounded like one.

"Who was the father?"

Either Mother didn't know or she wasn't telling. Or maybe she thought if she ignored my question, the cat would slink back into its bag and I'd forget I ever saw its furry face.

Not likely.

"You know the story of the Prodigal Son?" Mother asked.

"Of course." We heard it from the pulpit at least once a year.

"I hate that story." She glared at the one piece of art in the room—an innocuous print of a soothing beach. "The Prodigal Son comes home not because he's seen the error of his ways." Some of the starch leaked out of her posture, and she leaned against the back of her chair. "He comes home because he's out of money."

Mother shifted her glare to me. "None of the things he's done matter. All is forgiven. Meanwhile, the other son, the one who followed the rules, is practically forgotten."

In a million years, I would never have suspected that Mother harbored such resentment for Aunt Sis. Disapproved of her lifestyle? Absolutely. Disliked her clothing? Certainly. But this—this venom? "It's a story about forgiveness," I ventured.

"Nonsense." She wielded the word like a knife.

What to say? I had no idea.

Thank God, Greg pushed open the door. His skin looked pasty and his eyes were red-rimmed. His gaze shifted between Mother and me, and his tongue darted out of his mouth as if he could taste the tension in our little waiting room. "Marjorie wants to see you."

Mother stood.

"Both of you."

I stood as well.

"Ellison, go find your father. He'll want to see Marjorie."

"There's a limit of two visitors at a time, and she asked for the two of you."

Did Marjorie really want to see me, or had Greg made that up to thwart Mother? I suspected the latter.

"Fine." Mother disappeared through the door, somehow intimidating the slow hinges into slamming behind her.

Greg sank into a chair.

I paused and patted his shoulder. As gestures went, it was awkward, ineffectual and insufficient. It was also all I had. "How is she?"

"Mad at me."

Had he expected that getting shot would mellow her?

"How is she feeling?"

He sank his head into his hands. "Right now she's feeling no pain."

That made one of us.

I offered up another awkward pat and a platitude. "Things will look brighter tomorrow."

Greg snorted. "They won't."

Not with that attitude, they wouldn't. I glanced toward the door. "I've got to go. If Mother is holding the elevator, she'll be livid with me. You'll be all right?"

He sunk his head into his hands.

I'm not good with raw emotion. I didn't grow up with larger than life displays of grief of anger or happiness. Grief was meant to be personal and private. Anger found surrogates like golf balls or wide swaths of paint. Happiness called for Shirley Temples with two cherries or, as I got older, a glass of Champagne. I have no skills when it comes to comforting a man who has screwed up his marriage so badly that he radiates anguish. But I couldn't just leave him. "What can I do?"

"Nothing." He lifted his head and sat up straight in his chair. "Go."

"I'll call or see you here tomorrow." I hurried down the hallway to the elevator.

Mother had left me.

Of course.

She doesn't enjoy being kept waiting at the best of times. These were the worst of times. That argument with Sis...Mother had peeled back the carpet and revealed the creepy crawlies that hid beneath.

I know a thing or two about sibling rivalry, and I wasn't about to judge Mother for nursing her resentments (even if she had been overfeeding them).

I took my time getting to Marjorie's room, in no hurry to deal with Mother in her current mood.

I lingered outside Marjorie's open door and considered what I might say to my sister.

How are you feeling?

Who shot you?

Did he mean to shoot me?

Mother's voice carried into the hall. "What seems to be the problem?"

Marjorie mumbled something.

"Well, he's not my favorite. But divorce? What's wrong with you and your sister that you can't make your husbands happy?"

Why did it have to be me standing outside Marjorie's room as Mother eviscerated her? Why couldn't someone else save her from Mother's epic snit? Greg was dissolving in a waiting room. Daddy was drinking coffee. Aunt Sis was in a cab on her way back to my house. Grace was at home. That left me. I drew a breath deep into my lungs and stepped into the breach.

Marjorie looked pale. It was hard to tell if that was from being shot or Mother's foul temper.

"What took you so long?" Mother demanded.

I answered with a pained smile, slipped past Mother and claimed Marjorie's hand. "How are you?"

"Tired."

"You should rest." I glanced at Mother. "We should go."

"We just got here."

Tap, tap, tap. Anarchy entered the room.

"What are you doing here?" Mother's lip curled as if Anarchy smelled like a just turned compost heap.

"I have a few questions for Mrs. Blake." Anarchy's mild tone belied the sharpness in his eyes.

"You'll have to come back. Now is obviously not a good time."

"Mother, Marjorie was shot. That's an attempted homicide. Anarchy is just trying to catch the person who did this."

She snorted. "Call Hunter."

"Marjorie doesn't need a lawyer."

"Don't be naïve, Ellison."

"She's a victim not a suspect."

Mother pursed her lips.

"I think you should have Daddy take you home. Put your feet up, have a drink, you've had an awful weekend." A couple of strong scotch and waters might take the edge off Mother's temper.

"That's an excellent idea." Daddy stood at the door with two cups of coffee in his hands.

"But—"

"No buts, Frances. You need to rest. We'll come back later." He handed Mother a cup, crossed the room, and dropped a kiss on top of Marjorie's head. "Looking good, sugar."

Was there no one in the whole family who could tell a convincing lie?

Mother joined him next to the bed, reached out, and stroked Marjorie's cheek.

"We'll be back soon, sweet girl."

My father led Mother away from the beeps and blips of the machines that surrounded Marji.

Mother stopped at the door. "I love you."

"Love you too, Mom."

Mom?

That one word defined the difference between Marji's and my relationship with Mother. My shoulders tensed. For a moment I returned to high school, a vision complete with Mother wondering aloud why I couldn't be more like my sister.

All things considered, I was glad I wasn't more like Marji.

Mother and Daddy left and Anarchy cleared his throat and looked at me expectantly.

"What?" My voice was too sharp

"I need to speak with your sister."

Marjorie shifted and the sheets on her bed rustled. "Please, can she stay?"

His coffee hued gaze shifted between Marjorie and me.

"Please?" Marjorie sounded so pathetic—looked so pathetic—there was no way he could tell her no. And even if he did, I wasn't going anywhere.

Anarchy rubbed circles at his temples as if we were giving him a headache. "Fine."

I settled into the Naugahyde chair next to Marjorie's bed.

Anarchy leaned against a window sill large enough to accommodate half a florist's shop. No doubt it would be filled by tomorrow. "Did you see who shot you?"

"No." Her voice was small.

"What were you doing there?"

Marjorie's gaze slid my way. "I met someone."

"Who?" The question slipped out. Anarchy's lips twitched as if he was amused and not annoyed by my interruption.

"A friend," Marjorie whispered.

Oh. Dear. Lord. Quin Marstin? John Ballew? Kinky? Who? This time, my question remained locked behind clenched teeth.

"You look like Mom." My sister's voice was stronger now.

I put my hands on my face and smoothed away whatever expression I wore that reminded Marjorie of Mother. I relaxed my jaw. Or tried to. Had she no sense? Marjorie couldn't have picked a more indiscreet place for a rendezvous.

"What happened?" asked Anarchy.

"My friend left and I walked back to Ellison's car."

"You were alone in the parking lot?"

"I thought I was. I didn't see anyone."

"Can you think of anyone who might want to hurt you?"

A tear escaped from the corner of Marjorie's eye and she scratched the tip of her nose. "No." No doubt about it, my sister was the worst liar in a family of bad liars.

Anarchy's slightly indulgent expression morphed into something harder.

"You were wearing your sister's coat?"

"Yes."

"And driving her car?"

"Yes."

"Can you think of anyone who might want to hurt her?"

"No." This time, Marjorie didn't scratch her nose.

A nurse bustled in, took one look at Marjorie's pale cheeks, and said, "You have to go."

Anarchy flashed his badge.

"I don't care if you're with the FBI. Mrs. Blake needs to rest."

He pushed away from the window sill. "One more question. Is there anything you can think of, anything that seemed off?"

Marjorie closed her eyes. She really was pale, nearly as white as the hospital sheets. "The tapping." Her voice sounded tired.

"The tapping?" Anarchy leaned forward.

So did the nurse. "Out!"

"I'll be back, Marji." I patted her hand. "Is there anything I can bring you?"

She fingered the hospital gown. "A nightgown and bed jacket."

"Of course."

"My makeup and the pig bristle hair brush."

"Certainly."

"My moisturizer. I can't do without that."

I nodded. "Nightgown, bed jacket, makeup, hairbrush and moisturizer."

"And—"

I shook my head. "Five items is my limit unless I can write them down. I'll bring anything you want first thing in the morning. If you think of something else, call."

The nurse herded us into the hallway. As the door closed behind us, I heard her ask, "Would you like a warm blanket?"

"I need to call a cab." Exhaustion reached out and grabbed me. If Marjorie didn't want a warm blanket, I'd be happy to take the bossy nurse up on her offer.

"No, you don't. I drove your car here."

My hero.

Anarchy led me to the parking garage and Henry's car. He even opened the passenger door for me. "I'll get your purse from the trunk."

Perfect. I didn't have to go back to the club tonight. He really was a hero.

Although...the club served dinner. There was nothing at my house but frozen pizza. My stomach rumbled in protest.

Anarchy climbed into the driver's seat.

"Thank you for bringing the car."

"You're welcome."

We drove in silence for a few blocks.

"Who would want to kill your sister?"

That's the question I should have been pondering. Instead, I'd been wondering how long it would take the Chinese restaurant to deliver fried rice and Moo Shu. "I don't know. We don't talk often. Do you have siblings?"

"A brother."

"Do you get along?"

There it was again—that amused smile. Barely visible in the dark car but still potent enough to make my empty stomach flip.

"We do best when there's half a country between us."

I understood completely.

"I have to go back down to the station. Do you think you could avoid trouble for the rest of the night?"

All I wanted was dinner, a large glass of wine, and the comforts of my bed. "I think I can manage that."

The best laid plans...

THIRTEEN

Grace sat curled in the corner of the couch holding a plate.

Max sat at her feet and watched with rapt attention as a slice of pepperoni pizza traveled from the plate to her mouth.

Aunt Sis sat in an easy chair clutching an industrial-sized glass of wine. She looked blurry, as if the glass was not her first.

The television was tuned to the NBC Mystery Movie. Peter Falk, wearing a rumpled raincoat and carrying a camera, asked Dick Van Dyke a seemingly innocuous question.

"Dick Van Dyke's the killer?"

Grace, her mouth full of pizza, nodded.

If only it were so easy to identify a killer in real life.

"Did you take a cab home?" Not only did Aunt Sis look blurry, she sounded blurry.

"Anarchy brought me."

Two gazes shifted from the television to me.

"He had Henry's car."

This comment helped with the gazing not one bit.

I frowned at Aunt Sis. "Would you like something to eat?"

"The only thing you have is frozen pizza."

"I can call for take-out."

Aunt Sis snorted into her wine. "I'd like to go out."

She was in no shape to go out.

"I insist," she said. "My treat."

From her spot on the couch, Grace nodded. "Mom, you should take Aunt Sis to Luigi's. I bet she'd love it."

Half-bar, half-restaurant, Luigi's was nearby and an enormous bowl of noodles might soak up some of the Blue Nun sloshing around Sis's stomach. My own stomach rumbled at the mere thought of lasagna. "Fine. Sis, are you ready?"

My aunt lurched to her feet.

Oh joy.

Luigi himself led us to a table which was nice of him since the place was surprisingly full for a Sunday night. Perhaps it was the baseball game on the screen above the bar.

"Who's playing?" I asked.

Luigi tilted his head and looked at me as if I might have a few screws loose. "The Dodgers and the A's. It's the World Series."

Who knew?

Apparently a bar full of men.

"Who's winning?" asked Aunt Sis.

"The Dodgers, one to nothing."

We sat and Luigi put menus in our hands.

With her menu still closed, Aunt Sis said, "A glass of Chianti, please."

Really? Water might be a better choice—and not a glass but a pitcher.

My aunt squinted and cocked her head. "You look just like your mother when you make that face."

Oh dear Lord. "Make that two glasses."

"Just make it a bottle," Aunt Sis amended.

This little excursion had the makings of an epic disaster.

I was seated facing the bar and that's where Luigi's gaze was glued—television high. "Of course. Your waiter will be with you shortly."

Epic, I tell you. We'd be lucky if we ate before midnight.

Apparently the waiter wasn't a baseball fan—he arrived promptly, took our order and delivered a bottle of water to the table. He even poured Aunt Sis a glass.

She didn't take the hint. "The man who seated us was going to bring a bottle of Chianti."

"I'll check on that for you, ma'am." The waiter departed.

Waiting on liquid courage would be cowardly. I took a sip of water and asked, "What were you and Mother arguing about at the hospital?"

"Frances." Aunt Sis pronounced Mother's name as if it was a new version of an old-fashioned four-letter word. "She's been like that since we were girls."

"Like what?"

"You know. Something doesn't go her way and she's an absolute witch for a few days." She lifted her left brow. "Don't tell me you've never noticed."

I'd noticed. "There was more to that argument than Mother being in a foul mood."

Aunt Sis pretended a sudden interest in baseball and swiveled her head to see the game.

"What was going on, Aunt Sis?"

"Leave it alone, Ellison." She scanned the small restaurant. "Where's that waiter with our wine?"

"You had a baby?"

"I said leave it alone." Her voice was loud enough to draw the attention of a few baseball fans.

If there was indeed a family secret kept hidden for decades, discussing it at a neighborhood restaurant at decibels more suited to a Grand Funk concert wasn't the best idea. I fell silent.

The waiter arrived with our wine and Aunt Sis kept him pouring until the level in her glass neared the brim.

"How's Marjorie?" she asked.

"The doctors say she'll make a complete recovery."

"I'll drink to that."

As if she needed a reason.

"I felt sorry for Greg today." She sat back in her chair and cradled the bowl of the wine glass in both hands. "I always got the impression they were happy."

"I think they're both having mid-life crises."

"Another woman?"

I shrugged. She wasn't the only one who could keep secrets.

"Another man?"

Another shrug.

"They should both just buy sports cars."

Excellent advice that came too late.

Our dinners arrived and we tucked in, eating in the companionable silence shared by anyone who's ever missed a meal then been served excellent Italian.

Aunt Sis demolished half a bowl of pasta before she stopped for breath. "This is delicious. What are you having?"

"Lasagna."

She turned her fork in the midst of her pasta, wrapping strands around its tines. "I didn't mean to be rude."

"Rude?"

"Some things are better kept secret, dear."

That was God's own truth. "I understand." I also understood that somewhere along the line Aunt Sis had had a baby. Had she given the child up for adoption? Or had she kept the baby? Did my cousin have a health problem? Was that why Sis had spent so much time alone in hospital waiting rooms? I swallowed my questions with a sip of Chianti.

Aunt Sis wiped her mouth with the linen napkin. "Would you excuse me a moment, dear? Where's the—"

"The ladies' room is just past the bar."

She stood without lurching—a huge accomplishment given the much lower level in our bottle of Chianti—and staggered off toward the bathroom.

I gazed at the bar and immediately regretted it.

Quin Marstin gazed back. He was the owner of a gaze that made a woman feel as if she needed a bath when finished looking.

Worse, he hefted himself off his bar stool and approached. "Hey, foxy lady."

Foxy? I choked on my wine.

Quin fancies himself a ladies' man—open collar, gold chains, expensive watch, hair that defies description (well, expect to say that not all of it was his). The only lady who'd be interested would have to be blind, deaf, and without a sense of smell. The scent of his Aramis whacked me over the head from a few feet away.

Maybe that was how he got women back to his place. He forced them to hold their breath until they passed out.

I smiled at him anyway. Quin had been on the steps when the bust fell. Had he looked up from Marjorie's cleavage long enough to see anything? If so, I wanted to know what it was.

But foxy? I gulped my wine. "You always were a sweet talker, Quin."

For an instant, he looked surprised that I hadn't told him to get lost. For an instant, he looked like a real person, one with insecurities and feelings. Then his lips curled into an oily smile and he slid into Aunt Sis's chair. "It's not sweet talk, babe. It's true. All the stars in the sky have been captured in your eyes."

Did women actually fall for such drivel?

He leaned forward, nearly dipping one of his chains into Aunt Sis's pasta. "If I said you had a beautiful body, would you hold it against me?"

Somehow, I kept my lasagna down. Somehow, I made my eyelashes flutter. "The other night, when that statue fell, you were on the stairs, weren't you?"

He leaned back, draped one arm over the chair, and adjusted his gold chains. "Yeah, babe."

"Did you notice anything before it fell?"

"Just you walking down the stairs."

Liar. His gaze had never shifted from the deep vee of Marjorie's dress.

"It was so brave of Kenneth to save me."

"Kinky?" With a wave of his hand, Quin dismissed Kinky's heroics. "He just got lucky."

"Lucky?"

"We were all talking to Marji and his wife came up to us and asked for a word with him. She looked mad as hell." Quin's half-laugh was fully admiring. "Kinky's never let little things like marriage or his wife interfere with chasing tail."

That the tail was my sister didn't occur to him.

"He didn't go?"

"Nah. But after that he was off his game. That's why he saw the statue falling."

The wine and the lasagna burbled in my stomach. This was what the sexual revolution had brought women? A game? The right to be objectified as tails?

"You want to get out of here?"

Hell, no. "I'm here with my aunt."

"We can drop her off on the way to my place."

"I think not." My voice was frosty.

Quin paled.

A hand grazed my shoulder and I stiffened.

"Marstin." If my voice was frosty, Hunter Tafft's was frigid. His hand on my shoulder tightened in a show of possession.

Quin stood. "Nice talking to you, Ellison." He scuttled back to the bar—or the rock he crawled out from under.

"What are you doing here?" I asked.

Hunter lifted his hand from my shoulder and crossed his arms. "I called the house and Grace said you'd brought your aunt here for dinner. Where is she?"

"The powder room." I glanced at my watch. She'd been there a long time.

"Does Jones know about this?"

"About what?"

"That you went out?"

Luigi's wasn't "out"; Luigi's was a place you went when you didn't want to cook and were too tired to change out of your jeans. "I didn't tell him we were coming."

He looked half-gratified and half-irked. The gratification I chalked up to my not telling Anarchy my plans. The reason for his annoyance was a mystery.

"There have been multiple attempts on your life."

Mystery solved.

Hunter Tafft had worried for my safety. The glow emanating

from my stomach had nothing to do with the large glass of Chianti I'd downed when talking to Quin.

"I'm not so sure there have been," I said.

"Oh?"

"Wrong place, wrong time." It was the story of my life.

"The bust nearly fell on you."

"That bust came closer to falling on Kinky than it did on me. He was lucky he knocked me down or it might have landed on him."

"The firebomb."

That was harder to explain away. "It wasn't much of a firebomb."

"They shot at you, Ellison." He had a point.

"They missed by a wide margin."

"The poisoning?"

"Any one of nearly a dozen people could have sat in that chair." Plus, there existed the slim chance that Hammie was the intended target all along.

"What about today? I hear Marjorie was wearing your coat, driving your car..."

My eyes filled with tears. No doubt caused by too much wine and remembering the gut-wrenching panic I'd experienced in the parking lot when it looked as if I'd spend the rest of my life without a sister—even if she was a monumental pain in the wahoosy. "I wonder what's taking Aunt Sis so long. She's been in there forever." I stood. "I'm going to check on her."

Hunter followed me to the ladies' room.

I tapped on the door. "Aunt Sis? Are you all right?"

No answer.

I tapped louder. Had she passed out? Had she tripped over the hem of her caftan and hit her head on the toilet? Was she hurt? There was a murderer on the loose. Was she his latest victim? Was she dead? A surge of adrenaline sent my heart racing and I raised my voice. "Aunt Sis?"

"Let me." Hunter banged on the door.

Nothing.

He jiggled the handle. "Locked."

I raced back to the bar. "I need someone to open the ladies' room door. Something has happened to my aunt."

"The key's missing," said the bartender. "Haven't seen it in weeks."

"We need to open the door." My tone rose an octave with each word until I squeaked.

Hunter appeared at the entrance to the hallway that led to the bathroom and looked at me expectantly.

"No key."

He disappeared into the hallway.

Hunter is suave. Hunter is debonair. Hunter is always impeccably dressed. Hunter makes his living with his brain not his hands or his body.

I raced down the hall after him.

He crashed his shoulder into the door, grunted, and did it again.

The frame on the side of the door protested—a sound of nails and wood struggling to remain where the carpenter had put them. What if something had happened to Sis? What if it was my fault because I'd ignored Anarchy's warning to stay safe? My heart beat in my ears and fingertips and stomach. I bit the back of my hand to keep from screaming her name.

Hunter crashed again.

This time something gave way and the door swung open.

"Sis?" I cried.

My aunt's lower half lay on the bathroom floor. Her back leaned against the wall. Her head lolled onto her shoulder. Worst case scenarios flitted across my brain like the newsreels they used to show before movies. Was she dead? She wasn't moving.

My already abused heart quit working and stars danced around my head.

ZZZ-zzz-zzz-ZZZ.

Sweet nine-pound baby Jesus.

Aunt Sis was out cold. She'd passed out in the bathroom. I fell to my knees and wrapped my arms around her. When she woke up, I was going to kill her.

Hunter rubbed his shoulder. "I'll pull the car up to the back door."

"Pardon me?"

"Would you prefer that I carry her through the restaurant?" That Hunter Tafft, he's a problem solver even if he does have a sarcastic streak.

"Thank you." I patted my aunt's cheek. "Aunt Sis, wake up."

Nothing.

I glanced over my shoulder but Hunter was gone.

I patted harder.

ZZZ-zzz-zzz-ZZZ.

Nothing short of an open-palmed slap or a bucket of ice water was going to wake her. The slap was out of the question, but the water...

I patted again. I even shook her shoulder.

ZZZ-zzz-zzz-ZZZ.

I gave up, ceded defeat, threw in the towel, cried uncle—call it what you will. Aunt Sis wasn't waking up. I sat next to her and leaned my back against the wall. It was surprisingly comfortable for the floor of a public bathroom.

My aunt had set out to get this drunk, and I was the one paying the price. For now. In the morning, she'd be the one paying.

Hunter appeared in the doorway. "I paid your tab and the car's outside. Can you help me get her up?"

The bathroom was not a large one—just a toilet, a sink, a towel dispenser, and a glass vase holding patchouli scented joss sticks—but somehow Hunter and I managed to lever Aunt Sis off the floor.

Now it was just a matter of dragging her to the back door. If we each took a side...

In one dramatic sweep of his arms, Hunter picked her up.

If I had that kind of strength, I would have tossed her over my shoulder in a fireman's hold. Not Hunter. He cradled her in his arms like a newborn.

He loaded her into the backseat with equal care. He even fastened her seatbelt.

We drove the short distance home and he reversed the process. Except now when he lifted Aunt Sis into his arms, Vivian Leigh and Clark Gable came to mind. It was probably just the gracious sweep of the front stairs that made me compare him—favorably—to a swoon-worthy hero.

I followed them up the stairs. "Second door on the left."

Hunter laid Sis on the bed.

I removed her shoes and pulled a blanket over her. "Give me a minute." A stack of towels, a pitcher of water, what else might she need if she woke? I grabbed a bottle of aspirin and returned.

"You're very thoughtful," Hunter said.

"Me? You saved us."

He shook his head and the light from the hallway caught the silver of his hair. "Anyone would do the same."

He was wrong, but I didn't argue.

ZZZ-zzz-zzz-ZZZ.

Instead, I backed out of the room.

We paused in the hallway.

"You look tired." He brushed a strand of hair away from my face.

"I am. Thank you for—" coming to the restaurant to make sure I was okay, getting us home, taking such good care of my aunt— "everything."

Something electric passed between us—a frisson of excitement as we stood together, poised on the edge of the unknown.

The door to my room stood open and the large empty bed drew my gaze. His too.

It would be so easy. To be held. To be touched. To be cherished.

Seductive promises that would turn to dust in the morning light. "I'm not ready."

A smile touched his lips. "I told you, I'll wait."

"Why?"

"Mainly because you don't know why." He kissed the end of my nose. Would it be wrong to lean on him? He'd be sturdy and warm and safe.

He kissed the corner of my mouth and a tingle rippled through my whole body.

It was wrong to lean on Hunter. I did it anyway. I let myself go limp against him.

One arm circled me, holding me close against the softness of his cashmere sweater. He stroked my hair. "I'm here whenever you need me. No strings."

Were more seductive words ever spoken?

We stood there for I don't know how long. Until Max wedged himself between our legs. Until I relocated my spine. Until I stiffened said spine and pulled away, brushing my fingers against the chiseled perfection of his cheek. "You should go."

He didn't argue. Instead he took my hand and led me down the front stairs. "Is everything locked up?"

"Yes." I'd check after he left. If he stayed much longer...

He slipped out the front door, and I turned the lock behind him. Then I checked the kitchen and every window on the first floor. Finally, certain the house was secure, I trudged upstairs and fell into bed.

Maybe, just this once, the sleep gods would let me pass the night uninterrupted. A woman can dream...

FOURTEEN

The doorbell rang at an indecent hour.

Ugh. Aggie would answer the blasted door. I rolled over, pulled the covers over my head, and drifted back to sleep.

Tap, tap, tap.

Lord love a duck, what now?

"Yes." I *might* have sounded a teensy bit terse, but I'd had a rough weekend and now faced a Monday morning without near enough sleep.

"Mrs. Russell," said Aggie through the door. "I think you should come downstairs."

I sat—fast enough to make me dizzy. Among other things, the wit Dorothy Parker was famous for the way she answered the phone. I stole her line. "What fresh hell is this?"

Aggie cracked the door and the smell of coffee wafted in. "There's someone here. I think you'd better come."

"Who's here?"

Aggie pushed open the door, crossed my bedroom, and put the mug in my hands. She blinked a few times, but if she had comments on the state of my hair or the bags beneath my eyes, she kept them to herself. Instead she said, "You probably ought to get dressed before you come down."

I took a bracing sip of coffee. "Who is downstairs? Mother?"

She shook her head so hard that her earrings swung like pendulums. "I'm not exactly sure who he is."

"But he's worth getting up for?"

I doubted it.

She nodded. Life—or at least this particular morning—would be easier if I didn't trust Aggie's judgment so completely.

I sighed and threw off the covers. "I'll be down in ten minutes."

I made it in five.

Aggie, God love her, met me at the bottom of the stairs with a fresh cup of coffee. "He's in the living room."

"What does he want?"

"Your aunt. She's still asleep. I couldn't wake her."

Aunt Sis's night of too much wine—the gift that kept on giving.

I peeked through the door. A man around my age stood by the front window looking out at my lawn. His hands were shoved in the pockets of a pair of corduroy trousers and there was something about the way he tilted his head...He looked vaguely familiar—someone I should recognize.

"Did you get a name?" I whispered to Aggie.

"He wouldn't give me one."

A name would be easy and simple and straightforward. In other words, nothing like a Monday. I stepped into the living room. "How may I help you?"

He turned and I saw him full on. My jaw dropped as if held together by faulty hinges. Hinges that refused to spring back into place. I'd been right. Sis had definitely had a baby. A son. And he was in my living room.

"You must be my cousin." It counted as a victory that I actually closed my mouth enough to form words, squeaky though they were.

He crossed the room, his right hand extended. "David."

His handshake was firm, direct, and confident. Mine was limp from shock.

"I'm so pleased to meet you. Won't you sit?" I waved toward the settee. He might not need to sit, but I did. My knees, usually so reliable, were quivering like Aspen leaves in a strong wind.

People kept secrets. That I knew all too well. But this? A person? The man in my living room was the granddaddy of all secrets. And Mother had never said a word. Did my father know?

"My mother and I were supposed to meet for coffee this morning." His forehead wrinkled and worry lines formed around his mouth. "She didn't show up, and I've been worried that something happened to her."

I could put his mind to rest on that score. "Your mother had one too many glasses of wine last night. She's sleeping in."

"Really?" His brows drew together. "She doesn't usually drink much."

Be that as it may..."We had a rough weekend." No need to tell him about Hammie Walsh's murder or Marjorie being shot or Sis's fight with Mother. "We all needed a glass of wine last night."

His mouth tightened and silence ensued. What to say to a man you didn't know existed? David stared at the paintings on the walls. I stared at a crack in the ceiling, made a mental note to call the handyman, and sipped my coffee.

Coffee.

What kind of hostess was I? "Would you care for coffee?"

"I never touch the stuff."

Maybe we weren't related after all.

"Tea?"

"No, thank you. Your housekeeper already offered. Besides, I can't stay."

Why not? Curiosity burned in my stomach like an ulcer.

I shifted on the sofa. Every single question that popped into my head seemed too personal, but if he was going to leave, I might never get another chance to ask. "I...I didn't know about you until this weekend."

The skin around David's eyes crinkled and for a half-second he looked like a thinner version of my grandfather as a young man—almost exactly like the photograph that sits on Mother's desk. Except for his eyes. In the photo, my grandfather's eyes are dark. David's eyes were a hue caught somewhere between chill grey and ice blue. I'd only seen one other person with eyes like that. Ever.

There was that question answered.

I crossed my ankles and straightened my spine.

"This is going to sound corny, but where have you been all my life?"

"Majorca." He pronounced it like a native-speaker.

"But you're here now."

"I am," he agreed.

"Why?"

A cloud flitted across his face, the promise of a coming storm. "It's complicated."

I expected nothing less. When are things ever simple or easy? Especially on a Monday? My hands tightened around my mug. "How complicated?"

"My mother came to ask something of my father." David crossed his arms low on his rib cage, his fingers splayed. "It's incredibly important, and if he says yes, I need to be here."

Whatever Aunt Sis had planned on asking David's father, now wasn't the best of times. Not while he lay in a hospital bed and his wife lay in the morgue. Unless...Had Hammie been an impediment?

My blood ran cold. Was Aunt Sis the kind of woman who'd commit murder if someone stood between her child and whatever they needed? A moment passed.

"Are you all right?" David asked. "You look pale."

"I'm fine." I shifted on the couch. A few years ago, in front of a crowd in the clubhouse bar, Connor Penning accused Worth Lawrence of shaving his golf score. The silence that followed was the most awkward I'd ever heard. Until now.

"Mother tells me you're a painter." At least my cousin retained the ability to make polite conversation.

"I am." I latched onto that bit of dialogue like a three-year-old who's afraid of the water latches onto floaties. "I have an opening in New York in late November."

"You must be terribly busy."

"My work hung in a gallery here. That gallery closed so there are a fair number of canvases available."

"Still...it can't be easy to get ready for an opening and have a house full of guests."

Especially not when they got drunk or shot or left their husbands. "What do you do?" I asked.

"Investments." He shook his head. "Nothing as creative or exciting as painting."

"What kind of investments?" Thank heaven my ability to make polite conversation had returned.

"I match investors who are interested in medical research with companies that are developing promising devices or drugs." His voice was flat.

I blinked. Twice. David was the first investments man I'd ever met who didn't ask me if I was interested in parting with some cash within a few minutes. He didn't want to talk about his work. I got it. I searched for another topic. "Where are you staying?"

"The Alameda."

A popular place.

"Aggie, is there coffee?" Aunt Sis's voice floated in from the foyer.

David froze, caught between his Mother's voice and a sunbeam. For an instant, his skin looked almost yellow in the morning light.

"Right. I'm not supposed to know about you." My voice was low, barely more than a whisper, perfect for keeping secrets.

"No. I only came because I was worried. There's been a lot going on around here."

My cousin was a master of understatement. "Why can't I know about you?" I asked.

He opened his mouth but no words came out.

"Don't tell me." I held up my hand. "Let me guess. It's complicated."

He grinned, an expression that transformed his lean face. "It is."

Aunt Sis's footsteps faded.

"She's gone to the kitchen. I can let you out the front."

"Thank you." He sounded truly grateful. "It's just that..." His voice faded. More secrets.

We hurried to the front door.

"I'd like to see you again," I said. Awkward silences aside, the man was family.

"I'd like that. I've been curious about you for so long. I'm staying at—"

"The Alameda. You told me. I'll call."

"It was nice meeting you, Ellison." He bent and brushed a kiss against my cheek, slipped through the door, and jogged down the drive to a car parked at the curb.

I watched him drive away then climbed the stairs to a shower (visions of sitting on the floor in a public restroom still danced in my head) and a change of clothes. Where I was going, a pair of jeans would not pass muster.

Fortified by Aggie's pancakes and a third (and fourth) cup of coffee, I stashed an overnight case for Marjorie into the backseat of Henry's car, drove to my favorite florist, and bought a Swedish ivy and a vase brimming with bronze football mums. Then I drove to the hospital and parked.

Ivy or mums? I grabbed the ivy first. I had questions.

Walking the hospital's sterile corridors with the plant clutched in my arms, I rehearsed those questions in my head. Did David's father know he had a son? Had Hammie known? Randolph Walsh had some answering to do.

I heard his hospital room before I saw it.

Damn. I'd planned my session of questions and answers without taking into account an essential fact. It is a truth universally acknowledged that a widower in possession of a good fortune must be in want of a wife.

I peeked through the open doorway. Hammie wasn't in the ground yet and already there were three widows circling round Randolph like vultures waiting for some poor animal to gasp its last breath.

Anne Lattimer, Jane Stark and Mary Fienes did not look glad to see me. Neither did the two divorcées, Elizabeth Fielding and Kitty Ballew. They all donned saccharine sweet smiles, as if my arrival was the best thing to happen since Lilly Pulitzer designed her shift dress. What was going on? Animosity from Kitty I understood, but the other women were usually quite friendly.

Then it occurred to me—a horrible notion. I was a widow too. They thought...they thought...I shuddered so hard I nearly dropped the ivy.

I'd watched Hammie die and Randolph Walsh was older than my father. Did they really think I was husband hunting in a hospital room?

Those sugared smiles that didn't reach their eyes said they did. Oh. Dear. Lord.

"Good morning." I smiled at Randolph. "It looks as if you have plenty of company. I'll just leave this." I put the ivy on his tray table.

Five sets of tight smiles got even tighter.

"Mother asked me to check on you. I'll be sure and tell her that you're well looked after."

Four of the thinly-veiled and slightly desperate expressions softened. Not Kitty's. I'd expect nothing less of the woman who used to...have relations with my late husband.

I took a step toward the door.

"Ellison." Randolph's voice sounded old and weak. "Has that police detective discovered anything about..." Tears filled his eyes.

"I don't know, Randolph. If I see him, I'll ask him to call you."

The man in the bed nodded. "Thank you."

"You're welcome." I slipped into the hallway and paused. My heart thumped in my chest as if I'd just escaped a hungry pack of lionesses. All of whom were trying to cozy up to the lion. None of whom wanted me around.

No wonder people hated hospitals.

I returned to my car and grabbed the small suitcase and the mums.

Those I carried to Marjorie's room.

In contrast to the Grand Central Station that was Randolph's room, Marjorie's was empty. Not even Marjorie was there. I deposited the flowers on the sill and the case on the bed, picked up her discarded morning paper, and settled into a chair.

Not a single word about a shooting at the club was printed on the newspaper's pages. How much had that cost? And who had paid?

I dug a pencil from the depths of my purse and began the crossword. A twelve-letter word for liar? That was easy. P.R.E.V.A.R.I.—

"Isn't this nice?" said the nurse who pushed Marjorie into the room. "We have a visitor."

"*We* do not have a visitor. *I* have a visitor. *You* may leave." Marjorie sounded as if she was in a *marvelous* mood.

Oh goody.

Given her pleasant expression, my sister's ill humor made not a whit of difference to the nurse. She parked Marjorie's wheelchair next to my chair. "I'll check on you in a bit."

Marjorie watched her disappear through the door then grabbed my wrist. "You have to get me out of here. I swear to God, there was someone poking me or prodding me, hour on the hour, all night long. I haven't slept, I hurt, and they won't bring me a decent cup of coffee." The last bit brought tears to her eyes. She released her hold on me and wiped them with her sleeve.

"I'll bring you some coffee."

"You won't bust me out of here?" She sounded forlorn.

"I can't. Mother would kill me."

Marjorie tilted her head. "It might be worth it."

"For you. I'd be the one who was dead."

My sister grinned.

I patted her hand. "I'm glad you're not dead."

She pushed the hair away from her face. "You know, nearly dying puts all sorts of things into perspective."

I was familiar. My brushes with death had reminded me just how precious my daughter was. I treasured every moment I had with her. "You're going back to Greg and the kids?"

"Don't be silly. Carpe diem."

Seize the day?

I'd rather seize her throat and shake some sense into her. Her children needed her. "Perhaps you might do that after your children are grown."

"Don't be ridiculous, Ellison. I could die tomorrow. That bullet at your house nearly hit me and now this. You have to grab life, because you never know when it will end."

My lips thinned and I looked away. Marjorie was Marjorie, dramatic, selfish, self-centered, and my sister. I loved her despite it all.

"Knock, knock." Two dozen pink roses concealed whoever stood in the door.

Greg strolled into Marjorie's room and put the flowers on the window sill. He'd somehow managed to pull himself together. His hair was combed, his eyes twinkled, and his clothes looked freshly pressed. He adjusted the vase so an enormous bow faced the room then bent and kissed his wife's cheek. "You look better, darling. Are you feeling better?"

"I thought you were going back to Akron," said Marjorie.

"I decided to stay."

"Why?" Her voice was harsh.

"I'm not giving up on us."

"I am."

"Nope."

"Pardon me?" Marjorie's voice was arctic. I guess I'm not the only daughter who can channel Mother.

"I'm not giving you a divorce," Greg said, his tone matter-of-fact. "I made mistakes. You made mistakes. We're going to put them past us."

Marjorie stared at him as if he was a stranger. "I don't love you anymore."

Greg's eyes sparkled. "But you will. I can be very charming. Now, I left something in the hall. I'll be right back."

She reached toward me as if she meant to grab my wrist again. "Don't you dare leave me." Her words came in a desperate rush.

I jerked my arm away.

"Here it is." Greg crossed the threshold again, this time holding a large to-go cup. The scent of good coffee filled the room.

How could Marjorie resist a man who brought her coffee?

Her expression hardened. "I don't want it."

"Of course you do," said Greg. "Hospital coffee is awful."

"Take the coffee," I said. "You know you want to."

Her face scrunched as if her thoughts were causing her physical pain. Or maybe that was just the face of a caffeine addict tempted with a fix. "Fine," she huffed, extending her hand. "But this doesn't change anything."

Greg caught her waiting hand, brought it his lips and pressed a kiss onto her skin. "Everything is going to change for us. Trust me." Then he put the coffee cup in her hand.

While this newly confident, charming Greg had a better chance of winning Marji back, I made it a personal policy never to trust a man who says, "Trust me." I stood and walked toward the door. "I'll leave you two alone."

The evil gaze Marjorie fixed on me rivaled the one I'd received from Kitty Ballew. It was a very good thing looks couldn't kill.

I hurried into the hallway and ran smack-dab into a very hard chest. Hands circled my upper arms. I tilted my head and saw Anarchy Jones. "What are you doing here?" I asked.

"I have questions for your sister."

"She's with her husband and they're not fighting. Could your questions wait a little while?"

"Of course, if you'd care to answer a few."

An idea popped into my head. A terrible, wonderful, fiendishly good idea. "I'll answer anything you want. But first, let's go see Randolph Walsh." There was no way Anarchy would give Randolph an update in front of a room full of women. And with the lionesses gone, I could ask a few questions of my own.

FIFTEEN

If possible, Randolph's room seemed even more crowded than before. A nose count revealed six women. Six! The addition of Susan Archer meant the widow/divorcée ratio was even. The zeal they brought to their task was skewed. The widows were casting lines, seeing if Randolph bit. The divorcées looked more determined, their hooks baited with flashes of cleavage and smiles so sweet they made my teeth hurt.

Elizabeth and Kitty and Susan had married and settled into a life of relative leisure—one where the mortgage was paid along with the country club bill. A life where they asked for cash back when they wrote a check at the grocery store then complained about the price of milk if their husband noticed that they'd spent more than usual. A life with a clothing allowance, a station wagon, and the assurance that someone else was doing the worrying. Then they got divorced, and that life disappeared faster than a golf ball in the drink.

"May I have a word, Mr. Walsh?" Any surprise Anarchy felt at seeing Randolph's room packed to the gills with chattering women was hidden behind his "cop" face.

"Of course, detective." Randolph sounded eager, as if he realized that questions from the police meant the departure of his visitors.

"Ladies," Anarchy addressed the room, "if you'll excuse us?"

Several resentful glances landed on me. I donned a bland expression. After all, I was practically blameless.

Getting a half dozen women to collect purses and wraps and

gloves is not the work of a moment—or even five moments. They chattered, they said goodbye to Randolph and promised to return, they said goodbye to each other, and Kitty Ballew dropped her glove.

Not only did she drop the glove, she used her foot to push it under Randolph's bed.

A strategically forgotten item that would require her return.

"Kitty, you've dropped your glove." I pointed to the leather fingers just peeking out from beneath the bed.

"Thank you, Ellison." The words came from behind gritted teeth and she looked as if she wanted to throttle me.

She bent, picked up the glove, and faced five icy stares. None of her competition would soon forget or forgive her sneaky maneuver.

Randolph's guests filtered into the hallway and Anarchy followed them. Presumably to make sure they didn't linger outside the door.

"Thank you, Ellison. They were driving me mad with all that chatter."

"Would you like me to have Mother fix this for you?"

"How?"

"She'll put out the word that it's too soon, and that you think the women who're visiting are ghouls."

"But that's true."

A bonus.

"It will give you a few days' peace."

"A few days is all I need. Katie and her husband are on their way back from London now. She can run interference as soon as she gets home."

Hammie and Randolph's daughter was well capable of protecting her father. I claimed the room's sole chair. "In the meantime, just tell anyone who stops by that you're tired."

"They don't take hints."

"Then tell them to leave."

"I can't." He shook his head. "I can't be that rude."

Anarchy walked through the door.

"They're gone."

"That's a blessing," said Randolph.

Anarchy's cop gaze landed on me. "You can go too." Apparently he had no problem telling a woman to leave.

"Can she stay?" asked Randolph. "Please?"

Anarchy leaned against the packed window sill and nodded. "Mr. Walsh, are you sure your wife didn't have any enemies?"

"Everyone loved her. Everyone." Part of dying is being sainted. Already Hammie's flaws were disappearing into the mists of time while her good points were polished to a high shine—a saintly shine.

"I understand Mrs. Randolph could be quite direct."

"You're saying she was tactless."

"No, sir. I'm saying she spoke her mind and that's not always appreciated." Spin it as Anarchy might, Hammie had been tactless. He'd seen it himself. "You're sure there's no one she might have offended? No one who would hold a grudge?"

Randolph's eyes, a shade somewhere between chill grey and ice blue, filled with tears. "Of course not. That's not how we operate. Tell him, Ellison."

If by "we" he meant the women with whom Hammie played golf and bridge and tennis, he was dead wrong. The surface might look smooth as glass but underneath lay something sharper— women with long memories and short tempers, women who nursed perceived wrongs and their associated grudges like sick children in need of their mommies, women who traded veiled insults like ten-year-old boys traded baseball cards. For them, Hammie was an anathema.

Hammie, who said what she thought when she thought it, hadn't really understood that the ripples of a snub could be infinite or that a woman excluded from a cookie exchange might plot revenge. Between the size of Randolph's checkbook and a handful of loyal friends, she hadn't needed to.

"Of course it isn't." I patted his hand. If Anarchy wanted to talk about sharp edges, he needed to speak with Mother not Randolph.

"Your wife hadn't received any threats?"

"No!"

Anarchy nodded. "When you got to the table, did you or your wife move the place cards?"

"Of course not." Randolph sounded offended by the idea.

"I noticed everyone at the table was a bit younger than you and your wife..."

"We bought the table for Katie and Porter. This was months ago. They invited their friends then discovered that Porter had to be in London. We decided to take their places and donate our table."

"Donate your table?"

"They paid for it but didn't use it," I explained.

"I see. When was that decision made?"

"Weeks ago. Hammie hadn't invited anyone to join us yet, and it just made sense to sit at the table that was missing two and let Frances use the money for our table as a donation."

"So you knew everyone at the table?"

"Of course. The only surprise was when Ellison and Hunter joined us."

"Who was supposed to be seated next to your wife?"

"No idea. I believe Libba's date was indisposed and they had his place removed. That probably shifted everything."

Could it be that easy? A small gasp escaped my lips.

Anarchy turned his gaze on me. "Something to contribute?"

"Nothing that won't keep," I said.

"Does anyone have a grudge against you, Mr. Walsh?"

A few charged seconds ticked by.

"No." Randolph wadded a bit of blanket in his hand. "No, of course not."

"You're sure?"

Randolph glanced my way. "Positive." He shifted his gaze to Anarchy. "Do you know what killed Hammie?"

"It appears to have been a poison called Cantharidin."

"Cantha-what?"

"Cantharidin. It's more commonly known as Spanish Fly."

Randolph blinked and his eyes filled with tears. "She suffered terribly." A single teardrop trickled down his cheek. "Do you have any other questions for me, detective? I'd like to rest."

"Not right now." Anarchy pushed away from the window sill. "If you think of anything, you'll call?" He took a business card out of his wallet and laid it on the tray table at the foot of Randolph's bed.

"Of course."

"Randolph, I was wondering..."

Both men looked at me.

"I have a question."

"Yes?" said Randolph

"It's personal."

Anarchy gave me a speculative glance. "I'll wait in the hall."

I got up and shut the door behind him.

Randolph looked slightly confused, as if he couldn't imagine a question that required a closed door. How could he not?

"I met David," I said softly.

"David?"

"David, your son."

His hands scrabbled at the blanket, grabbing fistfuls of cotton and wadding it into balls. "How? Did Sis? She promised she'd never...it's part of the agreement..."

"Aunt Sis never said a word. I met David. He has your eyes."

Randolph turned his head and his eyes away from me.

"What happened?" I asked.

For a moment it seemed as if he wasn't going to answer me. "It was such a long time ago."

I waited.

"Hammie was the love—" his voice cracked "—of my life."

"But you got my aunt pregnant?"

"We didn't mean for that to happen."

No one ever does.

Another moment passed.

Randolph loosened his hold on the blanket. He even smoothed out a few wrinkles.

"Hammie and I were engaged."

Which begged the question—what had Aunt Sis been thinking?

"When Sis told me she was pregnant..." He shook his head, his gaze focused on a scene forty years in the past. "She told your grandparents. She had to. They arranged for her to take a trip to tour Europe...no one would ever need know. The plan was for her to give the baby up for adoption."

"But she didn't."

"She refused."

"And?"

"Somehow she convinced her father to allow her access to the trust his father had left her. She stayed in Europe."

"And you got off scot-free."

"No! It wasn't like that. For eighteen years, I sent support checks."

"But you've never met your son."

"No."

Shame flavored the air around him.

"You should. He seems like a nice man. He's in investments. Something about medical procedures or devices."

Randolph snorted.

"What?"

"The only procedure he's interested in is one where I give up a kidney."

I walked out of Randolph's room in a daze.

David had juvenile diabetes and his kidneys were giving out.

Randolph being his father was a potential match.

But, for Randolph, keeping secrets from Hammie had been more important than his son's life. He'd refused to consider undergoing such a surgery.

If ever anyone had a reason to want Hammie dead, it was my Aunt and cousin.

"Ellison!" Anarchy's voice was loud as if he'd had to say my name more than once.

"I'm sorry. What?"

"You walked right by me."

"Did I?"

"What did you talk to Walsh about?"

"It's personal." There was no way I was serving up any member of my family as a murder suspect.

"You look pale."

I felt pale. "I haven't eaten." Not if you didn't count that stack of Aggie's pancakes. "Pie?"

We rode the elevator to the first floor and found a table in the snack shop.

A waitress with a gravity-defying beehive approached. She put two water glasses on the table. "What'll it be?"

I didn't need the plastic covered menu stuffed behind the paper napkin dispenser. "Banana cream pie and coffee."

"What about you, hon?" She held her pen poised above her pad and looked at Anarchy like men who've played eighteen holes on a scorching hot day look at their first cocktails.

"Coffee."

She sashayed her way to the kitchen. The swing in her hips was wasted on Anarchy. He was too busy glaring at me to notice.

That wasn't good.

I shook the glass until the crushed ice settled below the rim. "Something Randolph said made me think."

"Oh?"

"About where people were supposed to be seated the night of the gala."

The furrows between his brows relaxed. Slightly.

"When Libba and I went into the ballroom, we asked Hector to remove Yancy's place."

"We tracked him down. That's exactly what he did."

"Then Libba should have been seated next to a woman."

He frowned. "What do you mean?"

"Let me show you." I stood and collected four sets of salt and pepper shakers from the empty tables surrounding us. These I added to the set already at our table and formed a circle where salt and peppers alternated. "The salts are women. The peppers are men. This one here—" I pulled a pepper out of the circle "—is Yancy." The space between the two salts seemed enormous. I rearranged the salts and peppers and created a smaller circle.

Anarchy rubbed the bridge of his nose. "But Libba was seated between Tafft and Martin Davis."

"Exactly."

He stared at me. "What are you saying?"

"When my sister snuck into the ballroom and switched the place cards, she grabbed Cassie and Kinky's cards and put down Hunter's and mine."

"Yes."

"She saw Libba's card and put Hunter next to her."

He favored me with a duh look.

"A woman should have been in that seat. Marjorie put the cards down incorrectly. Kinky LeCoeur—" I tapped a pepper "—should have been in my seat."

"You're sure?"

"Reasonably."

"So either someone came in after the cards were switched and meant to kill you—"

"Or they were trying to kill Kinky," I finished. There was no point in mentioning that my aunt had a good reason to want Hammie dead.

"Here's your pie, hon." The waitress put the plate down in front of me then eyed the salt and pepper shakers. "You need all of those?"

My show-and-tell was completed. "I believe we're finished with them. Thank you."

She deposited our coffees and collected the extra shakers.

This time Anarchy watched her walk away. "Who would want to kill LeCoeur?"

"No idea."

"What do you know about him?"

"He graduated high school with Marjorie, so he's a year older than I am."

Anarchy dug in his pocket, pulled out a small notepad and flipped through the pages.

"He owns a paper company." I glanced at the ceiling. "Quin Marstin says he cheats on his wife."

"Who is Quin Marstin?"

"Someone who's impressed by the amount of—" I took a sip of burning hot coffee "—*tail* that Kinky chases." I didn't add that they'd been competing over my sister's tail.

"He sounds charming." Anarchy's tone wasn't dry. It was desiccated and it contrasted nicely with the sudden sparkle in his eyes.

I stacked the little plastic creamer containers into a pyramid. Mainly because looking into Anarchy's eyes when they sparkled was a dangerous activity—at least for me. Was there any actual cream in the containers? I removed the top of my pyramid and squinted at the label.

"Ellison?"

"What? Oh. Right. Charming. You have no idea."

"What else can you tell me about, LeCoeur? How did he get his nickname?"

"Kenneth Keye. Ken Keye. Kinky. Beyond that I am not certain. If you want to know for sure, I'll have to ask Marjorie." Oh dear Lord, that made it sound as if—"Not that she would have firsthand knowledge, but they dated..." This wasn't getting any better. "In high school..." I ceded defeat and sealed my lips

"Do you think there's a chance they reconnected?"

"Kinky and Marjorie?" God, I hoped not. Kinky was...well, Kinky was Kinky. Not the type of man that women dreamed of. Especially now that middle age had thickened his waist and thinned his hair. Even when he was in high school I found him...icky. My nose wrinkled.

"What can you tell me about his wife?"

Cassie was a nice enough woman but not from Kansas City. "She's from some little town in Arkansas." Kinky met her in college and the talk around the bridge table when he first brought her home wasn't kind—small town pretty with an unfinished degree in home economics. A few ladies, Mother among them, might have speculated that in small town terms, Cassie had hit the mother lode. "She's pleasant."

Twenty plus years later and Cassie fit in—sort of. She played golf and tennis and bridge. None of them particularly well. She was a tireless committee member who'd never been asked to chair an event. Her children, twins, were seniors at Grace's school. And sometimes, if she'd had one too many glasses of wine, you could still hear the small town twang in her voice.

"She's friends with Randolph's daughter?"

"No. I mean...they're friendly, but it's Katie's husband and Kinky who are friends. They graduated high school together." I took a bite of pie, closed my eyes and moaned.

Pie more than made up for having to visit Marjorie in the hospital.

Pie with Anarchy across the table from me? Well...

SIXTEEN

Lasagna. Pancakes. Banana cream pie. Good for my taste buds, terrible for my waistline. Exercise was required.

In the summer, I'd have swum. In October, the pool was closed. If I was lucky, a jog around the park would burn off the monumental number of empty calories I'd consumed and unsnarl the tangle of my thoughts.

I tied my shoelaces and stretched. Max happy danced around me like a dog who hadn't gone for a run in days.

It was Monday. It had been days.

"Sorry fella. I didn't realize." I rubbed behind his ears, clipped the leash to his collar and we jogged down the drive at a warm-up pace.

Together we ran to Loose Park and did two laps around the perimeter. The leaves were turning—crimson and umber, saffron and gold—and looked impossibly brilliant against the soft gray of a mist-filled day. The park was near empty and I took off Max's leash. He ran next to me for thirty seconds or so, then raced ahead, chased a squirrel up a tree, and waited for me to catch up, his pink tongue lolling out of his mouth. Four squirrels later, he was ready to head for home.

The steady slap of my sneakers against the damp sidewalk kept tempo with my heartbeat, and for the last mile or so I forgot the problems that beset my family. It was heaven.

And it had to end.

Libba's car was parked in the driveway when I got back to the house. She's never let a little thing like my absence get in the way of making herself at home.

"Look, Max, Auntie Libba is here."

He wagged his stubby tail.

I walked through the front door, let Max off his leash, and followed him to the kitchen. We both needed water.

Libba sat at the island with a can of Tab in front of her, talking on my telephone. She was dressed to the nines in a plummy tweed suit and a silk blouse. She waved her fingers at me and spoke into the phone. "Toodles, dear heart. Gotta go. Ellison's home." She handed me the receiver.

I looked at the receiver in my hand then at my so-called best friend.

"What? You're up. Besides—" Libba directed my attention to a pair of Ferragamo flats that exactly matched the purple of her blazer "—I'm breaking in new shoes and my feet hurt."

I hung up the phone without even a tinge of sarcasm. There's no point in wasting smart remarks on those who don't care when they've been zinged.

"You've been running." That Libba, she's an observant one.

"I have."

"You smell." Libba wrinkled her nose. She doesn't like to sweat unless there's a tennis racket involved. She'd no more go running than I'd go on a date with…with Quin Marstin.

"It's hard to smell like L'Air du Temps after a run. Where is everyone?"

"Grace is upstairs doing homework. Aggie went to the dry cleaners, the post office, the grocery, and the seamstress. She said to tell you that everything you need for tonight's salad is prepped and in the fridge. All you have to do is mix it together."

"Where's Aunt Sis?"

"I don't know. She said she had an errand and climbed into a cab."

Max lifted his head from his water bowl, allowing the excess water to drip from the sides of his mouth onto Aggie's clean floor. "Must you?" I asked.

He grinned at me.

I grinned back. It could have been worse. It could have been toilet water he was dripping all over the kitchen.

I opened the refrigerator door, noted the sealed Tupperware bowls filled with chopped vegetables and grilled chicken, and grabbed the water pitcher. Maybe I could drink without dripping.

Libba watched me gulp a glass of water and pour a second. "We could have played tennis."

"Not in the mood for the club parking lot."

"I guess I can't blame you."

"Besides, it's misty outside. What are you doing here? Like that?" I pointed at the suit.

"Lunch with my trustee." She smoothed her lapel. "And I haven't seen you since Saturday night. How are you holding up?"

"Fine."

"You are a terrible liar."

She wanted the truth? Generally when people asked they wanted platitudes. "Not fine."

"That I'll believe. How's your sister?"

"The doctors say she'll make a complete recovery."

"That's a blessing." She drummed her fingers on the countertop. "I've been thinking about everything that's happened in the past few days. Have you noticed that whoever is trying to kill you is completely incompetent?"

I choked on a sip of water.

"I mean it." Libba pointed a manicured finger my way for emphasis. "That bust might have hurt if it landed on someone's head but...it didn't. They missed when they shot at you the first time. I went outside and looked at where the soot is and where the bullet hole is. They're not even close."

I wasn't about to argue.

Libba tapped the tip of her nail against the Tab can. "Who leaves poison in a glass that anyone might drink?" She shook her head. "Seriously, who does that? And now they've shot the wrong Walford. Incompetent."

That or I wasn't the target.

I wasn't the target.

I wasn't.

Still, I shuddered to think what Anarchy would say if he learned I'd gone running alone. He did not share my faith in Max's protective powers.

I drank more water. So did my canine hero. Enough to make small puddles on the floor. I'd somehow managed to forget all about murder when I was running, I didn't want to talk about it now. I cast about for another topic. "Speaking of incompetent, I saw Quin Marstin at Luigi's last night."

"Did he hit on you?"

That was like asking if golf courses were green in springtime. "What do you think?"

Libba shook her head. "Poor guy."

Not the response I'd been expecting. "What do you mean, 'poor guy'?" The one thing Quin wasn't was poor.

Libba adjusted the bow on her blouse—fluffing. "He's almost forty and he hasn't done anything meaningful since he graduated from college. Too much money."

She was right on all counts, but how did that earn him a "poor guy" sobriquet?

"His friends have started families and companies and law firms. He clips the coupons off municipal bonds once a quarter and calls it a job well done."

"And you feel sorry for him?"

"I do. He's terrified everyone will see him for what he is so he pretends to be a player."

Who knew Libba had such observational skills?

"We talked one night."

"Talked?"

Was "talked" a euphemism for—

"Don't wear that face. It makes you look like your Mother. *All* we did was talk—one night at the bar at the club. I think he considers me a kindred spirit."

"Why?"

"I haven't exactly accomplished anything either. Then again, I'm a woman so no one expects me to."

"That's not true. You've accomplished plenty."

She waved her hands in front of her face as if the movement could wipe away what she'd just said—that or erase my assertion that she wasn't wasting her life. "It is true. In two years, I'll be forty and I have three divorces and a great shoe collection to show for it."

"Libba, that's simply not true."

"It is true. I can show you the divorce papers and my shoe collection is fabulous."

"You started a charity that provides daycare for working mothers who can't afford childcare."

"Ferragamos." She ticked off a finger.

"The luncheon you chaired for the museum raised more money than any before or since."

"Boots from The Chelsea Cobbler." She ticked a second finger.

"Your friends adore you."

"Boots from Hermès." She tapped a third finger.

"Grace thinks of you as a second mother."

Libba looked up from her count. "She does?"

"She does."

"That's very nice of you to say, Ellison."

"It's true."

Libba didn't say word. Instead she adjusted her bow a second time, smoothed her hair and sat up straighter on her stool. When she finally spoke, she said, "At any rate, poor Quin was drinking because his latest girlfriend had cheated on him."

"With whom?"

"Kinky."

I set my water glass down too hard.

"Really?"

She nodded. "Really. Quin was upset about it." She tilted her head to the side. "Not so much about the woman. I don't think she mattered to him. He was furious that Kinky poached on his territory."

"Was this recent?"

"A few weeks ago."

Had Quin been upset enough to slip poison into Kinky's glass? That didn't feel right. Surely a man with injured pride would call out his rival. Although, Quin seemed to fancy himself a lover not a fighter…

And who was this woman who'd slept with Quin and Kinky? How did one make choices like that? The mere thought of either one of them in bed made me shudder. "What is it about Kinky?" I asked. "I just don't see it."

Libba looked down at her Tab and her cheeks flushed nearly as pink as the can.

"You didn't." There's no way my voice could have sounded as scandalized as I felt. "He's married." And he was Kinky.

"I know." She kept her gaze on the suddenly fascinating soda pop. "It was just once."

"When?"

"A couple of years ago."

"And?"

"And he lives up to his name."

"That's not what I meant. How?"

"It's really been too long if you don't remember. You put tab A in slot B and then—"

"Libba! How did you end up in bed with Kinky?"

"He has this way of talking to a woman as if she's the only one he'll ever want."

"But what about Cassie?"

"That's why it was just once. I blame the martinis."

My late husband cheated on me with reckless abandon. We weren't in love. We weren't even friends. And each incident hurt me. I compared myself to the women he chose. What was it about Kitty Ballew or Madeline Harper or Prudence Davies (the mere thought of her tightened my jaw) that attracted him? "Does Cassie know?"

"About our one night? I doubt it."

"In general?"

"I think she pretends not to." Libba looked up from the can of soda. "Stop staring at me as if you disapprove."

"I do disapprove."

"It's not as if they're still in love."

What had Quin said? That Cassie was angry with Kinky for flirting with Marjorie? That sounded like a woman who still cared. "I think she is."

Libba considered this for a moment then whispered, "Damn." She returned her gaze to the Tab can. "What's done is done. It's not as if I can apologize to her."

"No," I agreed. I yanked a length of paper towels off the roll and dropped them on the floor near Max's puddles.

"Are you mad?"

"Not at you." A small lie. Given a few days to cool off, it wouldn't be a lie at all.

Per Aggie's instructions, neatly written and left next to the refrigerator, I made the salad. Grace and I ate it together at the breakfast table.

"Where's Aunt Sis?" she asked.

"No idea."

"She's very cool."

No arguments from me.

"Why do you think she decided to live in Europe?"

"I'm not exactly sure." I wasn't sure—not exactly.

"Is Aunt Marjorie coming home tomorrow?"

"Tomorrow or the next day."

The back door opened and Aunt Sis breezed in like a spring gale. "Oh good. I didn't miss dinner."

I stood. "I'll fix you a plate."

"Don't be silly. Sit down. I'll get it." Aunt Sis filled a plate with salad and joined us. "Where were you all day?"

"The hospital. Marjorie needed a bag. I also visited Randolph."

The fork traveling from Aunt Sis's plate to her mouth froze briefly. If I hadn't been watching, I would have missed it.

"Oh?" she said. "How is he?"

"Inundated with lonely widows and desperate divorcées."

"Already?" Her shoulders slumped slightly—a tiny movement. A tiny movement I would have missed if I weren't observing her like...like Anarchy observes a suspect.

Grace wrinkled her nose. "He's old and he smells like cigars."

"Randolph and I are the same age." Aunt Sis pronounced the words with a high degree of asperity.

My teenager, who probably thought thirty was ancient, shook her head. "No you're not."

"I assure you, we are."

"Nope." Grace was having none of it. She speared a bite of chicken and waved her fork at her great-aunt. "You stayed young. He got old."

"Ellison, you raised an extraordinarily charming daughter."

"Thank you, I know."

I also knew that in the weeks before Grace's birthday her charm increased exponentially.

My daughter raised a last bite of salad to her mouth then put down her fork.

"May I please be excused? I still have homework."

"Of course."

She picked up her empty plate and carried it to the sink (Grace hadn't quite figured out that putting the dirty dishes in the dishwasher part was an integral part of the process). "I'll talk to you later, Aunt Sis."

"Of course, dear."

"Dishwasher," I insisted.

The sigh of a deeply put-upon teenager echoed through the house, but she opened the dishwasher and put her plate inside.

The sound of her footsteps on the back stairs faded and I stared at my aunt. "We need to talk."

She laid her fork down on the edge of her plate.

"You and Randolph had a fling."

The blusher on her cheeks suddenly looked too bright—swathes of orange on pale skin. "A long, long time ago. How did you find out?"

I was the one asking the questions. "He was engaged."

Aunt Sis shook her head and her lips pursed. "Hammie broke things off."

That gave me pause. Two sides. One story. "What happened?"

"I'd had the biggest crush on him in high school. I came home from college that summer and he was so wounded. He needed someone. I stepped in."

"Then Hammie changed her mind."

Aunt Sis scrunched her face as if the past still hurt her. "He dropped me like a hot potato."

"Did Hammie ever know?"

"That we dated? I'm sure she did. I've often wondered if she changed her mind about Randolph because he found someone else so quickly." She lifted her water goblet. "It was a long time ago. Water under the bridge."

It wasn't.

"I know about Dav—"

"Don't say another word, Ellison." My aunt looked every bit as old as Randolph in his hospital bed. Older.

I reached across the table and laid my hand on top of hers. Upsetting my aunt wasn't part of my plan.

She used her free hand to wipe her cheek. "Water. Under. The. Bridge."

If in fact the water had passed under the bridge, I would have dropped it. But the water had a room at the Alameda. And it was only a matter of time before Randolph Walsh figured out that my aunt and my cousin had a reason to want Hammie dead. If Anarchy found out about my cousin, he'd make the connection in seconds.

"I met David."

The hand beneath mine turned ice cold.

Aunt Sis yanked her hand away from my touch. "We will not talk about this." She stood, knocking her chair over backward.

"But—"

"We will not."

"Aunt Sis, someone killed Hammie. The police are looking for people with motives. You have one."

"I had nothing against Hammie. I didn't kill her." Too bad she scratched her nose. "Besides, that water glass was at your place not hers. Who wants to kill you?"

"No one."

"Then who was supposed to be sitting there?"

Life would be much easier if we knew for sure.

Aunt Sis drew herself up and donned a *grande dame* expression so close to Mother's that for a moment I was struck speechless.

"The bust, the fire, the poisoning and the shooting. You are the common denominator. Just because you refuse to believe someone is trying to kill you, doesn't mean it's not true." With that she spun away from me in a swirl of caftan and outrage and marched out of the kitchen.

SEVENTEEN

Once upon a time, people hosted balls in their homes—large elegant parties with dancing and punch and the possibility of romance. They needed ballrooms.

I do not.

One of the first things Henry and I did to the house when we moved in was convert the third floor ballroom into a studio (this was when Henry and I fancied ourselves in love and he thought my painting was an amusing hobby).

My studio was the best possible place to spend a Tuesday morning. Bar none.

Besides, I'd made a deal with God. I owed the school auction a painting.

A landscape of Loose Park the way it was yesterday—a study in gray brightened by autumn leaves would have to do. I daubed paint onto my pallet and began sketching out a scene.

"It's nice to see you safely at home." Anarchy Jones stood just inside the door.

"What are you doing here?" Not exactly a polite reply but my studio was mine. No one entered but me and Grace (and that was only in the case of fire or blood).

"Your aunt sent me up." Aunt Sis was still furious with me— had she realized sending someone to my studio was a sure way to get even?

Anarchy took a moment, his sharp gaze taking in the mason jars filled with brushes, the cans of turpentine, the blank canvases stacked between two windows, and the battered pine table covered with art books and trays of acrylics. He stared for a moment at the lone club chair, shabby and comfortable, and the numerous abandoned coffee mugs that needed to be returned to the kitchen. "There's plenty of light."

Windows on three sides and multiple skylights insured that on a sunny morning, the studio was positively flooded with light.

He approached my easel and looked at the rough outlines of trees on the canvas it held. "I expected something...neater."

He stood too close. I could smell soap and the very faint scent of bay rum, as if he'd worn cologne the last time he'd donned his jacket.

I stepped away from the canvas, from him, and straightened an already neat pile of books. "Sorry to disappoint you."

"I'm not disappointed. I find it enlightening."

"Oh?"

"It's like seeing another side of you."

Exactly what I didn't want. "What can I do for you?" It sounded better than *why the hell are you here?*

"We got the ballistics reports back."

"Ballistics?"

"The bullet we dug out of the back of your house and the bullet they removed from your sister came from the same gun."

"What does that mean?" It was a stupid question, one I wanted back as soon as it left my lips. "Never mind. I understand what it means." One gun. One shooter.

It wasn't as if there'd ever been much doubt.

"We also got this." He pulled a folded sheet of paper from his inside coat pocket and handed it to me.

"What is this?"

"We took down every license plate in the parking lot when your sister was shot. That's a list of the owners."

I scanned—John Ballew, Brooks Foster, Kenneth LeCoeur, Quin Marstin, Harlan Stokes, Wright Thomas...the list went on and on. "Everyone on here is a club member."

"Look more closely. Someone is trying to kill you."

"Or Marjorie." I wanted that comment back too.

"Who would want to kill your sister?"

"No one." Too bad my voice squeaked. My brother-in-law, idiot though he might be, was the only person in Kansas City I could think of who might want my sister dead. I preferred that Anarchy remain convinced someone was trying to kill me rather than investigate Marji and Greg's sordid problems.

"Who?" he insisted.

I breathed deep. "No one." This time my voice sounded as if it belonged to me and not a five-year-old with a helium balloon. "I don't know why I said that."

What had Aunt Sis said? I was the common denominator?

Well, Marjorie had been present for three out of four attempts on my life. Maybe she was the target. Maybe Hammie's death was something entirely random—I'd simply been in the wrong chair at the wrong time. Nothing more.

If that was true, there were two killers.

I scouted the studio for the cup of coffee I'd brought upstairs with me. There. Next to the wooden mannequin. It still retained a bit of warmth. I wrapped my fingers around the mug and held it tightly.

Anarchy stepped closer to me. "What are you hiding?"

I took a sip of tepid coffee. The bitterness coated my throat. "Nothing."

"I worry about you." He took the mug out of my hands and returned it to the table.

"I'm fine."

"There have been multiple attempts on your life."

"I'm fine." If you say the same thing too often, it sounds ridiculous. *I'm fine. I'm fine. I'm fine.* Ridiculous.

"You're not." His fingers grazed my cheek.

My cheek tingled. My toes tingled. Everything in between tingled.

Tingling was bad.

Tingling led to tab A in slot B.

Tab A in slot B led to heartache.

I knew this but I didn't move away. I stood there, hypnotized by coffee brown eyes and a mere touch.

His fingers moved from my cheek to the nape of my neck and his hand warmed my suddenly chilled skin.

He was just inches from me—lean and handsome and nearly impossible to resist.

Thank God for nearly.

I pulled away from him.

"You know, I'm nothing like your husband."

"I know." Knowing a thing and believing it were entirely different.

"Do you ever wonder what it would be like to really kiss me? What would happen if we took our time? If no one interrupted?"

I was wondering that right now. "No." Too bad it was the five-year-old with the helium who answered for me.

A slow smile cracked his face, he stepped closer to me, and his lips brushed against mine.

His lips brushed across mine.

There was no tingling. Tingling is a gentle sensation. The lightning that seared my body was not gentle. It burned everything in its path. Reason. Responsibility. Doubts. Common sense. Every thought or feeling I had that might have protected me from the onslaught of Anarchy's warm, firm lips turned to ash.

I kissed him back.

We took our time. Each touch, each sigh seemed like a seismic shift, breaking apart the hard crust that protected me.

Our lips parted.

"Ellison," he said my name as if it was a prayer and a promise rolled into one.

Breathless. When a man like Anarchy Jones whispers a woman's name like that, it leaves her breathless. Or at least that's what his whisper did to me.

Maybe it was the lack of oxygen. Maybe it was a shift in light. Maybe it was some small, sensible part of my brain restarting or the realization that while he tasted of mint, I probably tasted like stale coffee. I put my hands on his shoulders and pushed away.

"We shouldn't." The five-year-old with the high voice had run off for a game of hide-and-seek. My voice sounded like a frog with laryngitis.

"Why not?" His brown eyes were seductive, his voice whiskey rough.

Because kissing Anarchy Jones made the world spin out of control. I preferred a well-controlled world, a world not fractured by sensation. A world without the kind of risk embodied by Anarchy.

"Ellison." This time when he said my name it sounded like a plea.

"It's too soon. I'm sorry. I just can't." I wiped my palms on my paint shirt as if I could wipe away the way his hair and his skin felt beneath my fingers—as if I could wipe away the memory of that kiss.

I wasn't that lucky. The memory of Anarchy's lips on mine was going to haunt my nights. Exactly the sort of off-kilter thinking I couldn't handle. "I think you should go."

He scowled. "I can't fight a dead man."

"Pardon?"

"I'd fight Tafft for you, but I can't fight your husband." He meant it—he'd tighten his hands into fists and battle Hunter for me like some modern-day knight entering the field with his lady love's token tucked near his heart.

"I have to fight my husband." No one—especially not a man—could vanquish Henry or the wounds he'd left behind. I had to triumph on my own.

Anarchy rubbed the pad of his thumb across my swollen lips. "Hurry up and win."

"I don't think this is something that can be rushed." The five-year-old was back from hiding and she'd found a fresh balloon. Oh goody.

"Where will you be today?"

I cleared my throat. "Here. Painting."

"Stay safe? Promise me."

Staying safe would mean staying away from him. I merely nodded.

"This isn't over."

Exactly what I was afraid of.

I chose the club for dinner.

Not the smartest choice I've ever made. In my defense, showing David that not all of his family was determined to keep him a secret was my motivation.

I didn't think about consequences.

We followed the hostess to our table, leaving a swell of speculation in our wake. I nodded politely to a few of Mother's friends and a few of mine.

Finally, we reached our table. Too bad it sat next to Beverly and Carter Byrd's.

Carter stood, forcing me to stop and chat. "Mrs. Byrd." I smiled at Beverly. "Mr. Byrd. What a treat to see you both. Please sit down."

Carter ignored my request.

"How is your mother holding up?" asked Beverly.

"It was a very trying weekend and, of course, she's devastated about Hammie."

It was far better that Beverly be curious about Mother than David. I wiped my metaphorical brow.

"And how is your sister?"

"She'll make a full recovery."

"That's a blessing." Beverly covered her heart with her hand. "It's absolutely terrifying that something like that could happen *here.*"

"Indeed, it is." My unknown escort was positively dull in comparison to a shooting in the parking lot.

"And just to steal her purse." Betty shook her head as if the world was coming to an end and she'd been appointed to watch the destruction. "It was stolen, wasn't it?"

Marjorie's purse had been found, untouched. It was truly amazing the stories the gossip mill could manufacture. "The police have asked me not to talk about their investigation."

"Of course they have, but you can tell me."

"Really, Beverly, I can't." I nodded. "I promised to keep my lips sealed." A story about a stolen purse was preferable to a story about how someone was trying to kill the Walfords.

A satisfied smile spread across her face.

"I've kept you from your dinner long enough. Have a lovely evening."

Apparently murder and attempted murder trumped any interest the Byrds might have in David. Carter sank back into his seat and David and I moved on.

We sat.

The hostess put menus in our hands. "Would you care for a drink?"

That's when disaster struck.

Mother and Daddy walked into the dining room. My stomach plummeted past my ankles and through the carpet. It ricocheted off an I-beam and whizzed past the basement's stone walls before splatting against the concrete floor.

"A martini. Dry. Hurry."

"Nothing for me, thank you," said David. If he'd but known what was coming, he would have ordered straight scotch.

The hostess hurried toward my waiting parents, said something, and Mother's gaze landed on me then shifted to the man with whom I was dining, a man without silver hair, a man who was not Hunter Tafft.

I read her lips.

"We'll join my daughter."

Damn.

She made her way across the crowded dining room—Tuesday being prime rib night; the club was busier than usual. Mother lifted her nose, set her eyes straight ahead, and pretended not to hear the sudden hush followed by a rush of whispers.

Nothing and no one could stop her.

Where was the waiter with my drink?

"Ellison, what a surprise."

David and I stood.

"Mother, I could say the same thing."

"I didn't feel like cooking."

Mother seldom feels like cooking. That is why my father employs a housekeeper who can also roast a chicken.

I didn't point that out in front of David. People who live in glass houses...

"Who is your friend, dear?"

Mother looked at David more closely and, well—

Grace has this *thing* that sits on her desk—almost like an hourglass but flat. And instead of sand, there's liquid inside. When it's turned, the colors run and fade and end up at the bottom. That was what Mother's complexion did. The flesh tones ran and faded until she was ghostly white.

The dining room at the country club was probably not the best place to introduce her to her father's doppelganger.

She swayed and Daddy pulled out a chair.

Mother sank into it.

She whispered something to my father and he waved over a waiter. "Scotch. Neat. Two of them."

I knew this encounter was going to call for scotch. Hopefully the waiter would bring my martini as well.

"Mother, Daddy, I'd like you to meet David." I pitched my voice low, but Mother still glared at me as if I'd just yelled *This is my aunt's bastard!* across the dining room.

"A pleasure." My father extended his hand and David shook it.

Mother looked ill. "Ellison, may I please speak with you in the ladies' lounge?"

"No."

That got her attention. Daddy's too.

"We'd be delighted if you'd join us for dinner." I extended an olive branch.

Daddy laid a hand on Mother's arm as if a simple gesture could keep her from—from making kindling. "We'd love to." Then my gentlemanly father turned to David and said, "How are you finding Kansas City?"

"It's beautiful. I'm staying on the Plaza and it reminds me of Seville."

The waiter brought our drinks. Thank God.

Mother, Daddy and I all reached for our glasses immediately. Drank immediately.

Somehow small talk carried us through dinner. Daddy's explanation of the local parks system saw us through the salad course. The rules for football proved enough to get us through our entrées. An explanation of the difference between Spanish and Italian olives kept silence at bay while we drank our coffee. Who knew some olives were treated with lye? I might have to rethink dirty martinis.

When we stood, Mother sank her talons into my arm. "Ellison, a word."

Daddy shrugged. It was beyond his power to save me now.

"I need to take David back to his hotel. Perhaps another time."

"I'm sure David won't mind if I steal you for a minute." The smile she gave him was truly terrifying.

He actually stepped back. "Of course not."

Judas.

Mother, her talons still deep in my arm, dragged me into the ladies' lounge. She let go of me—but only to ascertain that we had the room to ourselves. "What in the hell were you thinking?"

"I was thinking that David might enjoy a dinner out with someone besides Aunt Sis."

She planted her hands on her St. John clad hips. "Have you no sense of decorum?"

I didn't bother answering. Anything I said would feed her anger.

"Your family has stood by you through gossip and infidelity and murder and now you do this? Invite derision?"

"David is family too."

"It's not the same."

"Tell that to Aunt Sis."

Mother crossed her arms and softened her tone. "I'm only trying to protect you."

"From what?"

"Scandal."

Oh dear Lord. "I've weathered scandal. Trust me, no one cares if Sis had a baby out of wedlock but you." Not exactly true but...

"What about Katie Walsh Woods? Do you think she'll care?"

"She might be delighted to have a brother. I'm delighted to have a cousin. And if you cared about family half as much as you say you do, you'd be delighted to have a nephew."

I might as well have slapped her across the face.

Her eyes narrowed. Her lips pinched. Her hands curled—the talons were back. She opened her mouth, closed it, then turned on her heel and stalked out of the lounge.

I exhaled slowly.

Mother wasn't talking to Aunt Sis. Aunt Sis wasn't speaking to Mother. And now neither of them were speaking to me.

EIGHTEEN

Marjorie refused to go home with Greg. "Home" being a relative term. She refused to stay at the Alameda with Greg. *My home* was just fine.

Her adamant refusal meant I was the one at the hospital loading bouquets and plants into the back of Henry's car. For someone who didn't even live in Kansas City, she'd amassed an impressive amount of flora.

"I'll take that one." From the passenger seat, Marjorie pointed to an enormous bouquet of orchids and roses.

The nurse who was helping me handed the arrangement through the door.

Marjorie settled the vase between her legs.

Ostentatious. Expensive. Gorgeous. So many flowers it was nearly impossible to see Marjorie behind them.

"Who sent those?" I loaded the last bouquet into the back seat and closed the door.

Marjorie flashed me a smile through the roses. "A friend."

Great. Perfect. "Who sent them?" I added an edge to my voice.

"None of your business."

I slammed her door shut, walked around the car, opened the driver's side door and got in.

"There's no need to be testy," said Marjorie.

Testy? "Do you see the police car behind us?" My fingers tightened on the wheel.

She didn't turn. Apparently being shot in the shoulder makes glancing behind painful. "Yes."

"It followed me here. It will follow us home."

"What has that got to do with my flowers?"

"Maybe nothing." Probably nothing. "But there are too many secrets in this family."

"What's that supposed to mean?"

"Mind your own business." Petty? Yes. Childish? Undoubtedly. Incredibly satisfying? Absolutely. I started the car and pulled away from the curb.

"I think we should talk about something else." My sister stuck her nose in a full blown rose and inhaled deeply.

Good idea. "Did you see anyone in the parking lot before you got shot? Notice any strange cars?"

"I don't want to talk about that. The police have asked me those questions a thousand times."

"Now I'm asking."

"No. I did not see anyone. Aren't you driving a bit fast?" For someone living a fast lane lifestyle, Marjorie was a veritable Granny when it came to speed. "There is a policeman following you."

I eased off the gas. "What exactly happened?"

"I got dropped off."

"By whom?"

She hid her face behind her flowers. "Not telling."

"Fine. You got dropped off by the man who sent you those flowers, and...?"

"He left."

"He didn't wait to see you safely in your car?"

"Oh, please. It was the country club parking lot, not the ghetto."

And she'd been shot. "Did anyone follow you up the drive?"

"I don't think so."

"So whoever shot you was already at the club."

"I guess." She took another whiff of rose.

Someone had shot her. You'd think she'd be more interested in catching them than inhaling fragrance.

"And you didn't see anyone?"

"Don't you think I would have said? I wasn't looking for a lunatic with a gun."

"You said you heard a tapping."

"Yes."

"Like golf spikes on concrete?"

"Sort of. Not quite. Definitely steps. They stopped, there was a bang and the next thing I knew I was in an ambulance." She cast me a sideways glance. "You were crying."

"The last time I was in an ambulance with someone, they died."

"You were worried about me." She smirked.

"Of course I was worried about you. You'd been shot."

Anarchy had gone running at the sound of that shot.

Presumably a gunshot at the club had stirred at least a few men to investigate. Had someone opened the door to the parking lot? Was that why the killer hadn't taken a second shot? Why hadn't he made sure Marjorie was dead?

I thought back to the parking lot.

If I was the target, the killer had had ample time to realize their mistake and shoot me too.

The thought gave me pause. Why hadn't they?

Was Marjorie really the target?

Where had Greg been? Was he a killer? I had only his word for when he'd arrived in Kansas City. For all I knew he could have been staying at the Alameda for days. Or, if he was clever, he could have stayed at some anonymous hotel downtown for a few days and then checked into the Alameda when he wanted us to know he was in town. Could Greg have shot his wife?

I shook my head. Greg loved his wife. I was sure of it. He wouldn't try to kill her.

"The light is green." Marjorie interrupted my musings.

"Oh." I pressed the gas pedal. "Sorry."

We drove in silence for a moment.

"You're going to divorce Greg?"

"Yes."

"And marry the man who sent you the flowers?"

"Yes."

"Has he asked you?"

"No. But he will."

"You're sure?"

"I'm sure. I'm the only woman in the world for him."

"Really?"

"You don't have to sound so doubtful."

"I don't trust men." Who could blame me?

"Just because things didn't work out with Henry, doesn't mean you can't find happiness with someone else."

I kept my eyes on the road.

"Maybe Grace would like a new father."

"Grace is still mourning the old one." Death and divorce were hard on kids. "What are you going to tell your children?"

"That their mother is following her bliss."

"What?" Somehow I kept my eyes on the road. I couldn't keep the incredulity out of my voice.

"I went to a lecture by this man named Joseph Campbell. He says that if you follow your bliss, you put yourself on a path that has been waiting for you—the life you ought to be living. If you do that you'll find happiness."

"Do children or responsibilities appear on this path of yours?"

"My children want me to be happy."

"Your children want a mother."

"I need this. I've never done anything on my own."

"And you're not now. You're trading one husband for another."

Marjorie turned her head and looked out the passenger's window. "You don't understand."

I understood all right. Marjorie was borrowing or twisting a philosophy to justify whatever she wanted to do. I hit the turn signal hard enough that my fingers hurt. "I don't want to fight with you, Marji."

"But..."

She knew me well.

"Until your kids are out the door, their happiness should be more important than yours."

"How did that work out for you, Ellison?"

We drove the rest of the way home in silence. I pulled into the drive, parked, and got out of the car. I opened the back door and wrapped my arms around a Swedish ivy identical to the one I'd given Randolph. "I'll send Aggie out to help you."

Marjorie didn't reply.

Perfect. Now I wasn't on speaking terms with my mother, my aunt, or my sister.

Aggie opened the front door before I could fit my key in the lock. "Mr. Tafft called. He'd like to take you to dinner tonight."

"Does he realize I have guests?" Wait—I had guests who weren't speaking to me. "Please call him and tell him I'd be delighted."

Aggie grinned. "I already did."

I glanced over my shoulder. My injured sister still sat in the car, hidden behind a veritable rosebush. "Would you please help Marjorie?"

"Of course." Aggie stepped out onto the drive.

I've said it before, I'll say it again—Aggie is worth her weight in gold.

"Aggie, you're sure you don't mind?" Between my houseguests and my sister being shot, I'd forgotten all about my bridge game. Thank God I'd looked at my calendar. But leaving Aggie with Marjorie hardly seemed fair. I glanced at my watch. If I wasn't careful I'd be late, but guilt kept me in the kitchen.

"Go. Have a nice time." Aggie took a bowl of grapes out of the refrigerator.

"She hasn't asked you to peel them for her, has she?"

"Of course not. Go." She put the grapes down on the counter and reached for a can of Tab and a lime.

"I can find a sub."

"Go," she repeated. "Your sister and I will be fine."

I drove to the club with the policeman right behind me.

I parked, got out of my car, and approached him.

He rolled down the window. "Yes, ma'am?"

"I'm going to play bridge. I'll be three hours."

"Yes, ma'am."

"I'm telling you this in case you want to use that time to go catch a criminal."

"I'll be right here, Mrs. Russell."

Of course he would. Anarchy had sent him.

I walked into the clubhouse and headed straight for the card room. Libba and Jinx had already claimed our usual table. I hung my purse over the back of a chair. "I'm sorry I'm late."

Libba glanced at her watch. "Two minutes."

"Late is late." Late was inconsiderate. "Where's Daisy?"

"Taking one of her brood to the doctor's office. She says they're coughing up green gunk." Jinx wrinkled her nose. "Dorothy Howland is subbing for her."

I sat, claimed a deck of cards, and shuffled. "How's her divorce going?"

"Well," said Jinx.

"Marjorie's back at your house?" asked Libba.

"She is." My tone did not invite further questions.

"How's she feeling?"

"She'll live."

"Well, I think it's absolutely terrifying," said Jinx. "The police finally removed the crime scene tape from the parking lot this morning."

Dorothy hurried into the card room. "I'm so sorry I'm late. It's...there's a *police car* in the parking lot and I thought something else had happened."

I had no intention of admitting to a police escort. "I bet he's just keeping an eye on things after the shooting."

"Now, that's a good idea," said Jinx. "I feel better already. Do you think he might escort us to our cars?"

"Shall we play?" I fanned the deck across the table and drew a ten of diamonds.

Libba won the deal with a king of hearts.

We played a few hands. Part-scores. Nothing exciting.

"Did you hear about Kitty Ballew?" asked Jinx.

"What?" I asked.

"John is selling the house and insisting that Kitty get a job."

No wonder she'd looked so desperate in Randolph's hospital room.

"Well, I think that's awful," said Dorothy.

Dorothy and I weren't close. She didn't know that I considered Kitty public enemy number two (second only to Prudence Davies).

"So unfair," she continued. "Kitty gave John her youth and now what does she have?" No one said a word. "She has no skills. What kind of job is she going to find?" Dorothy had me confused with someone who cared.

"Are you and Kitty friends?" asked Libba.

"Not at all. I just think it's shameful that men walk away from a marriage with everything and women are left with nothing."

Perhaps her divorce wasn't going well after all.

"I'm sure he's going to have to pay some kind of alimony," said Jinx.

"He's selling her house. Even with alimony, she'll end up living in one of those tiny little apartments to the west of the Plaza. You know the ones; the bedrooms are the size of our closets. Kitty will get a job selling shoes to women with bunions or spritzing perfume at unsuspecting shoppers at Harzfeld's."

Jinx, Libba and I all shifted in our chairs. None of us would be sorry to see Kitty on her knees fitting shoes on strange women. "Whose bid?" I asked.

"Mine," said Libba. "One spade."

Dorothy frowned at her cards. "Pass."

"Three spades," I replied.

"Pass," said Jinx.

"Four spades." Libba went to game.

Dorothy played the ace of diamonds.

I laid down the dummy hand. A hand that included four spades instead of three.

"Poor Kitty." Dorothy shook her head. "I just hate hearing stories like this one."

Frankly, I hoped Kitty got the bunion job. That, and I hoped that every pair of feet she helped slide into pumps smelled.

Libba pulled the three of diamonds from the board.

Jinx threw the five of diamonds.

Dorothy stared at Jinx's five. "It's not just Kitty. What skills does a woman who's been married for twenty years have? She can run a house and take care of children and drive from school to piano lessons to football practice. How does that translate to the workplace?"

I didn't argue. Dorothy brought up excellent points. Points I should bring up with Marjorie in case her Prince Charming turned out to be a frog. Of course, Marjorie was one of the lucky ones; she'd never have to shoe-horn any feet but her own into Ferragamos. The trusts my grandfather had established ensured that.

Libba trumped Dorothy's ace.

"I saw Kitty the other day. She was visiting Randolph Walsh in the hospital." There was no need to explain the implications of such a visit.

Libba led back to the board with a low spade. "She didn't waste any time."

Dorothy played the ten.

"There were six women there," I said.

"See!" said Dorothy.

"See what?" said Libba, her tone mild. She played the jack from the board.

"She has no hope of finding another husband. The competition's too steep."

"Maybe for Kitty." Jinx laid down the nine. "Ellison doesn't have any trouble accumulating beaux."

The dummy's jack had won. Libba pulled the five of hearts from the board.

Jinx covered it with the king.

Libba took the trick with the ace.

Dorothy threw the seven of hearts. "Second hand low."

Libba and I focused on the cards lying on the table. Libba even caught her lower lip between her teeth. It wasn't the best of ideas to criticize Jinx's playing skills.

"I'll keep that in mind." Sure, Jinx sounded harmless, but I could tell she was annoyed—Dorothy and her sub-par skills would not be subbing for Daisy again. "If you had to get a job, what would you do?" asked Jinx.

"Stewardess," said Libba.

"Aren't you too old?" Jinx asked with an evil smile

"Bite your tongue. You might be aging. I'm getting younger. What about you?"

"I don't know. I've always enjoyed baking. Maybe I'd open a bakery. What about you, Dorothy? What would you do?"

Dorothy shook her head. "I have no earthly idea. I do know this; it wouldn't be selling shoes." Then she looked my way. "What about your sister? I hear she's getting divorced. Will she get a job?"

"Marjorie?" Good lord, had the gossip started already? Small wonder—the way Marjorie had been carrying on. "Where did you hear my sister was getting divorced?"

Dorothy rubbed her chin. "One of those parties. Maybe the ball?"

"As far as I know, Marjorie and her husband are not getting divorced." It wasn't a lie. Not exactly. Not as long as Greg refused to give her one.

"If she did get divorced, would she get a job?" asked Jinx.

"Lord, no."

"Does she have a good lawyer?" asked Dorothy. "A good lawyer makes all the difference."

Libba snorted. "She has a good trustee."

"Whose deal?" asked Jinx.

"Would you excuse me a moment?" Dorothy pushed away from the table.

I watched her walk away. "Sounds as if Dorothy is worried about spritzing perfume at Harzfeld's."

"Agreed." Libba cocked her head. "About your sister..."

"Yes."

"I bet there's another man."

I knew there was another man.

Quin Marstin?

Kinky LeCouer?

I crossed my fingers for John Ballew.

NINETEEN

"Have you heard anything about Hammie Walsh's funeral?" Jinx stared at her hand. "One no-trump."

Libba shook her head. "Pass."

"Don't let's talk about Hammie." Dorothy slid back into her chair and arranged her cards. "Her death upsets me so. Two clubs."

"Were you friends?" asked Libba.

"No, but I was seated at the table near hers when she died. It was awful." Dorothy shuddered.

"I was at her table," said Libba, unimpressed. "Ellison was sitting next to her."

At least she hadn't added that I'd shared my glass and poisoned her.

"Pass," I said. "And I agree with Dorothy on this. Let's talk about something else."

"Excuse me, Mrs. Russell." A waiter stood next to my chair. "There's a phone call for you."

I rose from my chair so quickly I saw stars. "Is everything all right?"

"I believe it's your housekeeper on the line."

I hurried to one of the oak paneled phone booths.

The waiter, who had followed me, said, "She's on line two."

"Thank you." I pushed the red-lit button. "Aggie?"

"I'm so sorry to disturb you." Aggie sounded harried.

"What's wrong?" Had something happened to Grace?

"Your sister is bored and she'd like a needlepoint project." Aggie kept her voice neutral. Unbelievable. In less than three hours my sister had driven my unflappable housekeeper to distraction.

"Oh, Aggie, I'm so sorry I left you with her."

"I called The Studio, that needlepoint store in Brookside. They'll stay open until you get there."

I glanced at my watch. "I'll go now." I'd have to break up the bridge game but somehow I didn't think Libba or Jinx would mind. "Thank you for calling."

Poor Aggie.

I hurried back to the card room. "Girls, I have to go. Marjorie is driving Aggie round the bend."

"Is there anything I can do?" asked Libba.

"Industrial size bottle of valium?" I grabbed my purse. "I'll talk to you later."

The policeman followed me to Brookside. He even found a parking space next to mine.

I waved at him then pushed open the door to The Studio and was met by a cheery jingle. Painted needlepoint canvases covered two walls. Yarn covered the third. The window that faced the sidewalk was filled with completed projects—belts and pillows and tote bags with needlepoint monograms.

Jane Prewitt, her hair pulled back in a bun, her readers perched on her nose, was seated at a large table in the center of the room pulling a forest green strand through a tiny canvas hole. She looked up from her project then put it on the table. "Ellison, you're here."

"Thank you for staying open. This is so kind of you."

"It's no problem at all. Someone is coming in for an interview in a little while. You need something for your sister?"

Would Jane be shocked if I asked for a scarlet "A"? "I do. Maybe a pillow?"

"What colors?"

"She's been wearing a lot of ice blue lately."

Jane stood, walked to the far wall, and considered the canvases hanging there.

"What about this one?" Jane pointed to a canvas with bright

colors and clean lines that looked as if Frank Stella might have painted it.

"Perfect. I'll take it."

"I'll just collect the yarn." Jane pulled this skein and that one from the wall.

The bell attached to the door hinge jingled and I turned.

Kitty Ballew stepped inside.

She stopped when she saw me and we barred our teeth at each other in vicious excuses for smiles.

"Kitty—" Jane looked over her shoulder "—you're early. I'll be with you in a few minutes."

Kitty was interviewing for a job? Chalk one up to Jinx's grapevine.

"What are you doing here?" Kitty asked.

"Shopping. You?" I added an extra dose of saccharine to my voice.

Kitty flushed slightly.

"Ellison picked out a project for her sister," said Jane.

Kitty stepped closer to me. "I hear she's been sniffing around John." Her voice was so low I could barely hear her. There was no way Jane could.

I just smiled. Sweetly.

"John might take her on a test run but, he'd never get serious about someone like that."

"Like what?" Marjorie on her worst day (today?) was better than Kitty on her best. My sweet smile now required effort.

"An adulteress slut."

Before he died, my husband developed a predilection for whips and handcuffs and apparatuses that resembled medieval torture devices. I had it on good authority that he'd strapped Kitty to those devices and whipped her. In that moment, I hoped every stroke of Henry's whip had hurt like hell. "Well," I said, "after being married to you, anyone John dates can only be an improvement."

"I need to run into the back for the last skein." Jane was oblivious to our whispered conversation. "I'll be back in a jiff."

With Jane gone, Kitty spoke louder. "I hear you've had a couple of near misses lately. You should be careful. Maybe next time whoever is trying to kill you won't miss."

"Are you threatening me?"

Kitty curled her lips. It was the kind of smile Genghis Khan smiled before invading China, the kind of smile Julius Caesar smiled before conquering Gaul, the kind of smile Attila the Hun smiled before pillaging the Balkans. It said she'd like to destroy me.

Before Kitty took up with my husband, we never had a problem. We weren't the best of friends—more like acquaintances who made a point of being pleasant. And then came Henry. Kitty chose to cheat on her perfectly nice, very dependable husband with a man who made alley cats look faithful (my husband). Yet it seemed as if she blamed me for her problems. There was no way I going to let Kitty Ballew see that her destructive smile bothered me. I yawned. "So, are you interviewing for a job? I'll have to put in a good word for you with Jane."

The smile flickered.

I wouldn't sabotage her chances of a job—not when she needed one—but she didn't need to know that.

"Genevieve Harney recently bought the same canvas." Jane's voice carried from the back room. She followed it into the shop with a bag in hand. "That won't be a problem, will it?"

"Of course not." Hopefully Marjorie and her duplicate needlepoint project would return to Ohio soon. "You keep records of who buys what?"

Jane nodded. "I do."

She wasn't the only shopkeeper to do that. Dress shops kept records. Wine sellers kept records. Florists kept records.

I had a call to make. I glanced at my watch. Too late. I'd call in the morning.

"Shall I bill you?" asked Jane.

"That would be lovely." I took the bag from her, went outside, and threw Marjorie's new project on the passenger seat. "I'm going home now," I told the policeman.

I arrived home to a flustered Aggie, an aunt who'd disappeared a few hours ago, a daughter who'd taken refuge in her room, and a sister who somehow managed to terrorize the entire household (even Max was in hiding) from the comfort of my favorite chair.

I walked into the family room and thrust the bag of needlepoint supplies into my sister's lap. "Have you lost your mind?"

"No."

"How dare you treat my housekeeper this way? You were raised better than this."

"I don't feel good." When Grace was five and had the flu she sounded more mature saying those words than Marjorie did now.

"I don't care how you feel." I glared at her. "Getting shot does not give you leave to treat people poorly." Especially not Aggie.

Marjorie lifted her nose as if she intended to look down its length—hard to do when she sat and I stood. "I think I liked it better when you weren't speaking to me."

"I'm not speaking to you now. This is a special circumstance."

"Humph."

I lifted a finger and waved it at her. "Aggie is the best thing that has happened to Grace and me all year. If you can't behave yourself, you can leave."

"You'd pick your housekeeper over your own family?"

"Aggie was around when Henry died. Where were you?"

"I knew you'd throw that in my face one day."

"You went to a swim meet, Marjorie." Perhaps—just perhaps—I might still be harboring a bit of anger over that.

"That meet was important to Harper."

"Having a mother is important to Harper. Missing a swim meet is not."

"Maybe I should leave." She spoke in a poor-poor-pitiful-me tone that invited argument.

If she expected me to argue with her she destined for disappointment. "Shall I call Greg?"

"Greg?"

"Your husband. You remember him, the father of your children. Maybe he'll pick you up."

"There's no need to flip." She seemed to sink farther into the chair—that or she was shrinking.

She stared at Walter Cronkite's face on the television and a moment passed. "I'm sorry."

She wasn't. She just didn't want to leave with Greg.

Her eyes closed, she chewed on her lower lip, and her shoulders slumped. "I should have come. Greg and I were having problems and the kids had so much going on. It just seemed easier—" She shook her head slowly. "I should have come. And I shouldn't have said what I did in the car. I'm sorry."

What she'd said in the car had angered me because it hit too close. I should have divorced Henry. I'd made a huge error, and I'd made it trying to protect Grace. Now it seemed as if I was urging the same mistake on my sister.

I half-collapsed onto the corner of an ottoman. "Marjorie, do you remember Bathilda?"

"The Nazi nanny? How could I forget her? She frightened us half to death."

"What about Estancia? Do you remember her?"

"She was worse."

Actually she wasn't. She was just dramatic. In a family where low-key elegance was a daily goal, big emotions left us confused.

"And Yvette?" The French girl had mostly ignored us. "Do you remember her?"

Mother had hired the United Nations of au pairs.

She nodded.

"What's your point?"

"We had nannies. We wanted Mother. I don't care if you leave your husband, but don't leave your kids."

Marjorie dropped her head into her hands. "When I think about going back and restarting my marriage...plus, the carpools and the brown bag lunches and the rides to practice and what's-for-dinner? I just feel so exhausted."

"I think all mothers feel that way from time to time. Please, think about your children. They need you."

She lifted her head and tears stood in her eyes "I will."

"I'm supposed to go out to dinner with Hunter. Do you want me to cancel?"

"No."

"You're sure?"

"Actually—" she lifted the bag of canvas and yarn from her lap and put it down next to her chair "—I'm very tired. I think I'd like to go to bed." All that trouble for a canvas that would most likely go untouched. I ought to set up a lunch date with Kitty for her.

I swallowed my frustration. "Whatever you'd like." I wasn't going to argue with her—not when she showed signs of listening to me. "Come on. I'll help you upstairs. I need to change."

Thirty minutes later, Hunter picked me up. "Where would you like to go?"

"Someplace where I won't see my family or anyone who knows my family."

He reached across the front seat of his Mercedes and took my hand in his. "That bad?"

"Awful. But we can't go too far away. Marjorie may decide to terrorize Aggie again."

"Aggie can take of herself."

I shook my head. "You don't know Marji when she doesn't feel well."

He drove us to a Chinese restaurant near the Plaza. "This okay?"

Everyone's favorite spot for take-out, it was a rare occasion that anyone we knew actually ate there. "Perfect."

"Does the policeman want to join us?" There was an edge to Hunter's voice as if it was Anarchy who'd followed us from my house and not a man in a squad car.

"No, but he'd probably like some take-out."

Hunter grinned at me—all white teeth and raw strength. "We'll send him some fried rice."

The hostess led us to a quiet table without him having to ask.

"Do you still have that dollar I gave you?" The last time I'd been a murder suspect I'd retained Hunter for the grand sum of one dollar.

"I do."

"So anything I say to you is privileged? Or do you need another dollar?"

"We're good."

"I'm worried that Greg may have tried to kill Marjorie."

"I thought it was your mother who harbored those suspicions."

"She told you?"

He nodded.

"And you're telling me?"

"She didn't give me a dollar. Besides—" he reached across the table and took my hand, "—I wouldn't take her money if she offered. There's a potential conflict of interest."

My heart fluttered. Any woman's would.

"Anar—Detective Jones thinks someone is trying to kill me. I'm not so sure. I think Marjorie is the target."

Hunter kept my hand.

"Tell me."

I told him. How far the bust was from hitting me. How much closer the shot in my backyard came to hitting Marjorie than me. How I'd sensed a killer in the parking lot but no one had shot at me.

"The only problem with your theory is Hammie's death. Marjorie was never supposed to be seated at that table."

"What if it's unrelated?"

He claimed my hand again and his thumb rubbed a gentle circle on the back. "I just don't see it. Either someone, thank God an incompetent someone, is trying to kill you or there are two killers and two targets and you just happen to be around for each attempt."

Well, when he said it that way, my theory did sound far-fetched. But...there was no reason for anyone to want me dead. Not love, not money, not jealousy, not sex.

"I think Kinky LeCoeur was supposed to be in my seat at the ball."

Hunter's lips thinned.

"Or maybe the cards got shifted and Hammie was supposed to be there." I'd thought about those damned place cards so much that in my mind they got up on little place card feet and moved themselves.

"Who would want Hammie dead?"

"Privileged?"

He nodded.

"My aunt."

"Pardon?"

"It's true. She and Randolph had an affair years ago and she had a baby."

Hunter's handsome face remained expressionless. Whatever he was thinking, I couldn't read it there. No wonder he made such a good lawyer.

"The baby, David, is forty now. He has diabetes and he's going to need a kidney."

"So that's why your aunt came home."

"It is."

"Have you been tested yet?"

"Tested?"

"To see if you're compatible."

"No. Aunt Sis hasn't asked." I hadn't thought of it, but I'd offer as soon as I got home. "She's been focused on Randolph."

"Randolph's too old. She's focused on Katie."

"Whatever her focus, Randolph didn't want Hammie to know about David."

"And now Hammie is dead."

I nodded.

"My aunt had a motive."

Hunter stroked his chin. "There are lots of people with motives who don't commit murder. Besides—" he gifted me with an everything-is-going-to-be-all-right smile "—I bet it was Kinky who was supposed to be in that chair. There are no end of people who'd like him dead."

I don't know why that made me feel better, but it did. They say a problem shared is a problem halved. Finally, I understood what they meant.

We ordered. Kung Pao for me. Moo Shu for Hunter. And combination fried rice for the policeman.

I might not trust Hunter with my heart, but I did trust him with my secrets.

TWENTY

There are probably lots of good florists in Kansas City. I know of three. And really, with a list of three florists who can work magic with only a few flowers, why would I ever need to call anyone else? I crossed my fingers that whoever had sent that enormous bouquet to Marjorie thought the same.

I sat cross-legged on my bed and picked up the phone, my finger frozen above the dial. I wasn't invading Marjorie's privacy. I wasn't. I was calling from my bedroom, as opposed to the kitchen, so no one would interrupt. It had nothing whatsoever to do with not wanting Marjorie to hear me.

I dialed my favorite florist first. "This is Ellison Russell calling."

"Good morning, Mrs. Russell."

"I'm hoping you can help me."

"Of course, Mrs. Russell."

"We moved my sister home from the hospital yesterday and somehow lost the list of who sent what." I scratched my nose. "She'd like to write thank you notes today and we're in a pickle. Would you please tell me what you sent to Mrs. Blake and who paid for it?"

"One moment, please."

I stared at my bedroom walls, tapped my pen against my notepad, and examined my cuticles.

Finally, the voice came back on the line. "I have that list for you, Mrs. Russell." The woman on the other end of the line proceeded to tell me about Swedish ivy, stargazer lilies, an order called in from Ohio for yellow mums and daisies in a white compote dish, a wooden duck filled with roses, and a fern.

They'd been responsible for the duck? I might have to reconsider my favorite florist.

"My sister received a lovely arrangement, a large one, with pink roses and orchids. Did someone send that?"

"No, ma'am."

"Thank you," I said. "You've been most helpful."

I dialed the second florist. More ivy, more modest floral arrangements, more ferns—no duck, a point in their favor.

I dialed the third.

The girl who answered the phone remembered the orders that went to Marjorie. A fern and an enormous arrangement of roses and orchids.

"Who sent those?" I asked.

"Let me pull the ticket. Would you hold please?"

"Of course."

Someone in my house picked up an extension.

"Hello," I said. "I'm on the phone."

"Would you let me know when you're done?" asked Marjorie.

Call it bad timing. The flower shop girl came back on the line. "Mrs. Russell, a Mr. Kenneth LeCoeur sent those flowers."

Lord love a duck—and not a tacky wooden one with a scooped out back filled with flowers. Kinky? Really? I thought Marjorie had better taste. Maybe she didn't. Maybe she liked the wooden duck.

"Thank you." I hung up the phone and waited.

Not long.

My bedroom door flew open. Marjorie stood in the doorway flushed with righteous anger. "How dare you?"

"I needed to know."

"Why?"

Multiple attempts at murder. One of which was successful. I pursed my lips.

"Why?" Her high-pitched tone made Max cover his ears.

"What was your plan, Marjorie? Divorce Greg for Kinky?"

Without conscious effort I twisted Kinky's name into something contemptible. "How did this start?"

"None of your business," she snapped.

I shook my head. "We're not doing that again."

She responded with a mulish expression and crossed her arms

If she wanted an argument on a five-year-old level, she could have it. I upped the ante. "I'll tell Mother."

"You wouldn't."

"I would." The threat hung in the air like a cartoon balloon—that or a fresh-hewn hatchet.

She caved. "Our high school reunion. We reconnected. We're in love."

Oh dear Lord. I didn't want to know any more. Already my imagination supplied whispered phone calls and stolen weekends. Thanks to Greg's idiocy, Marjorie wasn't even cheating.

But Kinky was. On his wife and on his girlfriend.

"He's cheating on you."

"What?" She squinted at me.

I unfolded my legs and stood. "Kinky is cheating on you."

"Don't be ridiculous."

"I'm not. He slept with some woman Quin was seeing."

"I don't believe you."

"It's true. It was a couple of weeks ago. Why would I make that up?"

"Because you want me to go back to Greg."

True. But it was also true that Kinky was a cheater. "Call him. Ask him. Or call Quin."

"It can't be true." She sounded less certain.

"Why can't it? He's cheating on Cassie by being with you. It's not as if you picked someone of strong moral fiber." Ugh. I sounded exactly like Mother. I softened my tone. "Marji, he's a cheater."

"He loves me."

"Maybe he does." He didn't. "But according to Libba, he's been cheating on Cassie for years."

"That's not true. I'm the only one."

What else had Libba said? That Kinky could make a woman feel like she was special? My sister had bought that hook, line and sinker.

"You're not the only one. There's Libba, and the woman from a few weeks ago, and God knows who else."

"Libba?" Marjorie's chin quivered.

"Libba."

Marjorie stumbled all the way into my room and sank into a chair. "You're sure?"

"I'm sure. Libba told me before I ever dreamed you'd—"

"I don't believe it." The mulish expression settled back onto her face.

If she wouldn't take my word, I'd prove it. The phone book lay on the bed. I flipped through its pages. Marstin.

Calling Quin Marstin wasn't something I ever dreamed I'd do.

He answered on the third ring.

"Quin, it's Ellison Russell calling."

"Ellison. Babe."

Two words and already I felt queasy.

How does one ask a man about the woman who'd cheated on him with his friend? "Quin, I don't quite know how to say this."

"It's cool, babe. I get it. How about drinks tonight? Then we can come back to my place. Or if you want to cut to the chase, we can have drinks here."

He couldn't think—

He didn't think—

"I've been expecting you to call. I knew Tafft was too uptight for a stone fox like you."

He could.

He did.

Quin thought I was calling him for a date. No—not a date—a rendezvous—for sex. I closed my eyes and ignored the heebie-jeebies crawling on my skin. "I think you have the wrong idea."

"I have all sorts of ideas. We can try them out tonight."

I shuddered.

Marjorie tilted her head to the side.

"What?"

I waved her off. "I heard a rumor that—"

"It's true. Ten inches."

What?

"All for you, babe."

Sweet baby Moses in the bulrushes.

"Quin." My voice was as sharp as affronted sensibilities could make it—that is to say, razor sharp. "I did not call you for sex."

"Then what do you want?"

"You were seeing a woman."

"I see lots of women."

"Recently."

"You're not narrowing the field much, Ellison."

"This one cheated on you with Kinky."

Ten seconds passed. When you're holding a phone ten seconds seems like an eternity. "Quin, are you there?"

"How did you hear about that?" That on-the-make teasing quality in his voice had disappeared, replaced by something cold.

"It doesn't matter."

"It does."

"Is it true?"

"Why do you care?"

"I'm trying to convince someone that Kinky isn't worth her time." Maybe Quin would talk about the woman who'd cheated on him if it meant ruining Kinky's chances for—I crossed my fingers—"tail."

"Marjorie?" he asked.

Now it was my turn to be quiet.

"Put her on," he said.

I held the phone out to my sister.

She looked at it as if I was holding out a rat. But she took the receiver and she held it against her ear.

"When was this?" she asked.

Whatever Quin said brought tears to her eyes. She sank onto

the edge of my bed and lowered her head. "Who?" Her voice was thick with unshed tears.

I couldn't hear his answer, but Marjorie's spine straightened. "You're kidding?"

She listened to Quin's answer.

"And Kenneth told you about it?"

Whatever Quin said took a long, long time.

"That must have been very difficult for you. Thank you, Quin. You've been most helpful." She stood and put the receiver back in its cradle. "You were right." She shook her head. "I can't believe he'd cheat on me with her."

"Who?"

"That hatchet-faced witch, Kitty Ballew."

Some might argue that Marjorie's description was kind. I, for one, could think of much more colorful things to call Kitty.

"You should get dressed," said Marjorie.

Last time I checked, jeans and a sweater counted as clothes. "I am dressed."

"Dressed for lunch. You have to come with me."

"I do?"

"I'm having lunch with Kenneth."

She'd just been released from the hospital and now she was traipsing off to lunch?

"Don't go."

"I have to go. I want the satisfaction of looking in his eyes when I tell him what a turkey he is."

Turkey? Surely Marjorie could come up with something better than "turkey." Her vocabulary needed expanding. "You don't need me for that."

"I do. Kenneth could sell ice to Eskimos. I need you there for moral support."

"Let me understand this. He lied to you?"

"Yes."

"He cheated on you?"

"Yes."

"And you need me around to make sure he doesn't talk his way back into your good graces?"

"Exactly." She leaned toward me. "Please."

I closed my eyes, counted to ten, and took a deep cleansing breath. "Fine." If lunch was all it took to keep Marjorie away from Kinky, I'd attend a hundred lunches.

"Where?"

"The Pam-Pam Room."

Was she kidding? "The Pam-Pam Room at the Alameda?"

"Are there two?"

"The Pam-Pam Room at the hotel where your husband is staying?"

"Oh." It was more of an exhalation than an actual word.

"Can you change the location?"

She glanced at her watch. "It's too late. I can't get in touch with him."

"Then stand him up."

"No." She shook her head. "I want this to be over."

This had all the makings of a disaster. I marched to my closet with all the enthusiasm of a condemned man walking toward a firing squad, opened the door and pulled out my favorite Diane von Furstenberg wrap dress. "Is this okay?"

"Fine."

"I'll be ready in fifteen minutes."

The police officer in the patrol car followed us to the hotel and into the parking garage.

Marjorie and I climbed out of Henry's Cadillac, and I approached the officer's car. "Would you please come inside?" The potential for ugliness was high.

"Yes, ma'am." He followed us to the lobby then found himself a chair.

Our heels clicked on the restaurant's parquet floor as the hostess led us to a table with a view of the Plaza.

"You're sure you want to do this?" I asked. "We can leave."

"No. We can't. There he is." She sounded slightly breathless as if she was talking about Mick Jagger or Warren Beatty and not a philandering putz she'd known since first grade.

Kinky claimed a chair next to Marjorie. "Ellison, this is a surprise." Then he waved the waitress over. "A martini. Wet. Girls, what do you want to drink?"

I'd passed out of girlhood twenty years ago. "Nothing, thank you."

He stiffened at the tone of my voice. "What about you, Marji?"

"Tequila sunrise."

"Marjorie, you're on pain meds."

She ignored me. "A tequila sunrise."

Kinky took my sister's hand in his. "Marji, how are you feeling?"

He looked solicitous. He sounded as if he cared about her answer. The Eskimos might buy his ice, but I didn't believe him for a minute. Now was her chance to tell him he'd hurt her and to take his "turkey" ass right out of her sight.

She didn't. She sat and gazed at him with stars in her eyes.

"She was shot. She's tired. She's sore. And she shouldn't be drinking." I glared at them both.

"Ellison, don't scold."

Any minute now, Greg or David was going to walk through the door and a bad situation would get worse.

"I believe you had something you wanted to tell Kenneth."

The waitress arrived with their drinks.

Kinky took a sip of his martini. "What is it, doll?"

Marjorie played with the straw in her cocktail. "You've been seeing other women."

"I have not."

"Kitty Ballew."

"Kitty? She doesn't count. That was just to prove to Quin that anyone could have her."

I tried to follow that logic trail and ran into a brick wall.

Apparently Marjorie did too. "Did you stop and think how I might feel about it?"

"You?" Kinky sounded genuinely confused.

"I thought we had an understanding." Marjorie's voice was flimsy. Her chin quivered. She patted under her eyes with the pads of her fingers.

"Lighten up, Marji."

You'd think with all the women Kinky had slept with he'd have learned a bit about the female psyche.

Marjorie's chin stopped quivering. She left off fighting tears and narrowed her eyes. "I left my family for you."

"I said lighten up." Kinky smoothed his silk tie. "It's not as if we're married."

I refrained—barely—from pointing out that marriage didn't seem to be a hindrance to his cheating.

"So if we were married, there wouldn't be anyone else?" Marjorie's voice held an edge.

"Of course not." Kinky's promise fell from his lips, pretty as rose petals thrown at a wedding.

"Isn't that what you promised Cassie?" It slipped out. Not my fault.

Kinky glared at me. "This isn't your affair."

This isn't your affair—nothing but a slightly more polite way of saying *none of your business*. Telling Marjorie to lighten up was a gaffe, telling me to mind my own business was an epic blunder.

"Have you filed for divorce, or are you worried about how much Cassie will take you for?"

Again Kinky smoothed his tie—a pretty one, Hermès by the look it. "Cassie gets nothing. We have a prenup. My parents wouldn't let me marry a hick from Arkansas without protections in place."

Twenty years of putting up with Kinky and she got nothing? Well, nothing but a job at Harzfeld's spritzing perfume at women she used to call her friends. "That's not fair."

Kinky shrugged and looked deeply into Marjorie's eyes. "You're the only woman for me."

"And aside from Kitty, I'm the only woman you've been with?"

He hesitated, stroked her cheek, and ran his thumb over her bottom lip. "You know it, babe."

Couldn't Marjorie hear the truth in that hesitation?

She lifted her tequila sunrise, lurid in the afternoon light. "Promise?"

"Cross my heart. I could never lie to you."

In one fluid motion, Marjorie dashed her drink into Kinky's smug face. "Liar!"

Every head in the restaurant swiveled.

Marjorie was beyond caring. She grabbed his martini glass off the table and threw that too. "You. Are. A. Liar."

"Get ahold of yourself." Kinky wiped his face with a linen napkin then grabbed her arm and shook. He probably didn't mean to shake her so hard. He probably forgot she was recovering from a gunshot wound. He probably didn't notice her skin turning a delicate shade of asparagus.

"Let go of my sister!"

He sneered at me.

"Let go of my wife." Greg's fist connected with Kinky's chin. The resulting crash of body into table and china and cutlery would have given Mother a nervous breakdown.

I found the sound musical. Although...it was too bad about the tie.

Greg helped Marjorie from her chair.

She wrapped her arms around him and rested her head on his shoulder. "Oh, Greg, thank you. You saved me."

It was only then that the policeman appeared. Probably for the best...if a woman is going to depend on a white knight, he might as well be her husband.

The restaurant manager, a hand-wringing hotel manager, and all manner of waiters and bellhops circled the wreckage.

Kinky dragged himself off the floor. "Bitch."

Greg raised his fist again and Kinky retreated—retreated all the way out of the restaurant.

"I'll replace everything that's broken," said Greg. "I apologize for the mess and the commotion." He pulled out his wallet and withdrew a hundred.

The restaurant manager accepted the bill. "Thank you, sir."

"He insulted my wife."

The expressions of the men circling us changed from annoyance to respect. They nodded.

Marjorie's expression—well, she looked at her husband as if he was Superman.

I was definitely no longer needed. "I'm going home. Shall I have Aggie pack your things?"

Marjorie spared me a half second of her starry-eyed gaze—just long enough to nod. The policeman followed me to the garage and watched me slide behind the wheel of the Cadillac. I sat for a moment and breathed a sigh of relief. Finally, something had gone right. Things were looking up. At last.

TWENTY-ONE

I pulled out of the hotel's garage, circled the fountain some genius had stuck in the middle of the drive, and turned right.

Marjorie was back with Greg. They'd work things out. I actually smiled as I crested the hill. The traffic light was green and I pressed the gas pedal. Henry's land yacht surged forward and the light turned yellow. I pressed the brakes.

Nothing happened. Well, the pedal met the floorboard but the car didn't slow. Not one bit.

I whizzed through the red light followed by the blares of multiple horns. There was no time to worry about who I'd upset. The car was now headed downhill and picking up speed.

I white-knuckled the wheel as if holding it tightly might somehow restore the car's brakes.

Behind me the policeman turned on his siren.

Perfect. I needed another distraction.

Also perfect? What do people do when they hear a police siren? They slow down. I couldn't slow down. I jammed my foot against the brake pedal. Hard. Harder. There was no resistance. I might as well have pushed my foot into the floorboard.

The road ahead of me was littered with slowing cars—all intent on pulling over to the side. My car was intent on going faster and faster. I was intent on not dying.

Then it happened.

A woman in a Cadillac even bigger than Henry's stopped right in front of me. I jerked my wheel to the right, popped the curb with a bone-jarring bounce and entered Loose Park.

Branches whipped at the car's windshield. The tires bumped across uneven terrain. Smart people grabbed their children or pets and got out of the way.

I pressed the horn and held it. At least that worked.

The car was going to cross the walking path. An older gentleman and his basset hound stared at me, matching looks of horror on their faces as the car raced toward them.

I yanked the wheel, narrowly missing them and an oak tree.

The pond on the other side of the path I didn't miss.

Henry's car hovered above the water for a split second—long enough for me to pray. Oh. Dear. Lord.

The car dove into the duck pond like a seven-year-old leaping off the high board. The Cadillac made an enormous splash then sank like the tank it was.

Water already covered my ankles...my calves...my knees.

I tried the door. It refused to budge. I cranked the window. My hands, damp with sweat or the water already filling the car, slipped from the handle.

Dammit.

I refused to drown. Especially in Henry's Caddy.

I grabbed the handle again. Held tight. Circled once. Circled twice...Lower. Lower. Lower.

Ice-cold water poured in on me. My heart beat triple time.

I squeezed out of the opening, my dress catching on something.

I yanked, felt the fabric give, and kicked through the murky water toward the surface.

The policeman who'd followed me stood on the edge of the pond, his hand shading his eyes, his gaze fixed on the water.

If I live to be a hundred, no one will ever look as happy to see me as that man. He didn't have to tell Anarchy Jones I'd died on his watch.

I swam to the side of the pond, my arms suddenly heavier than lead, my legs so tired that the effort of kicking left me breathless.

The policeman hauled me out of the water. "You scared the

hell out of me." He wiped his forehead. "I don't swim. Are you hurt?"

I didn't answer. Instead I gazed at the last bubbles rising from the depths of the pond.

"Are you hurt?" he repeated.

The adrenaline that had replaced the blood in my veins vanished. I swayed on my feet. A few stars mixed with the bubbles.

"You're shaking. Where are you hurt?"

"She's in shock," said the man with the basset hound. His dog regarded me with drooping, red-rimmed eyes and barked in agreement.

I would have agreed with them but my teeth were chattering too wildly to speak.

"I'm going to call an ambulance," said the policeman.

I really ought to learn his name. He looked like an Alec. A not-so-smart Alec.

I sank onto the grass with the dead leaves and duck droppings and waited.

The sky was a pretty shade of blue. It was easier to look at if I lay down. I did that. What shade of blue? Royal? Indigo? Cerulean? The sky in Kansas City only achieved this saturated shade in October. I christened it October blue. After the darkness of the pond, it was the loveliest color I'd ever seen.

I closed my eyes.

"Ellison."

Damn it. I wanted to rest.

"Ellison!" I recognized that voice and it didn't sound happy. "Are you sure she didn't hit her head? Where the hell is the ambulance? How did this happen?" Nope. Detective Anarchy Jones did not sound happy.

"Don't y-y-y-yell at Alec. It wasn't his f-f-f-fault."

"Who's Alec?"

I opened my eyes. Anarchy and not-so-smart Alec loomed above me. I hate it when men loom.

How had he arrived so quickly? I'd only closed my eyes for—I glanced at my watch—note to self, Piagets and pond water don't mix. I squinted at the tiger's eye and diamond face. The hands didn't move.

I sat. A mistake. The remains of my breakfast objected. I added vomit to the dead leaves and duck droppings.

Anarchy crouched next to me and rested his hand on my shoulder. "Ellison, what happened?"

"No brakes."

"Had you been having problems with them?"

"No. The car is less than a year old."

Anarchy shifted his gaze to the police office who'd been assigned to protect me. "Get a team out here. Get that car out of the pond. Have someone check the brake lines. It sounds as if they were cut."

Good plan. I wiped my mouth with the back of my hand. "My purse is in the car." The car was in the pond. My dress was ruined. I was soaking wet. And I smelled like duck droppings, pond scum, and vomit. There are times when a woman's only recourse is to cry. I did that.

Not delicate tears but great wrenching sobs that shook my body, fat tears that soaked my face and melted my mascara. My nose probably turned a bright shade of crimson.

"I—" my voice quavered "—am t-t-t-tired—" I hiccupped "—of p-people—" I wiped my nose on the sleeve of my ruined dress "—trying to—" I hid my face in my hands "—k-k-kill me."

Anarchy ignored the dead leaves and duck droppings and vomit, sat on the ground, and pulled me into his lap. "You're shivering."

"The water was fr-fr-freezing." And I was soaking. The October breeze felt like a January gale. I snuggled closer to Anarchy's warmth.

His arms tightened around me but he addressed not-so-smart Alec.

"What's the ETA on that ambulance?"

"Three minutes."

"Ellison." His voice softened. "Can you tell me what happened?"

"The b-b-b-brakes didn't w-w-work." Talking would be easier if my teeth would stop chattering.

"Where had you been?"

"The Ala-la-lameda."

Anarchy glared at not-so-smart Alec "Weren't you watching?" His voice lost all of its softness. It sounded hard-edged and cop-like.

"N-n-n-not his f-f-fault. I asked him to c-c-c-come inside."

Anarchy's arms felt heavenly warm. Too bad they stiffened. "So your car was unattended. Did you lock it?"

"No."

"No?"

"I n-n-n-never do."

He must have caught a whiff of my pond scum hair because his face contorted. "Ellison, you have to be more careful. Someone is trying to kill you. You finally admitted it just a minute ago."

As men go, Anarchy is one of the good ones. But telling a drenched woman who's covered in pond scum and duck droppings—one who's contemplating the destruction of an expensive watch, the loss of her handbag and the sinking of her husband's car—*I told you so* is not smart. It is the equivalent of telling the woman to lighten up when she's upset about infidelity. Unfortunately, I did not have a tequila sunrise handy. "Or M-M-M-Marjorie. Someone might be trying to k-k-kill Marjorie. She went to the Al-la-la—" I swallowed. "She went to the hotel with me."

"You left her there?"

I nodded. "With her husband."

He stroked my wet, stringy, smelly hair. "We'll talk about it later."

Maybe *he* wanted to talk later but the implicit criticism—you didn't lock your car, you left your sister—set my teeth on edge. "Have you—"

The wail of the ambulance siren reached us, and I remembered where I was—sitting in Anarchy's lap, borrowing his warmth. He was right. Now was not the time to talk about brakes or Marjorie or murder. I shifted so that my head fit against his shoulder.

"I'm s-s-sorry about your coat." I'd marred Anarchy's jacket with damp and bits of leaves and probably some duck droppings.

"Don't worry about it. You're sure you're okay?"

I stared up at him. How was I supposed to answer that?

"You're not complaining about the ambulance."

"Lately, there's a certain inev-v-v-v—it's fate. I can't fight it."

He snorted.

The paramedics ran toward us.

Officer not-so-smart Alec extended his hand and helped me out of Anarchy's lap. I hated to leave it.

"Th-thank you."

Anarchy looked at me, his brown eyes warmer than coffee and twice as tempting. "You're welcome."

I allowed the paramedics to lead me to the ambulance and climbed inside. Silently I promised my heart to the first man who gave me a warm blanket.

I waited until we arrived at the hospital for that blanket and then it was a nurse wearing too much eyeliner and sensible shoes who wrapped me in warmth. My heart was safe.

As for the rest of me…well, Mother charged my little cubicle in the emergency room like an angry rhinoceros and glared at me as if the brakes failing in Henry's car was somehow my fault. "This has to stop."

I blinked.

Daddy followed her in. "She's not wrong, sugar. We talked about it on the way over here. Your house caught fire, your sister's been shot and now this…"

"How did you get here so quickly?" I asked.

"The hospital has instructions to call me whenever you're admitted," said Mother.

Really? Just because she was board chairman…If they didn't have such nice warm blankets, I'd consider another hospital.

"Now, tell me, what have you done? Who wants to kill you?" Mother demanded.

"I haven't done anything."

"Where there's smoke, there's fire." Her tone dared me to argue.

I wanted to argue—*where there's smoke, there's fire* being among my least favorite of Mother's expression—but I didn't have the energy. "It was nice of you to come, but I'm fine. Aggie is bringing me a bag. As soon as I can change—" my ruined Diane von Furstenberg dress lay in a trashcan and I wore a hospital gown in its place, "—I'm going home."

"I thought there was a policeman assigned to protect you." Mother's tone promised a call to the police commissioner.

"There was. There is."

"Then how did this happen?" she demanded.

"He kept an eye on me and not the car."

"Where were you?"

"The Alameda."

"Why?" she asked.

No need to tell her about the almost-lunch with Kinky. "Marjorie and Greg are back together."

Mother pursed her lips as she processed that tidbit. Her daughter had avoided a failed marriage. Her daughter's husband manufactured condoms. Was she pleased that they'd reconciled or disappointed?

"Marjorie is happy," I added. Surely that should tip the scales toward pleased.

"We'll see how long that lasts."

Too tired to argue, I leaned back against the blue plastic mattress covered with white paper and closed my eyes.

"We're here."

Aggie's voice had never been more welcome. *We*? I cracked my eyelids. My tiny little area now contained Mother, Daddy, Aggie, Grace and Aunt Sis. "Thank you, Aggie." I pushed away from the dubious comforts of the blue mattress and sat.

"Mom, what happened?" Grace's wide-eyed gaze took in my pond-scum hair and the hospital gown.

"The brakes on your father's car failed."

"But how did you end up in the duck pond?" Grace asked.

"It was that or hit a man and his dog."

"I suppose the car is ruined." Mother always liked Henry's Cadillac. "Such a shame. Such a lovely car. Did you have to drive it into the pond?"

"Yes." Would she have preferred that I hit the man?

"You're sure it's a total loss?" Mother shook her head sadly.

"You're not hurt?" At least Grace was more interested in me than the state of Henry's Cadillac. "You're certain?"

"Not a scratch," I assured her. Several bruises but not one scratch.

"I'm glad you're okay." Grace pushed through the collection of family and hugged me. Hard. Then she stepped away. "You smell."

"When I get home, I'm going to take a shower, then a bath, then another shower."

She wrinkled her nose. "Good idea."

I looked past her. Mother and Aunt Sis were eying each other like Muhammad Ali and Joe Frazier before a fight.

Daddy looked slightly bemused—women outnumbered him five to one.

"I'll just step outside so you can get dressed." Aggie's hint wasn't subtle. "Grace, let's give your mother a minute, then we can take her home." This second, even more blatant, suggestion fell on deaf ears.

Mother looked at Aunt Sis's flowing pants and tunic with evident distaste. "Why are you here?" Her first punch was a mere glancing blow.

"I was worried about my niece." Aunt Sis tilted her head and added, "As opposed to worrying about the car."

That was a direct hit.

Daddy cleared his throat.

Grace piped up. "You're right, Aggie. Let's give Mom a minute to change. Grandy, Gram, Aunt Sis?" She gestured toward the door.

Ignoring my housekeeper was one thing, ignoring Grace, quite another. "Good idea, Grace." Daddy draped his arm around Mother's shoulders and propelled her toward the door.

Aunt Sis followed suit, taking a few small steps toward the hallway.

Jeans, a t-shirt, and a ride home were within reach, as close as the travel bag that Aggie had deposited next to the bed.

"Just because I don't obsess over my children's health doesn't mean I don't care." Mother struck back.

Aunt Sis stiffened.

Daddy paused.

Grace and Aggie escaped into the hallway.

"Obsess?' Aunt Sis's voice was dangerously low.

Mother nodded.

"You listen to me, you spoiled, self-righteous termagant." Aunt Sis pointed her index finger and poked Mother in the chest. "Don't you dare belittle what I've been through. If you'd actually faced a challenge or two in your life, you'd be nicer to your daughters."

Mother opened her mouth but no words came out.

Daddy looked stunned.

"It's easy to sit on a high horse when things are good, Frannie."

Frannie?

"But life doesn't always work that way. It requires love and kindness and...forgiveness. Will your spotless reputation keep you company when you're old? Just how much derision do you think Ellison and Marjorie will take before they cut you off?"

Daddy squared his shoulders, ready to defend Mother.

"Enough." It was my voice that cut through Aunt Sis's tirade.

Three sets of surprised eyes stared at me.

"Enough," I repeated. "Both of you." I shifted my gaze from Mother to Aunt Sis and back again. "Stop before you say something you'll regret."

Sisters pulled and pushed and annoyed. They competed in

contests they didn't understand. They took each other's dresses and lipsticks and...boyfriends. They kept score and forgave debts. They destroyed each other and mourned over the wreckage. They resented each other and reveled in their closeness. The bond between them was warped and scarred and precious.

You'd think after sixty years, Mother and Aunt Sis would realize that.

Mother lifted her nose. "Take me home please, Harrington." She marched out my room without saying a word to me or Aunt Sis.

"Dammit." Aunt Sis's eyes filled with tears. "I've done it now."

The other thing that sisters do? They forgive.

"Don't worry," I told her. "I'll fix it."

How?

TWENTY-TWO

I got home from the hospital, took the longest, hottest shower in the history of showers, and then took another one. I sniffed my hair. The scent of Grace's Herbal Essence shampoo had replaced *eau de* pond scum. Thank God.

Still wrapped in a towel, I picked up the phone and called my sister.

"Ellison," she said. "Where have you been? I've been calling all afternoon. Has Aggie packed my things?"

I sat on the edge of the bed. "Not yet."

"Why not?" Unhappy two-year-olds sounded less petulant.

"I had a mishap after I left you."

"Oh?"

I could picture her eyeing her cuticles, maybe filing her nails.

"The brakes failed and I ended up in the duck pond at Loose Park."

"No you didn't." Her voice sounded strangled.

"I did."

"Obviously, you're all right."

"Yes, but—"

"I wish I'd been there."

That was rather sweet. "The pond water was freezing and dirty. Your wound might have gotten infected."

"No. No. Not in the car. On the banks. I can just imagine your face as you sailed into the water." She giggled.

My face had probably been contorted by fear. "It's not funny. Someone tried to kill me. Maybe you."

"Of course it's not funny." She'd be more convincing if she stopped laughing.

"I need your help."

"Just a minute. Greg—" her voice faded as if she'd covered the receiver with her palm "—Ellison drove Henry's car into the duck pond in Loose Park."

Greg mumbled.

"She's fine."

Greg mumbled again.

"Greg wants to know if you realize land yachts don't float."

The two of them could head back to Ohio anytime—except— "Marjorie, I need you to have dinner at the club tonight."

"Greg and I have plans."

She'd been a high maintenance houseguest for how long? She owed me this. "Cancel them."

"Why would I want to do that?"

Because I asked wasn't near reason enough.

"Mother and Aunt Sis had a set-to today. You and I are going to broker a peace." If said negotiations took place at the club, voices would be kept low and comments polite.

"I don't think I'm up to that."

She wanted me to beg? Fine. "Please, Marji. I need your help with this. Mother might listen to you."

"Fine." She drew out the word as if being part of a family was a huge imposition.

"Thank you. I'll pick you up at six."

"Fine." This *fine* lasted even longer. "Wait. How are you going to pick us up? We won't fit in your Triumph." She giggled. "I really wish I'd seen you in the pond."

She didn't realize the bone-chilling terror of being trapped in a car filling with water. If she did, she wouldn't laugh. At least that's what I told myself.

Greg mumbled.

"Greg says he has a rental car. We'll meet you there at six."

We hung up and I called my father.

I explained—eloquently—my plan.

"Are you sure this is a good idea, sugar?"

"It's better than leaving them at odds."

"This dinner of yours could make things worse."

I crossed my fingers. It wouldn't. "Just get her there."

At five minutes before six, Aunt Sis and I pulled into the parking lot.

Marjorie and Greg were just getting out of a sedan.

I parked next to them and got out of the car.

While Greg dutifully kissed Aunt Sis's cheek, my sister grabbed my arm, pulled me a few feet away, and whispered furiously, "In the history of bad ideas, this is the worst."

What was she talking about? Nothing had gone wrong...yet.

"That—" she jerked her chin toward a bright orange BMW "—is Kenneth's car."

I stared at the 2002i and something niggled.

"Are you coming?" asked Aunt Sis. She was already walking toward the double doors of the clubhouse.

Whatever was bothering me was sure to wake me up at two in the morning.

I waved at the policeman who'd followed us to the club (not not-so-smart Alec but a new man—this one looked like a George) and stepped inside.

The hostess led us to a table for six in the sparsely seated dining room—I'd hoped for more of an audience. At least Kinky LeCoeur was nowhere in sight. We sat, ordered drinks, and waited.

And waited.

"I believe I'd like to powder my nose," said Aunt Sis. She excused herself from the table, leaving me with Marjorie and Greg. They stared into each other's eyes like lovesick teenagers. While this was encouraging in regards to their marriage, it didn't make for scintillating conversation. I gazed across the room at Kizzi and Howard Standish.

They, like Marjorie and Greg, ignored me.

I glanced at my watch. Six fifteen.

Were they not coming? How would I explain that to Aunt Sis? Something like ice water trickled through my veins. Was Mother *that* angry?

I waved my fingers at the waiter—I needed something stronger than a spritzer—and spotted my father.

Daddy wore a sky-is-falling expression worthy of Chicken Little. He approached the table slowly.

"Where's Mother?" I asked.

"Your mother isn't coming."

Oh. Dear. Lord.

"Where's your aunt?" he asked.

"The ladies' lounge." She'd been there a long time. "Marjorie, let's go check on Aunt Sis."

Somehow, she tore her gaze away from Greg. "What do you need me for?"

"Mother isn't coming." Someone had to help me tell Aunt Sis.

"I told you this was a bad idea."

"You were right. I was wrong. Now, come on." I pushed away from the table.

With a put-upon sigh, she stood.

We entered an empty room. The ladies' lounge at the club is a study in wishful thinking—white on white, with glass topped lobster traps serving as end tables, Krill baskets to hide the tampons, and etchings of seashells. In the summer, the decor hints at distant ocean breezes. Now, in the fall, all that white seemed cold as a Nantucket winter.

"She must be in the bathroom," I said.

Marjorie, gifted me another I-told-you-so look and pulled a compact out of her purse. "You could do with some lipstick."

My favorite lipstick, a becoming shade of coral, now resided at the bottom of the duck pond. I pulled a gold tube of Guerlain out of my bag. The damned thing was cursed and the color, *Rouge Chaud*, wasn't flattering, but I'd spent too much on it to throw it away.

Of course I dropped it.

I bent, reached under the vanity, and felt a prickle on my neck.

Now?

I closed my fingers around the lipstick and stood.

Cassie LeCoeur was reflected in the mirror.

Niggling joined prickling. Kinky drove an orange BMW. *Niggle, niggle.* I hadn't seen an orange car the afternoon Marjorie was shot, but Kinky's license plate had come up...Odd since Marjorie said Kinky had dropped her off then left.

Niggle, niggle.

Cassie's car had been in the lot. Not Kinky's.

Why would Cassie try and kill me?

Duh. I'd been right all along. Marjorie—the woman having an affair with Kinky—had been the target.

"You." The word slipped through my teeth, ignoring common sense and self-preservation on its way.

Cassie reached into her purse and pulled out a gun.

Marjorie gasped.

"You can't have him." Cassie's voice shook.

"I don't want him," said Marjorie.

"Liar." Cassie's voice still shook but the hand holding the gun was steady.

"It's true," I said. "Marjorie and Greg are back together. He's in the dining room now."

Cassie shook her head. "Keeping up appearances. That's all anyone in this Godforsaken place does."

"No," I promised. "It's true."

"I'm sorry you got mixed up in this, Ellison." She aimed the gun at my sister's heart.

Behind her the bathroom door opened slightly.

"You shoved the bust?" I asked, stalling for time.

"It wasn't supposed to hit you. You walked into it."

"And the fire?"

She nodded. "I figured you—" she jabbed the gun in Marjorie's direction "—would come running. But you didn't. It was Ellison. When you finally stuck your head out the door, I missed."

"You killed Hammie Walsh," said Marjorie. "Why?"

I really wished my sister had kept her mouth shut. We might have been able to talk ourselves out of the numerous attempts on Marjorie's life. *We won't tell. Marjorie's going back to Ohio. You and Kenneth can work this out*...But Hammie's murder changed things. Cassie was going to prison. Why had Marjorie brought it up?

"That was an accident!"

The crack in the door behind Cassie grew bigger. What was Aunt Sis up to?

"Kinky was supposed to sit there."

She'd tried to kill her husband?

"I couldn't seem to kill Marjorie and he was going to leave me with nothing. Nothing!"

"And then I moved the cards," said Marjorie.

Cassie hands had shaken that night. I'd assumed she was upset because my sister was flirting with Kinky. I'd been half right. Her plan to kill her husband had gone awry. That meant someone else might die.

Poor Hammie.

"No one would question Kinky taking Spanish Fly."

She was probably right.

"Hammie was an accident."

"I doubt a jury will see it that way," said Marjorie.

Did she want to get shot again? I glared at her.

"What?" said my idiot sister. "She can't think she'll be able to shoot us and get away with it."

There was a door to the parking lot steps from the door to the lounge. Cassie could shoot us and disappear before anyone figured out where the shots had come from. At this range, not even an incompetent murderer could miss.

Aunt Sis slipped through the bathroom door. If Cassie wasn't glaring at Marjorie with such singular focus, she would've seen her.

"You cut my brakes," I said. Please let Aunt Sis get away. Please.

"I thought Marjorie would be in the car." Thank God Cassie's gaze remained locked on Marjorie. If Aunt Sis hurried, she'd be able to slip out of the lounge and go for help. "You know, no one in this town ever made any secret that they looked down on me. Just imagine how they would have treated me if they knew my father owned an auto repair shop. Yes, I cut your brakes."

Why wasn't Aunt Sis sneaking out?

Any second, Cassie was going to see Aunt Sis in the mirror.

"Did you notice the bruise on your husband's jaw?" I asked. "Marjorie's husband gave him that. There is nothing between Kenneth and Marjorie anymore."

"That might be true. But you figured it out. You knew I'd tried to kill Marjorie." Cassie cocked her gun. "You knew I'd killed—"

Aunt Sis leapt. The two of them fell to the floor in a tangle of caftan and .22 caliber gun.

"Run!" I said to Marjorie. "Go get help."

My idiot sister just stood there with her mouth hanging open.

Bang!

The shot echoed in my ears.

Cassie pulled away from my aunt.

Aunt Sis clutched her stomach.

Cassie struggled to her feet and backed toward the door.

"Sorry about this, Ellison."

Cassie cocked the gun.

My heart took flight, rising to my throat. Grace was going to be an orphan. I hadn't said goodbye, just left a note telling her I'd see her later. Had I even signed it, *I love you*? I held up my hands. "Cassie, please don't—"

Something black hit Cassie on the side of the head and she collapsed onto the floor.

A Ferragamo-shod foot kicked the gun out of her hand.

Marjorie swayed on her feet and gripped the edge of the vanity.

Mother rushed into the lounge and knelt next to Aunt Sis. Her large—and apparently very heavy—handbag thudded onto the carpet.

"What are you doing standing there?" Mother demanded. "Get help!"

Marjorie took off running.

I raced into the bathroom, grabbed every hand towel I could find and took them to Mother.

She pressed the towels against the crimson bloom near Aunt Sis's stomach.

"Don't you dare die," said Mother. "We have years of feuding left between us."

"How bad is—"

"Quiet! She'll be fine." Mother might have sounded convincing were it not for the tears streaming down her cheeks.

A few seconds later, the ladies' lounge was overrun with people. Including the policeman who looked like a George.

"She shot my aunt." I pointed at Cassie's prone figure.

He didn't question me. He just clasped handcuffs around her wrists. Thank God he was a not-so-curious George

A few moments later, Aunt Sis was loaded into an ambulance.

"I'm going with her," said Mother.

No one argued.

The ambulance flew down the drive. Lord only knew what Mother was saying to the emergency personnel inside.

Daddy, Greg, and Marjorie followed at a more sedate pace.

I called the Alameda. David needed to know his mother had been shot.

When I emerged from the phone booth, not-so-curious George was waiting for me. "Detective Jones would like to speak with you."

I bet he did.

"He can find me at the hospital."

I rushed out the front door of the club, climbed into my car and pointed it toward the hospital.

Please God, let Aunt Sis be okay.

TWENTY-THREE

Hospital waiting rooms—even private ones—are horrible. Who picks the colors? Do they also decorate gulags? How does one decide on congealed oatmeal as a paint color? What about sickly blue Naugahyde on the chairs? Who picks that?

I shifted on my sickly blue Naugahyde chair and checked my watch. Aunt Sis had been in surgery for an hour. In that hour, Mother had demanded an update six times.

Marjorie and Greg held hands.

David paced. He paused and asked for the third time, "My mother jumped someone with a gun?"

"Yes."

"Because that woman was pointing the gun at you and Marjorie?"

"Yes."

He resumed his pacing.

"She saved our lives," said Marjorie.

And then Mother saved our lives. "I thought you weren't coming to the club," I said.

She sniffed. "I changed my mind."

Anarchy Jones appeared in the doorway. Frankly, I'd anticipated he'd arrive sooner.

"A word, Ellison?"

I stood. "Fine."

"I'll need to speak with you too, Mrs. Blake, Mrs. Walford."

Marjorie nodded.

Mother ignored him.

"Coffee shop?" I asked.

We walked the hospital corridors in silence. We sat at our usual table in silence. We pretended to look at the menus in silence.

"Marjorie was the target," he said. "You were right."

"It happens." I shrugged. "I wonder what kind of pie they have." I didn't want pie. There was no way I could eat pie. Not until I knew Aunt Sis would be all right.

A waitress—this one with a flip instead of a beehive—approached the table.

"Pie?" Anarchy asked.

"Just coffee," I said.

"Two coffees and a slice of banana cream."

The waitress jotted our order down.

"Tell me what happened," said Anarchy.

I told him—first about Kinky and Marjorie.

He scowled at me. "That would have been helpful to know."

I shrugged. Sharing that a family member was an adulteress wasn't something any member of my family would do.

"What happened in the lounge?"

I told him about Cassie and the gun and Aunt Sis.

"Your mother hit Mrs. LeCoeur in the head with her handbag?"

"Yes."

"What does she carry in there?"

"I looked inside."

"And?"

"She had several rolls of quarters."

"Why?"

"She meant to go to the bank. She says trips to the hospital kept getting in the way."

"Thank God."

The waitress put down our coffee and the pie.

Anarchy pushed the plate into the middle of the table and put a fork in my hand. "Have you eaten today?"

I hadn't.

"Try it."

"I don't want any."

He used his secret weapon—that melting grin. "Just one bite."

I ate the entire slice.

Anarchy paid the tab and escorted me back to the waiting room where Mother, Daddy, and Greg waited.

"Any news?" I asked.

Mother shook her head.

"Where's Marjorie?"

"She and David went somewhere."

"May I call you tomorrow, Mrs. Walford?" asked Anarchy.

"Fine."

"Goodbye, Ellison." He dropped a kiss on my cheek. "Tell your sister I'll be in touch. I'll call you tomorrow."

Mother was too distracted to look annoyed by his tiny kiss. She didn't seem to notice when he left. "What if she dies?" She sounded bereft.

"She won't," said my father.

"You can't possibly know that." Mother snapped the end off each word.

"Harrington, I could do with a cup of coffee," said Greg. "Would you show me where the coffee shop is?"

We watched them go.

"That Greg has more sense than I gave him credit for."

"Oh?"

"I'm not fit company." Mother's gaze rested on a horrible painting of a woman in a field. "Your grandfather wanted to be a painter."

"He did?"

I'd never heard that before.

"His father wanted him in the family business."

Which is what he'd done. That and expand it exponentially.

"My father favored Sis. He said she had a poet's soul." Mother looked at me and smiled sadly. "He would have adored the woman you've become." She wiped her eyes. "Knowing that your father loves your sister better…it isn't something you get over. I've held it against Sis for most of our lives."

I didn't say a word. Mother and I were in uncharted territory, a territory where she revealed part of her soul.

"And now she might die, and I've wasted all these years being mad at her." She let the next few tears track down her cheeks. "The worst part is, she got hurt trying to save my daughters."

I waited for *Ellison this is all your fault.*

It didn't come. Perhaps because, this time, it wasn't my fault.

Mother sniffled.

I shifted to the chair next to hers and took her hand. "She won't die."

"You can't know that."

"I know." Now that our family had a chance to heal, Sis wouldn't die. I wouldn't let her.

Mother bowed her head and her lips moved but I heard no sound.

She was praying.

I joined her.

Maybe it worked. A moment later, the surgeon appeared. "Mrs. Walford, your sister is in recovery. She's going to be fine"

Mother dissolved in tears.

I *might* have gotten a little misty myself.

"Where's David? He'll want to know."

Mother was worried about David? What next? Flying pigs?

Daddy and Greg wandered back in, each carrying two cups of coffee.

My father saw Mother's tears, handed me the cups, and pulled her into a hug.

"Happy tears." Mother's voice was choked.

"Thank God," said Daddy.

"Where did Marjorie and David go? I'll go get them."

"We're here," said Marjorie.

"Your mother is going to be fine, David."

The green faded from his skin.

"We have news too." Marjorie looked like the cat that swallowed the canary.

"What?" asked Mother.

"I've decided to give David a kidney."

Everyone but David stared at her slack-jawed. My self-centered sister voluntarily undergoing major surgery?

I waited for Mother's argument—even crafted it in my head. But Mother didn't argue. She opened her arms wider and included Marjorie in her hug with Daddy.

That's the thing about families—at least mine. We keep secrets and fight and love each other. Sometimes, my family surprises me. I wouldn't change a thing.

JULIE MULHERN

Julie Mulhern is the *USA Today* bestselling author of The Country Club Murders. She is a Kansas City native who grew up on a steady diet of Agatha Christie. She spends her spare time whipping up gourmet meals for her family, working out at the gym and finding new ways to keep her house spotlessly clean—and she's got an active imagination. Truth is—she's an expert at calling for take-out, she grumbles about walking the dog and the dust bunnies under the bed have grown into dust lions.

The Country Club Murders
by Julie Mulhern

Henery Press Mystery Books

And finally, before you go...
Here are a few other mysteries
you might enjoy:

BOARD STIFF

Kendel Lynn

An Elliott Lisbon Mystery (#1)

As director of the Ballantyne Foundation on Sea Pine Island, SC, Elliott Lisbon scratches her detective itch by performing discreet inquiries for Foundation donors. Usually nothing more serious than retrieving a pilfered Pomeranian. Until Jane Hatting, Ballantyne board chair, is accused of murder. The Ballantyne's reputation tanks, Jane's headed to a jail cell, and Elliott's sexy ex is the new lieutenant in town.

Armed with moxie and her Mini Coop, Elliott uncovers a trail of blackmail schemes, gambling debts, illicit affairs, and investment scams. But the deeper she digs to clear Jane's name, the guiltier Jane looks. The closer she gets to the truth, the more treacherous her investigation becomes. With victims piling up faster than shells at a clambake, Elliott realizes she's next on the killer's list.

Available at booksellers nationwide and online

Visit www.henerypress.com for details

COUNTERFEIT CONSPIRACIES

Ritter Ames

A Bodies of Art Mystery (#1)

Laurel Beacham may have been born with a silver spoon in her mouth, but she has long since lost it digging herself out of trouble. Her father gambled and womanized his way through the family fortune before skiing off an Alp, leaving her with more tarnish than trust fund. Quick wits and connections have gained her a reputation as one of the world's premier art recovery experts. The police may catch the thief, but she reclaims the missing masterpieces.

The latest assignment, however, may be her undoing. Using every ounce of luck and larceny she possesses, Laurel must locate a priceless art icon and rescue a co-worker (and ex-lover) from a master criminal, all the while matching wits with a charming new nemesis. Unfortunately, he seems to know where the bodies are buried—and she prefers hers isn't next.

Available at booksellers nationwide and online

Visit www.henerypress.com for details

DOUBLE WHAMMY

Gretchen Archer

A Davis Way Crime Caper (#1)

Davis Way thinks she's hit the jackpot when she lands a job as the fifth wheel on an elite security team at the fabulous Bellissimo Resort and Casino in Biloxi, Mississippi. But once there, she runs straight into her ex-ex husband, a rigged slot machine, her evil twin, and a trail of dead bodies. Davis learns the truth and it does not set her free—in fact, it lands her in the pokey.

Buried under a mistaken identity, unable to seek help from her family, her hot streak runs cold until her landlord Bradley Cole steps in. Make that her landlord, lawyer, and love interest. With his help, Davis must win this high stakes game before her luck runs out.

Available at booksellers nationwide and online

Visit www.henerypress.com for details

LOWCOUNTRY BOIL

Susan M. Boyer

A Liz Talbot Mystery (#1)

Private Investigator Liz Talbot is a modern Southern belle: she blesses hearts and takes names. She carries her Sig 9 in her Kate Spade handbag, and her golden retriever, Rhett, rides shotgun in her hybrid Escape. When her grandmother is murdered, Liz hightails it back to her South Carolina island home to find the killer.

She's fit to be tied when her police-chief brother shuts her out of the investigation, so she opens her own. Then her long-dead best friend pops in and things really get complicated. When more folks start turning up dead in this small seaside town, Liz must use more than just her wits and charm to keep her family safe, chase down clues from the hereafter, and catch a psychopath before he catches her.

Available at booksellers nationwide and online

Visit www.henerypress.com for details

PILLOW STALK

Diane Vallere

A Madison Night Mystery (#1)

Interior Decorator Madison Night might look like a throwback to the sixties, but as business owner and landlord, she proves that independent women can have it all. But when a killer targets women dressed in her signature style—estate sale vintage to play up her resemblance to fave actress Doris Day—what makes her unique might make her dead.

The local detective connects the new crime to a twenty-year old cold case, and Madison's long-trusted contractor emerges as the leading suspect. As the body count piles up, Madison uncovers a Soviet spy, a campaign to destroy all Doris Day movies, and six minutes of film that will change her life forever.

Available at booksellers nationwide and online

Visit www.henerypress.com for details

CPSIA information can be obtained at www.ICGtesting.com
Printed in the USA
LVOW10s1508060516

487047LV00017B/518/P